Long Time Coming

JUDITH STAPONKUS

This book is a work of fiction. Names, characters, places and incidents either are products of the author's imagination or are used fictitiously. Any resemblance to actual events or locales or persons, living or dead, is entirely coincidental.

ISBN: 978-1-54396-094-5 (print)

ISBN: 978-1-54396-095-2 (ebook)

For Gregory and Carrie.

JUNE, 1964

ELIZABETH REALIZED THE GARBAGE CANS WERE STILL at the curb when she heard their old car rattle into the driveway. It was too early for Eddie to be home from the mill she thought, as she patted the lump of bread dough she had been kneading and covered it with a damp towel. Eddie would be furious that the cans were not put away, a job left undone by one of his daughters. She watched through the kitchen window as her husband stormed out of the car, his steps grinding into the gravel driveway as he marched back toward the street. Snatching one dented can in each hand, he dragged them down the corridor, metal bumping along the stones. When his heavy work boots thunked up the back stairs, Elizabeth, with a trembling hand, tucked a dark strand of hair back into place behind her ear.

She turned from the window to face Eddie as he entered the sunny, worn kitchen.

"You're home early," she said, smiling as she reached to welcome him with a kiss.

Eddie shoved Elizabeth away, his hand hammering against her chest.

"Mill's shutting down. Everyone's been laid off until further notice." His shoulders slumped as he dropped himself onto a chair at the kitchen table. With one sudden sweep of his arm, Eddie bulldozed the table, tossing the day's mail and smashing a Mason jar, filled with lilacs, onto the floor.

Stepping her way through the minefield of broken glass, Elizabeth moved to the refrigerator without a word, knowing Eddie would twist anything she said. After all, it was only a jar filled with flowers, hardly worth another thought, like Elizabeth herself, she figured. An old familiar, sinking feeling pulled her down into the deep and bottomless pit her life had become.

She tugged the handle upward and the refrigerator door trudged open, cold air escaping its frozen belly, no match for the cold, frozen heart pounding in Elizabeth's chest. Snatching three bottles of beer and the bottle opener, Elizabeth closed the door with her hip. She stepped over the strewn flowers and shattered glass, sat down to face Eddie at the kitchen table, and opened two bottles, pushing one toward her husband and raising another to her mouth.

"It's only a lay-off. You could get called back at any time, right?"

"Only a lay-off? A lay-off means no work, and no work means no pay. Besides, the union steward says not to count on being called back. Guess the mill has been on thin ice for too long, and we can't give up any more concessions, or we'll be paying the company to work there."

"Some of the guys are done and said they won't go back. They're thinking about heading north to Superior to work on the boats." Eddie tipped the brown bottle high, the beer dribbling from the corners of his loose lips. Elizabeth focussed on his Adam's apple, bobbing with each swallow, having learned long ago to allow Eddie's temper to run out of steam.

Elizabeth mentally moved through the house to locate their three daughters. She could hear the television in the living room playing the American Bandstand theme, timed to the soft thuds of star-struck, thirteen-year old Carol Jean, her strawberry-blond hair swirling as she danced barefooted in front of the TV, the girl's routine every afternoon.

Four-year old Nona's raspy voice carried into the kitchen. She would be in her usual perch, sitting with their dog, Lucky, on the living room sofa. Nona loved singing along with the music from the television and was mesmerized by Carol Jean's dancing. Elizabeth had no idea where Mince, her ten-year old, could be. She hoped the girl had enough sense to make herself scarce, since the job of retrieving the garbage cans that day belonged to Mince.

"Here's a thought," Elizabeth said. "The pickle factory is hiring. I could get a job there."

"Don't make me laugh." Eddie clenched his fists, the veins in his hands and forearms bulging like snakes.

"It would only be for the summer," Elizabeth continued, "or until you get called back to the mill." She hesitated, wanting to convince him but not sure what words would light that all too familiar fuse of Eddie's. "Lots of women work the season at the pickle factory. There's no shame in it." Afraid she had gone too far, she willed her shaking hands to place her bottle on the cracked formica tabletop.

Eddie, his first empty bottle shoved aside, cranked open the next, guzzled from it, eyes narrowing to a blade-thin squint. He belched and coughed out an icy laugh, sending shivers through Elizabeth, despite the sweat trickling down her back.

"You think you could survive for one week, no, make that one day, at a factory like that?" Eddie paused, then smirked. "Yeah, go ahead and apply. They'll never hire you, because you're a pathetic housewife. You never worked a day in your life."

Loosening his grip on the bottle, Eddie stood and swung the back of his hand toward Elizabeth. It was always the same dead end road for her. She could not unsay the words, could not run, could not escape.

Closing her eyes, Elizabeth steeled herself for his slap, but Eddie's arm somehow caught the top of the empty beer bottle standing in the center of the table. He knocked the bottle to the floor, bouncing it under the table.

"Leave the thinking to me, Lizzie." He towered above her, then moved his face in close to hers, his steely eyes imprisoning her. "Now, clean up this mess before somebody gets hurt."

Grabbing the opener and another beer bottle from the refrigerator, he headed towards the back porch. The screen door banged as Eddie went out, and slammed again, when he returned inside.

"Please forget about the garbage cans," Elizabeth mentally begged her husband. "Eddie, wait!" she pleaded aloud.

He shoved Elizabeth backwards, but she gained her balance and followed him into the living room.

"Where's Mince?" Eddie yelled.

Carol Jean froze mid-step, her face a familiar, fearful mask.

"She's not in here, Pops. Maybe she's outside somewhere." Carol Jean turned again to the television, but the dancing was finished.

Elizabeth directed her focus to Nona, who had buried her face in Lucky's furry neck. "I don't have her, Pops," Nona said.

Eddie grunted, turned, and collided with Elizabeth. "Get out of my way," he growled. Elizabeth froze in place, and Eddie continued his hunt for Mince.

"Get up, Minerva!" Eddie's voice was dripping with anger. Elizabeth rushed toward the hallway, arriving as Mince slumped forward, retching a string of yellowish drool onto the cracked leather of her father's work boots, the boots that had delivered a swift kick to the girl's stomach. Despite the blow, Mince righted herself and scrambled to stand, leaning against the faded wallpaper of the hallway, clutching her belly.

"Eddie, stop! It's not that important. Please, stop!" Elizabeth pleaded as she tugged at his shoulders and arms, attempting to move him away from their daughter.

"Butt out, Lizzie. This is between my girl and me." He shoved Elizabeth away, as he lifted Mince up by the front of her shirt.

"So, daughter, what do you have to say for yourself?" His hand was a vice, clenching Mince's chin to a milky white. Elizabeth wanted to help, to step in and rescue her daughter, but she was paralyzed, like so many times before. Whatever she did, it would make matters worse.

"Sorry, Pops." Mince's words were breathless, as though she had been running. "It's summer, and I forgot."

"My apologies. We wouldn't want to interrupt your summer vacation with things like doing chores!" Eddie reached behind Mince's head and jerked her long ponytail until her tear-filled eyes were looking into his.

Elizabeth swallowed a scream as she grasped Eddie's arm. "Please, let her go. It's my fault for not reminding Mince."

He threw off Elizabeth's hands and spit words into Mince's face. "There's a big part of the problem. You and your mother think it's okay to forget chores. It isn't ever okay, so you remember to do what you're told, when you're told to do it."

"I won't forget again, I promise, Pops."

"You bet you won't." He let go of her hair, and Mince crumbled to the floor. Eddie stomped past Elizabeth. Neither Elizabeth or Mince moved until they heard the screen door slam and Eddie's feet pounding down the back steps.

"Are you all right?" Elizabeth's slender arms reached for the girl, pulling her close.

Mince backhanded the tears moving down her face and leaned into her mother.

"Pops is mean and horrible," Mince said through clenched teeth.

Elizabeth rested her chin on Mince's dark hair and said, "I'm sorry, Love. It was wrong of Pops to hurt you . . . wrong, mean, and horrible."

WHITE GLOVES AND A PICKLE FACTORY

THE NEXT MORNING, ELIZABETH ROSE EARLY AND began scrubbing her way around the kitchen. By the time Mince and Lucky padded into the room, it smelled of bleach and summertime, and Elizabeth was standing at the counter, arranging her spotless, white cotton gloves, finger by finger.

"Good morning, Love. How's my girl?" She leaned over and kissed the top of Mince's tangled hair. "Is your stomach feeling good enough to eat some cereal?"

"I'm all right." Mince looked up at her mother. "Are you going to the A & P Store this morning?"

The plaid dress Elizabeth wore was reserved for the twice monthly trips to the grocery store. Cinched at her slender waist, the dress's leafy green color complimented Elizabeth's olive complexion and her long, dark hair. Imitation jade buttons running down the front of the dress matched her eyes.

"No, this is something much more important than shopping! I'm off to the Landers Pickle Factory. With so many folks out of work, I need to get there early to fill out an application."

Elizabeth straightened a string of creamy beads around her neck, and then her long, gloved fingers reached for a beige clutch purse. She pressed the bag to her fluttering stomach, nervous at the thought of applying for a job.

"It must be important to look your best when you go to a pickle factory, because you're wearing your Sunday church gloves," Mince said.

Laughing, Elizabeth placed a gloved finger beneath Mince's chin. "My funny child! Never forget . . . a girl should take advantage of every opportunity to be a lady."

The drive to the Landers' factory followed the river's journey past the paper mill at the edge of town. The two neighboring companies filled the entire northwest corner of the municipality, both straddling the much-needed water source. Elizabeth thought the color of the river, grey as smoke, was unusual for this time of day. Perhaps now that the paper mill had ceased operations, the river would become clean and usable again. Over the years, the condition of the river, and their entire town, had deteriorated.

Elizabeth twitched her nose at the unpleasant stench stretching upward from the lazy, ashen water, and she worried Nona would have a hard time breathing today. When Nona was born, she was diagnosed with a heart murmur, but it was later determined she had a disease called cardiomyopathy. Because of the disease, the contraction of abnormal muscle fibers in her heart caused fluid to back up in her lungs. She often suffered from shortness of breath, congestion, and coughing, especially on days like today when the hot, thick air hung heavy with noxious fumes. Instead of growing stronger with time as the doctor had predicted, Nona was becoming more and more fragile living where the air was unhealthy.

Cars filled the lot of the pickle factory, and the line of people waiting to apply for a job stretched out the front door, down the sidewalk, and around the building. By the time Elizabeth found a parking place and walked to join the line, it extended past the pavement to the lawn.

The other people waiting were mostly folks from town, many she had known all her life.

Elizabeth waved and said hello, recognizing they were her competition, desperate for a job, like she was. Beneath the unrelenting morning sun, Elizabeth stood with the others, the pickle smell prickling her nostrils, and the river fumes pummeling her lungs. There was a moment when Elizabeth thought she might keel over from it all, but she mustered the strength to stay upright.

Over two hours passed before Elizabeth was inside the building filling out an application. She had no real job experience, having been a housewife since high school, so completing the form was a quick, painful task. What she had accomplished in the past thirteen years occupied one single line in the work history section.

While she stood in line waiting to turn in the finished form, Elizabeth couldn't help but notice the applications others were submitting, line after line filled with past jobs and work-related experience, many having been employed for several seasons at Landers. Embarrassment and unworthiness demanded she escape, but there was no turning back. She needed the job, for the money, for her girls, and for herself.

When, at last, Elizabeth was at the employment secretary's desk, the woman smiled, raised her hand to halt the application Liz was handing to her, and stood to face the crowd filing into the office.

"I am sorry, but that is all the applications we are accepting today. Please check back with us tomorrow in case there are any positions left vacant." The woman turned away, dismissing Elizabeth and the others without another glance.

With the rest of the applicants, Elizabeth shuffled from the factory, everyone now silent and unsmiling. There was nothing to do but return home, and Elizabeth allowed herself a few indulgent tears on the way. Brushing them from her cheeks, she put on a cheerful face, hoping her daughters would not see through her fake smile.

Elizabeth pulled into the driveway and spotted the girls, whirling around the backyard, dancing with the hollyhock dolls they had made.

"Hello, dancing ladies!" Elizabeth stepped from the car and waved her white gloves. Mince and Nona ran to her, showing off their tattered and withering dance partners. Carol Jean followed along behind, hollyhocks tossed aside, face unsmiling.

"I see you've decided to prune my hollyhocks again!" Elizabeth laughed, knowing they were aware she didn't care as much about hollyhocks as she did about them having fun.

"Did you get the job?" Mince asked with a worried crease between her eyes.

"Will you be gone tomorrow, too?" Nona wanted to know. "Can I come along so I don't be lonesome?" She wrinkled up her nose. "Are you gonna smell like pickles every day?"

"What will you do all day at a boring, smelly pickle factory, anyway? Won't it ruin your hair and skin?" Carol Jean asked. The girl leaned to peer into the car's side mirror, examining her long, silky hair and creamy complexion.

"Hair and skin are the least of my worries," Elizabeth said, "and, no, I didn't get the job, yet. There were so many people waiting to apply, that I have to go back tomorrow to try again."

"That's a damn shame." Eddie sauntered down the driveway toward them.

"I figured you wouldn't get a job. Too much competition from folks who know how to work for a living."

Although talking back to Eddie was a mistake, Elizabeth felt compelled to say something, for her daughters' sakes.

"Landers accepted a certain number of applications on the first day and will take more when they figure out what positions are left."

"Keep telling yourself that, Miss Mary Sunshine. Seems like a waste of time and gas, driving over there for nothing." Eddie waved a disgusted hand towards Elizabeth, and she backed away, anticipating a slap. Instead, he marched into the house, the screen door bouncing against the doorframe.

"You didn't get the stupid job?" Carol Jean asked.

"Like I said, not yet, but you wait and see. I'll be working soon." Elizabeth shuttled the girls and Lucky up the back porch steps into the house, hoping her daughters did not sense how discouraged she was.

A JOB, NEW SHOES, AND
AUDREY LANDERS

AFTER THAT DAY, ELIZABETH RETURNED TO THE FAC-
tory three more times, each morning earlier than the one before,
until she was second in line when the office opened. The woman at
the counter accepted her form, along with five others, to fill two jobs
still available. Elizabeth stood waiting in the damp hallway outside
the office with the other applicants, their eyes avoiding one another
and focused on the floor. The cheerful chatter and friendly atmo-
sphere of previous days had vanished with the disappearance of the
jobs they all needed.

"Elizabeth, I didn't know you were applying to work here!"
Elizabeth glanced up to see, exiting from his office, Clayton Landers,
her old high school friend and owner of the Landers Pickle Factory.
The two had belonged to the same circle of friends, and, Elizabeth
recalled, were closer than most in the group.

"Like lots of other people, Clay."

"I heard about the mill and the layoffs. Tough times for so
many folks."

"We hope the men will be recalled soon. In the meantime,
unemployment compensation and maybe other temporary jobs will
keep everyone afloat."

"I hope so. Good luck and give my best to your girls." He walked back toward his office, shaking hands as he passed and exchanging wisecracks with the people standing in the hall.

Within minutes, the applicants were called inside. They were told the remaining positions were filled, and Elizabeth and another woman were asked to stay. The others who were dismissed shot angry looks and words at Elizabeth.

"Guess you gotta know the boss in order to get hired around here," a man in a plaid shirt and dirty jeans said.

"Wonder what else you gotta do to get hired?" a woman in a faded housedress asked.

Elizabeth realized Clay's attention gave the appearance of preferential treatment, but she didn't care. She needed that job, and she would take it any way she could get it.

At home, she rushed into the house to share the news with her daughters.

"I am now employee #137, shift number one, of the Landers Pickle Factory."

She smiled as she pinned a green, pickle-shaped ID tag with her name "Elizabeth Dembrowski, #137," onto her dress.

"I start tomorrow morning, working in the receiving area where I'll help sort and clean the loads of pickles being delivered by truck. I'll be gone from five or five thirty in the morning until four or later in the afternoon, and I will need you three to be at home with Pops to help take care of things. Do you think you will be able to do that for me?"

"I'm almost eleven, Mom. I'll finish all my chores and not fight, too much," Mince reassured her.

"I will close the screen door so bugs don't get in, 'cause I don't like bugs," Nona added.

"It's not fair. Because you are working at the stinky pickle factory, I have to be stuck here with my annoying sisters. Plus doing the extra chores. Plus having no free time for my friends," Carol Jean pouted.

"It will only be for the summer, and you know how fast summer flies by. Because we are a family, we all have to work together and make sacrifices, and if we do, things will work out fine. I need some work shoes for my new job tomorrow. How would you like to go downtown with me?"

Before they left to go shopping, Elizabeth and Mince went into the bedroom where Elizabeth reached high on the top shelf of her tiny, ordered closet. She retrieved her wicker sewing basket, where she kept, among other things, the money she had saved for two years to buy lace curtains at Lauermann's Department Store.

"But, you said you would never, ever spend the lace curtain money, no matter what," Mince said, watching the pressing out of the wrinkled dollars.

Her hands folding the bills, Elizabeth placed them inside the zippered compartment of her bag. "Things change, Love. Sometimes, you have to spend money in order to make money. Besides, I'm only using part of my savings. There will always be next year to buy lace curtains, and, if I have money left over today, I'll buy each of my helpers a popsicle."

The possibility of a popsicle brought a smile back to Mince's face. Downtown the four walked at an easy pace, for Nona was feeling breathless and tired, and Elizabeth was glad the one stoplight on the corner of Main Street and Madison turned red as they approached. Nona sat down on the curb, while Mince danced high and low along its concrete edge, and Carol Jean waved to a friend passing through the intersection. At the change of the light, Elizabeth surprised them by turning right, crossing the street towards Prince's Clothier.

"If I'm going to be a factory worker, I need factory worker shoes. This is the place to find them."

At the store, Elizabeth pushed the brass handle of the glass door, thick as a sheet of January ice. She ushered her three girls inside, where cool air greeted them. An air-conditioned store was unusual, but Elizabeth knew Julian Prince refused to allow his wife, Madeira, who ran the business, to suffer in the summer heat. What was more unusual was Elizabeth shopping in Prince's store at any time of year. Her clothes, and most of the girls' clothes, were either hand sewn by Elizabeth or by Marta, the girls' grandmother.

"Ladies, what brings you into the Clothier's on this sweltering summer day?" Madeira grinned with her square, pearly horse teeth as she approached them. Elizabeth recognized the perfume Madeira wore as Evening in Paris, and it arrived considerably ahead of the woman wearing it.

Elizabeth had known Madeira for a long time and admired her style. Although taller than most men in town, Madeira wore high heels, even in the grocery store. Quite willing to tower, she preferred straight black skirts and fitted sweaters dark as pitch to accentuate her long, stretch of a body, like a delicate, black licorice whip.

A man standing behind Madeira reached a pallid, thin hand toward them. "The Dembrowski ladies! What a pleasure." Julian Prince shook each of their hands with somber sincerity, looking from one to the other with his large, pale eyes.

Madeira was stunning and seemed an odd match for her husband, Julian, Elizabeth had always thought, at least at first glance. Madeira's dark eyes were set wide above high, rose- dusted cheek bones. Julian was short and slight, with reddish blond hair mowed across the top like a front lawn. His pale, freckled face was held together by thick, wire-rimmed glasses that magnified faint blue-grey eyes to an abnormally large and unsettling size. While Madeira had a loud voice that sounded masculine, Julian was soft spoken, requiring you to fine tune your listening to hear what he was saying. They reminded Elizabeth of the pieces of a puzzle that appear anomalous, and then snap together to form a complete and seamless picture.

"Thank you, Madeira, my dear, for a wonderful lunch." Mr. Prince pecked with thin lips against his wife's cheek. "Ladies, enjoy your shopping."

Elizabeth took Nona's hand and moved to the shoe section, where the two perched side by side in padded red chairs facing a mirrored wall. Carol Jean meandered through the shoe displays, her delicate hands fingering the soft leathers. Mince had wandered off as she had a tendency to do.

"Let's get that right shoe off and measure for the exact size," Madeira said.

When Madeira had finished measuring, she disappeared into the open doorway behind the shoe displays, and Elizabeth sat straight-backed, her legs crossed at the knees, nylon toes dancing in the air to the store's music. New shoes, even new work shoes, were a reason to be pleased. She could not remember the last time she had purchased shoes for herself. Glancing at their reflection in the mirror, Elizabeth was surprised to see her face relaxed and smiling.

Madeira returned, balancing a stack of shoe boxes. One by one, the woman slipped Elizabeth's foot into the shoes. Elizabeth paid close attention to the prices labeled on each box, and when the cost was out of her price range, the shoe did not fit for one reason or another.

"Let me take another look at what we have in your size," Madeira purred, as she carried the tower of shoe boxes back into the storeroom. Elizabeth was grateful for Madeira's discretion, but Carol Jean's face was pink with embarrassment. It pained Elizabeth to see how Carol Jean felt about being there with her, and Elizabeth was thankful they were the only ones in the store. She was disappointed when the door's bell jangled, and a flash of hot air signaled someone else had entered.

Madeira hurried from the storage room. "Audrey, what brings you out on a sweltering day like today? That sweet daughter of yours will melt in this awful heat."

Mrs. Clayton Landers waved a kerchief in a half-hearted greeting, then dabbed it across her upper lip and up the back of her sun-tanned neck, beneath her bleached blond page boy.

"Madeira Prince, as I live and breathe, you have the best job in this whole town! I swear, if my husband's pickle plant had air conditioning, I'd be there on the line myself."

At her side, Audrey Landers' daughter, Cynthia, a plump duplicate of her mother, stood sulking. Elizabeth wanted to disappear into thin air before Audrey could notice her, but even if that was possible, Cynthia would surely find Mince.

"We've been so lazy, lounging at the pool and at our cottage, I thought we should do something productive. What's more productive than shopping?"

Audrey laughed a deep, gravelly smoker's laugh, crinkly lines fanning out around her eyes as she scanned the room. "Is this the beautiful Carol Jean Dembrowski? Why, you've grown a foot since I've seen you last."

"Thank you, Mrs. Landers." The girl's eyelashes fluttered and her cheeks flushed. "Yes, I have grown up a lot, I guess."

Elizabeth understood Carol Jean was impressed with the wealth and lifestyle of Audrey Landers, and that her daughter enjoyed the woman's attention. Mince, on the other hand, had darted behind a rack of shirts. Poor Nona wasn't quick enough.

"Of course, this is little Nona. Aren't you the prettiest thing ever? What lovely brown curls and blue eyes, like a darkened Shirley Temple."

"Thank you ma'am," Nona sparkled.

Elizabeth stood, placing herself between Nona and Audrey, who was a magician at hiding an insult inside a compliment.

"Mom, there's Mince. Hi, Mince!" Cynthia waved. Elizabeth worried Mince would try to avoid Cynthia in order to avoid Mrs. Landers. Instead, Mince surprised her and walked toward the girl.

"Hi, Cynthia."

Like a snake on the strike, Mrs. Landers reached out and grabbed Mince's arm with her long, poppy-colored fingernails. "Minerva, you can't hide from me. Why, look at you, already brown as a walnut. I do believe you have more muscles than anyone I know, girl or boy!"

Rather than being insulted, Elizabeth felt Audrey had delivered a compliment to Mince, who prided herself on being strong and muscular. Calling her Minerva was another issue. It was her given name all right, but few dared say it out loud, or at least, to her face. Eddie used it sometimes in anger, but that's why he had named her Minerva in the first place. After Carol Jean, Mince was supposed to be a boy, Eddie's boy, for him to name and raise. Only Elizabeth and, in time, Mince, recognized that naming her Minerva was a punishment for both Mince, the baby girl, and Elizabeth, who should have produced a boy. Thank goodness for Elizabeth's father, William, who had held Mince as a newborn baby, admired her tiny face topped with dark, wispy hair, and declared she was as sweet as mincemeat pie. From that moment, everyone called her Mince.

Audrey's loud voice carried throughout the store. "Come along, Cynthia. You're practically bursting out of your shorts already this summer. I think we should cut back on your ice cream, darling."

Elizabeth breathed a sigh of relief as Audrey and Cynthia started for the girls' clothing section. To Elizabeth's dismay, Audrey turned around and strutted straight toward the counter where Madeira worked the register, and where Elizabeth stood waiting, purse in hand.

"I think these will work fine for you, and though they aren't leather and the crepe soles are somewhat thinner, they'll last for the summer," Madeira offered. "That will be $12.60 with the tax."

Elizabeth leafed through the pile of twelve one dollar bills in her hand, then placed them on the counter. "I think I might have the exact change." As she began shuffling through her purse, dagger-like fingertips tapped her arm.

"Such depressing news about the mill, Lizzie," Audrey said. "So many people out of work and no prospects for the future."

With her hands digging in her purse, Elizabeth looked straight into the woman's heavily made-up eyes.

"How sweet of you to be concerned, Audrey, but I'm not worried. Tomorrow, I start work for Clay, at the pickle factory."

"Clayton is nothing, if not generous, to those down on their luck. We have always prided ourselves on helping our community, and you, of course, are part of that community."

Elizabeth wanted to slap this crude woman who deserved none of what was in her life, especially Clayton. Instead, she lifted her chin and smiled. "Yes, he is generous. He personally saw to it I was hired, and I expressed my gratitude to him."

"Like I said, generous. Good luck at the factory. I know it is very hard work, but you are an old farm girl, so you should be able to handle all the smells, noise, and back-breaking labor." Elizabeth had ceased searching in her purse, aware she did not have enough money to pay for the shoes.

Audrey tossed a ten-dollar bill on the counter and beamed at Elizabeth. "Here, let me. A girl can't stand on her feet all day without the proper footwear."

Elizabeth looked at the money on the counter, her jaw tightening like a lock. "Thank you for your offer, Audrey, but that is not necessary."

Willing her voice to be steady and blinking back tears, Elizabeth said, "Madeira, I appreciate your help, but I think I'll pass on the shoes today. Good to see you both."

"Girls, time to leave," Elizabeth said. Carol Jean brushed past her and headed out the door without a word. Mince followed, and Nona reached for Elizabeth's hand as they left the store.

"I think we'll save those popsicles for another day," Elizabeth said.

When Nona whined in disappointment, Mince took her little sister's hand and skipped down the sidewalk toward Carol Jean, who was a block ahead of them. Elizabeth kept walking, discouraged because she hadn't purchased the shoes she needed, but a little proud of how she had stood up to Audrey Landers. Up ahead, Mince and Nona yelled for Carol Jean to wait for them, and when they caught up, the two older sisters put Nona between them, swinging their hands, and making Nona bubble with laughter. Elizabeth's face broke into a smile.

BAD NEWS

ELIZABETH WAS GRATEFUL HER FIRST DAY AT LANDERS was over. The factory was steamy and clamored with the noise of machines and people. Her eyes and nose burned from the brine smells and acidic air, her feet ached from standing in her old, worn shoes all day, and her hands were raw from handling the rough produce. Growing up on a farm, Elizabeth was accustomed to hard and dirty work, but the conveyor line was relentless and demanding, with none of the gratification and pleasure of the farm work she had grown up doing. Punching out, she hoped for the strength to return in the morning.

As she turned off Elm Street into her driveway, Elizabeth could see Mince and Nona waiting to greet her. Tilting the rearview mirror toward her, Elizabeth saw the exhaustion seared into her face, her cheeks shiny and red, like apples rubbed on blue jeans. Telltale tears began to tumble from her eyes, and she brushed them away, angry at herself for being so weak. It had been such a hard day, but it was the girls that mattered, and she needed to be strong.

"I'm so glad to be home," she said as she stepped from the car. "Look how beautiful you are." Elizabeth gathered them in a gentle embrace.

"Momma, Momma, we cleaned and weeded and danced!" Nona bubbled. "And we ate blueberries, but only ten each." Nona held up both hands, fingers fanned out. "Mostly we waited for you to come back."

Elizabeth touched Nona's flushed, pink cheeks. "Thank you, my darlings, for being so good. I am certain you did a wonderful job, so you deserved a few berries after working hard."

"Today was okay, except for Carol Jean being bossy," Mince said, "and grouchy."

"I'm guessing she's watching American Bandstand," Elizabeth said, understanding her oldest daughter was embarrassed by her mother's job at the pickle factory.

They walked across the yard, Lucky lumbering behind. Mince carried Elizabeth's lunch pail, a dented, rusting one Eddie once used to take to the mill.

Before they reached the porch, the screen door flapped open, and Carol Jean sulked out.

"The stupid phone's not working. You have to tell the phone company, because I cannot live without a telephone."

"I decided the phone is a luxury we can't afford this summer and stopped the service."

"How am I supposed to talk to my friends and do stuff this summer?"

"Stop your whining, Carol Jean. Now, let me get inside, and we'll talk about this later!"

"That's not fair. It's the one thing I had that my friends had, and now that's gone. I hate it here!" Carol Jean slammed back inside, stomping as best she could in bare feet.

Elizabeth looked at Mince and Nona, their faces deflated and unhappy. "She'll get over it in a day or two," Elizabeth said. "Now, tell me, is your father home?"

"He walked downtown to do something," Nona said.

"Apply for unemployment," Mince offered, "and he was real busy doing stuff all morning, working in the garage." Elizabeth was relieved to hear Eddie applied for unemployment compensation. With unemployment money and her wages, they might make it until the men were called back to the mill.

"Thank you, Mince." Elizabeth touched Mince's nose and lifted her chin. "Now, how about a glass of lemonade and a sit in the back-yard so you can tell me all about your day."

"Please, Momma, tell us all about the pickles," Nona begged, holding her nose.

"I will, and I promise it was not as bad as it smells!"

They were walking up the steps when a truck pulled into the driveway, and Eddie tumbled from the cab. He waved the pickup away, pounding the hood with his fist, laughing as the vehicle backed out, horn honking.

"Looks like the working woman is home from the salt mines." His speech was slurred, eyes red-rimmed and glassy.

"Hi, Pops!" Nona reached for her father to pick her up, but he side-stepped her and went inside, yelling, "Get in here before you let those damn flies inside."

"Girls," Elizabeth said, "stay outside. Let me change into some-thing that doesn't smell like pickles, and I'll get the lemonade. Take Lucky with you." Elizabeth felt a storm coming and sent her daugh-ters hurrying for cover.

Inside, Eddie was rummaging in the refrigerator, where he found a package of bologna in the meat drawer. He peeled several slices from the stack, rolled them, and stuffed them into his mouth.

"How was your big day at the famous Landers Pickle Factory?" he asked, bologna bits spurting out.

It was a loaded question with no right response. "It was about what you would expect, I guess. Hot, smelly, noisy, full of pickles. I earned a little bit, so that's something."

"What a relief, because I didn't earn one cent. Oh, and by the way, there is no unemployment money. Somehow over the years the insurance was underpaid or not paid at all, and nobody noticed." Eddie spun an empty beer bottle on the counter like the losing turn of a roulette wheel. "Now, the mill's being investigated by the government, which moves slower than shit in a constipated bull, so all financial records are stuck. Nobody gets any money until things are straightened out, and that could take months, maybe years."

Wanting to avoid an argument, Elizabeth said nothing. Without changing her clothes, she grabbed plastic cups and the pitcher of lemonade, and turned to go outside. Over her shoulder, she could see Eddie still spinning the bottle. If things went as usual, he would pass out on the couch for awhile, and she would be alone with her daughters. Outside, as she poured drinks for the girls, Elizabeth thought she was like one of those doomed pickles at the factory, moving along the conveyor belt, powerless to change their destiny, edging ever closer to the end of the line.

That evening, around the supper table, Nona and Carol Jean carried on in their usual way, laughing and jabbering about nothing in particular. Elizabeth encouraged the empty prattle, for the longer they talked, the less chance there was that Eddie could upset the meal. Most days, he was like a shook-up soda pop bottle, on the verge of blowing.

It wasn't always this way. Before Nona's condition worsened, before Eddie's drinking became a problem and the abuse started, before the mill stalled, they had almost been happy. She remembered a picnic at the County Park, where their family had shared a blanket, Eddie's arm resting around her shoulders. They had eaten cheese sandwiches spread thick with yellow mustard and had munched crisp dill pickles, the last jar from the season before. Mince played catch with her father, trying her hardest to be the boy Eddie had wanted her to be. While Carol Jean was hesitant to wade out into the cold water of the bay, Mince dove in head first, right behind Eddie. They both surfaced a few feet from shore, sputtering and hollering about how cold the water was. It had been a good day.

"Mom, you haven't told us about your first day at Landers," Carol Jean said, moving her uneaten creamed potatoes around her plate. Elizabeth stared at her oldest daughter, and ever so slightly shook her head in the girl's direction, hoping Carol Jean would get her message, but it was already too late.

"Yes, tell us all about your important first day at the pickle factory." Eddie's voice was coated with sarcasm.

"May I please be excused?" Mince bolted up to make a quick exit, like in a fire drill at school. Eddie was faster and pulled Mince back down to her chair.

"You all sit awhile and hear about this fascinating first day," he ordered, directing his words towards Elizabeth, who sat frozen at the end of the table.

Elizabeth cleared her throat. "There's not much to tell. I'm on the intake line in receiving, which means the conveyor belt where the produce is first dumped. The workers, including myself, sort through everything passing along on the belt to remove stems, blossoms, dirt and other foreign matter, and we remove damaged, rotten or over-sized pickles."

Her husband laughed. "That was fascinating, wasn't it? Such an important job, sorting through pickles all day. It's a wonder she qualified for the job, with all the skills it requires, right Minerva?" His rough, calloused hand still gripped Mince's arm.

Before Mince could reply, Nona reached for her glass of milk, knocking it over into the center of the table. Elizabeth bolted up, dabbing the puddle with her apron, as she soothed her youngest, who was in tears. "It's all right, Love. It's only milk."

"That's great," Eddie snarled, "letting them think it's okay to waste milk. Your daughters have no appreciation for anything! Stuff costs money, money we don't have, and money we're not going to get any time soon."

Summoning the girls from their chairs at the supper table, Elizabeth directed them out the back door. "I'll call you when it's time to do the dishes." She kept her voice light and cheery.

She watched through the screen door as Carol Jean and Lucky, with Nona trudging and wheezing, walked to the apple tree at the edge of the yard. Mince trailed behind, pausing to look back towards the house. Elizabeth waved and smiled.

"Last one up has to wash dishes tonight!" Carol Jean shouted back at Mince. Elizabeth could tell it didn't matter if Mince was last anyway, since it was her turn to wash.

Elizabeth watched as the girls reached the back of their yard near the river, where the ancient apple tree sprawled. Its muscled, rippling branches stretched out long and low, with a knack for growing together and spreading apart to form perfect perches, for sitting or hiding. It could be a hotel or a rocket ship, a school room or a stage. No matter what, her girls loved that old tree more than anything, except for Lucky. They scurried up with practiced abandon, leaving their dog circling the massive trunk, yapping at their aerial antics. Elizabeth felt her tired face smile, but the smile faded as she returned to the supper table.

Elizabeth, feeling relieved now that the girls were outside, poured Eddie a cup of coffee. Then she sat, not at her place at the other end of the table, but in Mince's spot, beside him.

"What's this really about?"

He turned the cup, its milky brown coffee rolling in lazy circles. "It's about getting our jobs back, that's what. The mill has gotta get back on its feet so we can start working again. Without that mill, we're done for."

Elizabeth raised a cup to her lips, green eyes peering over its edge. "We knew this day would come, Ed, and there's no denying it. They were running that mill purely for profit, with no regard for what's right or wrong or for what was happening to the town, the river, not to mention the air. Think about Nona. She's not getting any better and the conditions here are making her worse." Elizabeth's coffee cup remained at eye level, shielding her face.

He spoke, not to her, but to his calloused hands. "Running that mill for profit was what paid our wages, what kept us working. People will always get sick from one thing or another, whether its a dirty river, a hog bite, or a sneeze sprayed in your face. Right or wrong don't count for much when there's no food in the pantry or roof over your head. That's the road we're on, and it's a mighty short one."

When he stood up, Elizabeth pushed herself back from the table, placing her cup on its saucer. "At least we're on that road together, as a family. As long as we have one another, it'll all work out."

"Yeah, little Miss Mary Sunshine, let me know when it's all worked out. It'll probably be about the same time we stumble into that pot of gold at the end of the rainbow!" Her husband walked out of the house, the back screen door rattling on its rusting hinges.

Elizabeth followed Eddie outside and watched from the porch as he backed the car down the driveway. Across the yard, she could see the girls, carefree as they climbed the apple tree down by the river. On most days, she would have cautioned them to be careful, but today, she didn't have the strength to say the words. The exhaustion of working at Landers and realizing that there still would not be enough money to keep them going caused her to feel drained and unable to move.

HE MEANS WHAT HE SAYS

ELIZABETH AND THE GIRLS SPENT THE NEXT DAY AT the Sloan farm, picking strawberries with her parents. Working together harvesting the fruits and vegetables grown on the farm was a family tradition Elizabeth was proud to share with her daughters. Later that day, they set up a stand downtown in front of Prince's store to sell their portion of the bountiful crop. When they arrived home in the late afternoon, Elizabeth was hoping Eddie would not be there. Since supper the previous evening, she and Eddie had not spoken, and she wouldn't mind keeping things that way. Instead, when Elizabeth and the girls walked in the door, Eddie was waiting for them. He had baked the casserole Elizabeth prepared before she left that morning, and he had fixed a lettuce salad as well. He was smiling and talkative, a tactic often used to lull Elizabeth and their daughters into believing things were all right. Sometimes they were, but most times he was on the verge of exploding. She was suspicious of his good mood. It all seemed too easy.

"Good news," he informed them. "The mayor visited our picket lines today and thinks the governor is interested enough to talk to us."

Elizabeth understood it was unwise to let down her guard. Maybe there was no anger behind his cheery mood, but her past experiences with Eddie made it a long shot. Perhaps this one time, she thought, we will all share a civil, well-mannered meal in peace, like a real family.

"Is the governor like a sheriff?" Nona wanted to know. "I think he should arrest everybody at the mill. They took our money!" Her face was flushed with heat and fatigue.

"Such talk, Love." Elizabeth's hand, by habit, felt Nona's forehead and cheeks. "Everyone go upstairs and wash for supper. It looks like your father has given me a present tonight!"

"Is it your birthday, Momma? Can I help you unwrap it? Do we all get a present?" Nona loved presents.

Mince turned Nona by the shoulders, marching her towards Carol Jean, who was halfway up the stairs. "Not that kind of present. Pops has supper ready, and that's a present for everybody!"

Good moods hovered throughout the meal. Eddie felt progress might be possible if the governor became involved, giving hope that the mill would end the layoff. Until such time, the workers might receive their unemployment compensation benefits.

"There's no guarantee on when he'll take action, but it looks like we're on his list of places to visit. That will put the focus on all the jobs that are on the line and might get the mill running again."

"If they re-open the mill, will they make cleaning up the river a priority? Will they do something to help the town recover from everything the mill's done?" Elizabeth asked.

"Right now, we need our jobs back. All that other crap doesn't matter without a paycheck to cover our bills." Eddie's voice had that edge, the one like a knife blade, and his eyes locked onto her face with a frigid stare.

Elizabeth recognized the signals that Eddie was becoming agitated. Arguing was not helpful, so she changed the subject before he lost his temper.

"Tell Pops about your day selling berries," she said to the three girls.

"We made over fifty dollars!" Carol Jean said.

"And we sold all of the berries, except for one quart sort of left over, thanks to Mrs. Landers," Mince said.

"What did fancy-pants Audrey Landers do?" Eddie was in the middle of a mouthful of casserole.

"Nothing, really, and besides, she paid us twenty dollars when all she owed was about three dollars, and then she told us to keep the change!" Carol Jean added.

"But she probably ate up the difference in rescue berries, you know, what she needed to keep her from fainting," Mince said. "I think she was faking it so she could sit down and eat free berries." Mince had a way with recognizing motives, Elizabeth thought.

"It was pretty hot outside. Anybody could have felt woozy," Carol Jean reasoned.

"We did come out ahead on the money she paid," Mince said.

Elizabeth could feel Carol Jean and Mince's desperation as they struggled to explain away what had happened. Here they were again, falling deep into the dark pit where Eddie stored his anger.

"Let me get this straight. You saved Mrs. Landers from keeling over in the heat by feeding her free strawberries, and then she overpaid you for the produce you sold her? Sounds like everybody made out fine!" Eddie was smiling, but the girls were not. Elizabeth watched them waiting for the rage to follow, like wounded wild things, their eyes blinking and mouths chewing in silence.

It was Nona who did not know enough to remain quiet. "Why does she hate us so much, Momma? We always smile nice at her and act polite."

Before Elizabeth could answer her daughter, Eddie spoke, his voice part smooth, part jagged, like a saw blade. "See, it isn't you girls Audrey Landers has the problem with. It's your Momma. Yep, that's right. Your Momma's fan club is missing a couple of members, Audrey Landers being one of them."

"Ed, let's forget about it. We sold all the berries, we earned some money, so the day was a success, right girls?"

The girls didn't have a chance to respond, because Eddie continued in a loud voice. "Like an elephant, some folks don't forget a thing, ever. Take Audrey Landers, for instance. It's been years since your Momma and ole Clayton Landers were a couple, but his wife can't let it go."

"A couple is definitely something Clay and I were not, except for a couple of friends, and that's all."

"Besides," Carol Jean said, "she was YOUR Homecoming queen, right, Pops, because you were the captain of the football team?"

A lump formed in Elizabeth's throat as she recognized her oldest daughter's attempt to disarm the conversation and put her father in the spotlight.

"She sure was. Even though we were both elected on our own, when we sat together in that convertible during the Homecoming parade, your Momma took one look at me, and she fell head over heels in love with yours truly."

"You had a real convertible, Pops?" Nona's admiration was complete.

"It was a convertible, like a fancy limousine, with our very own driver, named Clayton Landers."

"Whose convertible was it, Pops?" Nona wondered.

"It was Clayton Landers' car, wasn't it, Pops?" Mince asked.

"He had the fancy car, but I had the girl. All he could do was drive that pickle-green convertible down Main Street, turning green with envy to match. Poor little Clayton Landers."

"Clayton Landers isn't poor, Pops. He has a pickle factory!" Nona proudly exclaimed, unaware of the fire she was igniting.

Elizabeth placed her hands on Nona's shoulders. "It's time to head upstairs for a bath, little girl." She was desperate to stop the discussion and escort her daughters out of the room, but Carol Jean had to add one more comment.

"He lives in a beautiful house with a swimming pool and everything." Elizabeth could hear the admiration in Carol Jean's voice.

Eddie's fist landed like a boulder on the table, rattling dishes, silverware, and the family seated there. Elizabeth flinched as her daughters jumped at the sound. They were wide-eyed and sat frozen in their chairs.

"You think he's so great, why not go live with Mr. Rich Guy. Come to think of it, you look an awful lot like that big shot. Maybe he's your real daddy. Let's see how much you admire him when he throws you out with the rest of the trash."

Carol Jean pushed away from the supper table and fled the room, her face pelted with angry tears.

"That's right, get out! All of you, get out of my sight and out of my house!"

"Eddie, you don't mean that. He doesn't mean that." Elizabeth was already moving Mince and Nona out of the room, to higher ground, away from the flood of their father's fury. When they reached the top of the stairs, Elizabeth heard a chair scrape the wood floor below, followed by Eddie's footsteps thudding toward the steps leading upstairs.

"Go ahead girls. Everything will be okay." Nona ran down the hall towards Carol Jean's bedroom, but Mince stood her ground.

"Go on, Mince," Elizabeth said, giving the girl a push. "Shut the door for now."

The fire in Mince's eyes told Elizabeth she was not going willingly, but when Elizabeth started walking towards her, Mince disappeared into the bedroom, slamming the door behind her.

From the bottom of the stairs, Eddie shouted, his voice echoing its way to Elizabeth.

"That's where you're wrong, Lizzie. I always mean what I say."

TREE CLIMBING AND A FISH FRY

IT WAS SATURDAY, THE ONE FOLLOWING ELIZABETH'S third week at the pickle factory. Being brought up on a farm, early rising was in her nature, so although it was her day off, she looked forward to the hazy sunrise of a summer morning. She sat down on the top basement step to put on her sturdy gardening shoes and was surprised when she felt Nona's warm hands cover her eyes.

"Guess who!"

"I guess it's Lucky!"

"No, silly, it can't be Lucky. He has paws, and these are fingers, see?"

Elizabeth opened her eyes to find the girl's fingers spread out in front of her face.

"I guess it's Nona." Elizabeth laughed, pulling her in close and kissing her cheek. "Come outside with me to see the beautiful morning sky."

The two walked hand in hand through the backyard's prickly grass, with Lucky snuffling behind them. They sat beneath the apple tree, the bare branches above providing only a crackling of shadow, but it was early, and they didn't need much shade. The river lumbered along before them, and though the air that morning was clear and lacked its usual pungent smell, Elizabeth would not allow Nona to get any closer to the water.

It was cooler outside than in the house, so Nona's flushed cheeks faded to pale. She liked to sing songs her grandmother or Elizabeth had taught her, making up words and rhymes and notes as she went along. Elizabeth joined in on occasion, but mostly she kept quiet, preferring to listen to her little girl sing, in a voice reserved for someone much older.

During the week, it was Mince who joined Elizabeth for an early morning breakfast of cornflakes and toast. Together they would make Elizabeth's lunch, stifling their giggles so they would not wake Eddie. By five thirty, Elizabeth would rush out the door, throwing kisses and last minute instructions at Mince. The girls were left to handle the household, working their way down the list of tasks Elizabeth had taped to the refrigerator door. She was thankful that today Mince was still sleeping, for a time relieved of the responsibilities the young girl accepted without complaint.

A yell through the screen door from Eddie pierced the morning's tranquility. "There's work that needs doing. Get those lazy daughters of yours out of bed." He clattered down the back porch steps, metal lunch pail in hand.

As Elizabeth and Nona approached the house, Eddie said, "I'll be on the picket line all day. Don't hold up supper for me." Elizabeth thought that, like every day since the layoff, he'd be with the other union men until late, ending the day drinking and playing dice.

"Bye, Pops! We love you! Don't be a stranger!" Nona called, waving and skipping down the gravel driveway after him. Lucky trotted along behind.

"Get back here, both of you. Pops has important business." Elizabeth tried to keep the relief from seeping into her voice. These days, with Eddie spending time on the picket line at the mill, things at home were going all right.

"Come on! I know two sisters who need waking!" Elizabeth, Nona and Lucky bounded into the house.

Later that morning, bending over the leaf lettuce in the garden, Elizabeth worried. She had watered as usual, but it never seemed to be enough. Everything looked wilted and pale, like a limp, faded dishrag. It was the heat, and even though summers were always hot, this year it was hotter than average and so dry. They hadn't had rain for weeks, and the winds blew searing, angry gusts, drying the life out of plants and trees. Listening to the rattling of the apple tree's sparse leaves, she wondered if there would be enough garden produce to sell now that their early summer moneymakers, the strawberries, were nearly finished for the season. If it would only rain, maybe their luck would change, and maybe good things would begin to happen.

"We're all done inside!" Mince called, galloping toward the apple tree. "Let's climb!"

Elizabeth straightened up from her weeding. "Be careful in that old tree, Mince. Stay away from the river side. Climb on this side where the branches are stronger." Elizabeth gazed past her daughter, following along the edge of the river's contaminated water. The land was barren and dead, and no vegetation, not even their beloved apple tree, could survive the poisons the water contained.

"Mince, wait for me!" Nona huffed, as her running slowed from a trot to a walk.

Elizabeth smiled as Mince came back, took Nona by the hand and walked with her toward the apple tree. Mince called Lucky to follow them, but Elizabeth was certain the old dog would avoid the heat. He had lifted one disinterested eyebrow as the girls passed, then remained stretched out in the shade of the garage.

Carol Jean sauntered from the house, blowing on her wet nail polish. "I'm only playing if we can be Hollywood stars and live in an apartment. I'm Kim Novak, and Mince, you can be Sandra Dee. Nona, you can be Audrey Hepburn." With parts assigned, Carol Jean strutted to the apple tree and began climbing.

"I'll have the penthouse on the top floor," Carol Jean called down to her sisters, "and you two can have your pick of any other apartment."

Carol Jean was strong and agile, and Elizabeth watched as the girl climbed with ease, her familiarity with each branch evident as she rose higher and higher.

Not far behind, Mince hesitated, then settled into the third crook of the main trunk as her older sister climbed. "I choose this spot right down here. It's the best place for an apartment."

Leaving the garden to keep a closer watch on Nona sitting in the first split of the lower trunk, Elizabeth squinted up into the sunlight sprinkling through the sparse leaves to where Carol Jean was spiraling upward to the river side of the old tree. The light flicked like camera flashes around her eldest daughter's silhouette, stopped near the tree top.

There was a crack, like the snap of a wooden rake handle, followed by the sound of Carol Jean, tumbling from above. Elizabeth watched helplessly as her daughter fell, tree limbs popping and groaning in her futile attempts to gain a hold. Landing on her back with a thud, Carol Jean was surrounded by broken sticks and dead leaves, beneath the jagged shaft she'd cleared through the tree branches up above.

"That's what you get for showing off!" Mince yelled. She leaped to the ground, with Nona close behind.

Elizabeth was already kneeling beside the fallen girl, who was struggling to breathe.

"Is she dead?" Nona whispered.

"Of course, she's not dead, goofy! Her eyes are open," Mince said.

Carol Jean moaned and inhaled a shaky breath, then moaned louder. "My arm . . . I think my arm is broken!"

"Don't move, Carol Jean!" Elizabeth ordered as she examined the girl's arm. "Nona, stay here with Carol Jean. Mince, come with me!"

Nona sat down next to Carol Jean and stroked her hair. "It'll be all right, Kim Novak. Remember, you are only make-believe. Your arm is only pretend hurt. I'll be your pretend nurse and will make you all better."

"Nona, don't touch Carol Jean's arm. Sit with her, okay? We'll be right back."

Elizabeth and Mince, with Lucky trailing behind, ran for the house. Once inside, Elizabeth began rummaging in a kitchen drawer as she gave directions to Mince. "Go to the bedroom closet and get the rest of the lace curtain money. Pick up my purse and the car keys."

"Wait," Elizabeth said, pulling out a halter apron. "Write a note telling your father to come to the hospital as soon as he can." She gave Mince a push toward the bedroom and then turned on the run, slamming out the back door.

By the time Elizabeth reached the apple tree, Carol Jean's moans were whimpers, and her face was the color of worn concrete. Nona sat cross-legged by her side, singing a song about a star named Kim Novak that fell from the sky one day. She patted Carol Jean's head in a soft rhythm.

"This will hold your arm in place until we get to the hospital," Elizabeth told Carol Jean as she folded the apron into a makeshift sling. "Try not to move it. Don't worry. Everything will be all right."

Elizabeth, Carol Jean, and Nona were making their way to the car in the driveway when Mince leapt down the porch stairs, her mother's purse in one hand and the car keys in the other.

Mince and Nona climbed into the back seat while Elizabeth helped Carol Jean into the front. As Elizabeth backed out, the car jostled with every graveled dip and bump.

"It hurts, Mom," Carol Jean said.

"I know, Love. We'll be at the hospital soon."

Pulling away from the house, Elizabeth gripped the steering wheel and accelerated, the tires spinning with the effort. She glanced another worried look at Carol Jean, then turned towards the back seat.

"Mince, is Nona okay?"

"She looks about normal." Mince paused. "There is one thing. I couldn't find the money."

"Did you look in the sewing box, underneath all the notions?" Even as she said it, Elizabeth knew.

"It wasn't in the sewing box."

"It's okay," Elizabeth said, telling a lie because the truth would not help.

Hours later, they returned home. As Elizabeth entered the driveway, she glanced into her rearview mirror. Nona was sleeping, her head on Mince's lap, and Carol Jean was resting against Mince's shoulder. Carol Jean's arm was in a thick, white cast reaching from her wrist to her upper arm.

"Mince, would you help Carol Jean upstairs?"

Mince nodded, and the two made their way toward the house. Elizabeth coaxed Nona awake and carried her up the porch steps. At the screen door, an anxious Lucky whimpered, lurching outside as soon as the door was opened.

"Nona, sit here and watch Lucky for a minute while I check on Carol Jean."

"Is Carol Jean going to be okay?"

"Yes, the doctor fixed her arm, and now, all it has to do is heal. Remember, stay put, and watch so Lucky doesn't wander out of the yard. I'll be right back."

Rushing through the house and up the stairs to Carol Jean's room, Elizabeth almost collided with Mince, who was closing her sister's bedroom door.

"She's sleeping. Told me to get lost, closed her eyes, and started snoring."

"It's the pain medication. For the next few days, she'll be sleeping quite a bit." Elizabeth opened the door and peeked inside where Carol Jean was deep in sleep. Together, Elizabeth and Mince went downstairs, arm in arm.

"We are a good team, aren't we?" Elizabeth asked. As they entered the kitchen, they encountered Eddie, his arms holding several bags.

"I'm home and smell the fish fry!" Eddie set down the brown bags dotted with oily spots and smelling of fried perch and french fries. "Where is everybody?"

"Here I am Pops! What did you bring us?" Nona had followed Pops inside and proceeded to pull up a chair to peer into the bags.

Elizabeth walked toward him. "Where were you, Ed? Why didn't you come to the hospital?"

Before he could answer, Mince interjected. "Yeah, Pops, I wrote you a note, see?" She tugged the paper from beneath the fish fry bags and handed it to him as he sat down at the kitchen table.

"How the heck was I supposed to read this, when I just got home? What happened now? Is Carol Jean all right?"

"She will be." Elizabeth's voice was soft, but her insides felt like granite. "Her arm was broken in two places. She'll have to wear the cast for several weeks, but at least she won't need surgery. Right now, she's resting."

Eddie leaned forward and grabbed Nona, hoisting her onto his lap. "You still didn't say what happened."

"We were movie stars in a 'partment," Nona offered. "Kim Novak, that's Carol Jean, had to have the henhouse, and she went way up high. That's when the tree broke." Nona's small hand patted her father's whiskered cheeks.

"That rotten old tree! It was only a matter of time before someone got hurt!"

"It wasn't the tree's fault," Mince said in its defense. "Carol Jean climbed up too far, and she was on the sick side of the tree, where the branches are bare and not strong enough."

"You kids stay out of that old tree from now on," Eddie said. "It's unsafe."

Then he turned to Elizabeth. "Lizzie, I make the decision about going to the hospital. I'm sick and tired of those crooks stealing my hard-earned money."

"Did you hear me say her arm was broken in two places, Eddie? There was no time to wait for you to make that decision."

"Next time, make time. We've wasted too much money on hospitals and doctors. We're not doing it any more." As Eddie spoke, Elizabeth watched Nona, hoping she had not connected his words with her many medical visits.

"Every time some little thing happens to one of those girls, you're off to get some sort of medical treatment, and nothing changes." Eddie dug into the bags, pulling out greasy cardboard containers.

"The food's here so we might as well eat it. You've already wasted enough money today. No sense throwing food away."

"Girls, go up to your rooms." Elizabeth pushed the two youngsters out of the kitchen. "I'll call you down for supper in a bit. Go on now, and do as I say."

"But the fish fry," Nona whined. "What about the perch and the french fries?"

Mince grabbed Nona's small hand and tugged her toward the stairs. "Mom wants to set it all up, you know, for a celebration. Let's go up and wash your hands and face so you are all clean."

Elizabeth walked to the sink and began scrubbing dishes under the faucet. Eddie crossed the room, leaning his backside against the sink. "Like always, you've taken the fun out of everything. I don't understand you sometimes, Lizzie."

She lifted her eyes, not to him, but to the unadorned window above the sink. "Understand this, Ed. I never have asked for much, and you know that. That money in the sewing box was put away for something special. I saved that money and now it's gone. Is that how you bought the fish fries, and the beer, and . . ."

Eddie grabbed Elizabeth's chin with his rough, calloused hand, forcing her to look at him. She raised her eyes, looking past the bristly stubble spread over his face. His nose was glossy and reddened, its pores dark like pepper. Her gaze reached his cold, blood-shot eyes and stopped.

"You listen to me. A man's got a right to all the money in his house. If I want to treat my kids to a fish fry or buy myself a beer, then, I will. I don't need your permission."

He looked down at her. "That money you saved was mine, earned by me, not you. Just because it went into the family pot doesn't make it less mine. Speaking of the family pot, where's that pickle paycheck of yours? Are we living in the lap of luxury yet?"

"My paycheck is gone, Ed, all gone, like the money in the sewing basket."

She pushed his hand away from her face and stepped back from his grasp. "Doctors and hospitals don't treat patients for free. I had to cash my check to pay for Carol Jean, so, I guess, the family pot is empty."

Elizabeth pulled dishes from the nearby cupboard and started setting the table, her hands shaking as she arranged the scratched, yellowed plates. When Mince and Nona returned from upstairs, they sat down at their places.

"Is this a celebration?" Nona asked, eyes moving from parent to parent.

"It was." Eddie began tossing food onto his daughters' plates.

The two girls studied what landed in front of them. Forks in hand, they poked at the cold, chewy perch and the greasy, limp fries.

"What's the matter? Food not good enough for you?" Eddie spoke through a mouthful of fish, scattering chewed bits onto the table.

"I don't like cold fish," Nona said, eyes staring at the perch on her plate.

"The cole slaw leaked onto the rye bread. The fries are icky," Mince added. She held up a drooping french fry, bending to the coming storm.

Eddie bolted from the table, hurled himself around behind his daughters, and grabbed each girl by the back of the neck.

"This food was bought with my hard-earned money, and you will eat it." He shoved their heads down, pushing the girls' faces into the food on their plates. "Now eat!"

"Eddie, stop, you're hurting them." Elizabeth was at his side, pulling his arms and shoulders backward. He flung her off with one swift toss, and she landed hard, her head cracking against the wall.

Elizabeth managed to sit up, braced against the wall now smeared with blood. She shook her bloodied head, trying to clear the cloud blocking her eyes.

What she saw first was the panic in Mince's eyes as the girl begged, "Pops, please. I'm eating, see?" Her words were garbled by the cold perch she'd been chewing. Nona, with short gasping breaths, sobbed into her food.

"Do not leave this table until your plates are empty!"

Elizabeth, still crumpled on the dining room floor, cringed as Eddie circled the table. He picked up Elizabeth's dinner plate and launched it across the room where it shattered against the wall above her head, sending her dinner, pierced with shards of glass, down upon her.

"Lizzie, don't you forget to finish your dinner." He laughed and walked out of the house.

WHAT EDDIE DID

DRY, CRACKLED BREATHS, SLOW AND LABORED, AWAK-
ened Elizabeth early the next morning. Squinting open her left eye,
Elizabeth struggled to see in the dim light. It was Nona, breathing
close to her face. With her little girl fingers, Nona pried open her
mother's other eye and looked into it.

"Are you awake?"

"What's the matter, Nona? Are you sick?" Her hands touched
Nona's face and pressed her tiny chest, gaging its rising and falling.

"I heard a clunking outside, like heavy feet walking. Will you see
what it is, please?"

"Do you promise to go back to bed if I check? It's too early to be
up, even if we go to the early Sunday service. Promise?"

Nona nodded her head up and down, her brown curls bouncing. "I promise. Could I sleep with you? Pretty please?"

Elizabeth reached toward Eddie's side of the bed. It was empty.
"All right. It's nothing anyway, but we will look out back, to be sure."

Protecting Nona from worry and agitation was crucial.
Unnecessary stress caused her weakened heart to become over-
worked and her breathing to be affected. Elizabeth took Nona by
the hand, and the two walked into the kitchen. The heavy wooden
back door was open to the screen, and together, Elizabeth and Nona
peered through it into the yard. There was the sound, a steady,
hard thunk.

At first, Elizabeth couldn't make out anything in the early river mist, its shroud reaching toward the house. They walked down the porch steps, and Elizabeth focused as far as she could until she recognized what it was. Eddie was swinging his ax against the girls' apple tree.

"I know what it is," Elizabeth told Nona in a quiet voice. "There's a fisherman paddling his way down river. You can't see him because of the mist."

"But, there are no fish in the river!"

"Sometimes people still go fishing in the early morning. If there are any fish, that's when to catch them. I can see him now, in a small rowboat. Look." She directed Nona's face towards nothing in particular off in the distance, and Nona nodded in puzzled agreement. Elizabeth turned the girl about and walked her back to the house and into the bedroom.

Elizabeth stayed with Nona until her breathing was even. The peacefulness of the moment was temporary, she thought, picturing how Eddie's actions would shatter the girls.

The dewy grass was cool and slippery as Elizabeth walked, barefooted, towards the river. There was Eddie, stripped to his waist, working the ax against what was left of the tree, now battered and ragged. Its limbs and branches were piled with abandon, reminding Elizabeth of a picture she had once seen. It was of a concentration camp during World War II, where human bodies were discarded in piles, arms and legs entwined in a heap. Elizabeth watched in disbelief as her husband finished his butchery, chopping the tree until it was a slaughtered stump.

"I can't believe you did this!" Elizabeth was standing only a few feet from Eddie when he noticed her.

"Get back in the house, Lizzie." He wiped a drop of sweat off the end of his nose. "This old tree was half dead anyway. It was only a matter of time before somebody got hurt, or worse, from falling out of it."

"The girls will be devastated."

"They'll get over it, if you don't make a big deal out of it." Eddie ran his hammer-sized thumb along the blade of the ax. Then, he walked past Elizabeth and the wounded tree stump, surrounded by its amputated and discarded limbs.

Coming through the mist toward Eddie were two small figures, Nona and Mince.

"Why did you do this!" Mince screamed the words. Elizabeth was surprised at the ferocity in her daughter's voice.

Nona stared ahead, her eyes focused and overflowing with tears. "Pops cut down our tree."

"How could you be so mean?" Mince asked.

Eddie pushed past his daughters, and for a moment, Elizabeth thought he would leave, but back he came, shoulders tense and face sizzling with anger.

"Eddie, don't make this worse!" Elizabeth stepped in to shield the girls, but the man tossed her aside like an old shoe.

With his hands, large as fry pans, he grabbed a handful of Nona's dark curls and Mince's loosened ponytail. They cried and squealed as he yanked until both girls were leaning against him.

"Do not use that tone with me. Speak only when I tell you to, and never, ever, question what I do. Understood?"

"Yes, sir, Pops," Mince managed to say, but Nona was unable to speak, her sobs interrupted by an occasional hiccup and gasp for air.

Releasing his hold on the girls, Eddie flung his faded work shirt over his shoulder. He sauntered past Elizabeth without looking at her, walked down the driveway and disappeared from sight.

"I hate him sometimes!" Nona said. Her breathing was labored and uneven.

"I hate him all the time," Mince said in a hollow voice.

Elizabeth should have admonished her girls for expressing hate for their father, but she could not say the words, because the girls' feelings were justified. She understood their hatred, and it was becoming more and more difficult to shield them from Eddie's anger.

It was after midnight when Elizabeth heard a car pull into the driveway. She closed her eyes and forced herself to relax and breathe deeply. If Eddie looked into the bedroom, she hoped he would believe she was asleep.

She heard him stumbling and cursing his way around the house, and when Eddie turned on the television and dropped like an anchor onto the couch, Elizabeth sighed with relief. After a time, she rose and went to the living room, where Eddie was sprawled, snoring, clothing rumpled and smelling like a tavern. Elizabeth turned off the television, checked to be sure no cigarettes were smoldering anywhere, and turned off the lights.

Tiptoeing back into the bedroom, she sat in the rocking chair, intending to read for a bit. Within minutes, she was sleeping a deep, exhausted sleep. It seemed hours had passed, when she felt warm breaths against her face.

"Wake up, Mom, please wake up."

Mince was next to her ear, whispering. Without a sound, Elizabeth placed a finger to her lips, silencing Mince. Rising from her rocking chair, Elizabeth shuffled to the bedroom door, closing it with a soft click, before she would allow another word. The last thing she needed was Eddie being awakened from his drunken slumber.

"Now, tell me!"

"It's Nona. I don't think she's breathing right, but not like her usual puffing." Mince's words fired like gunshots, punctuated with heaving breaths.

Elizabeth, still shaking off the webs of sleep, cradled Mince's haggard, worried face in her hands. "It's all right, Mince, everything will be okay. Slow down and tell me all that happened."

"I got up to go to the bathroom and looked in Nona's room like usual. At first, I didn't hear anything," Mince said, flicking a tear away from her face, "because she wasn't breathing at all."

Elizabeth, now wide awake, had taken a firm hold of Mince's shoulders.

"I watched her for the longest time. She did breathe, sort of, but short, far-apart breaths. I poked at her arm and hand. They felt real cold," Mince said with exhaustion. "She wouldn't open her eyes, even when I shook her."

No matter how many times Nona suffered one of her episodes, Elizabeth still felt stabbed in the stomach when it happened. The fact that Mince shared the burden of Nona's illness was sometimes more than the woman could bear.

Elizabeth pulled Mince close. "You did fine, Love. We'll take care of her, I promise." Grabbing her daughter's hand, the two moved past the living room where Eddie lay snoring, and tiptoed toward the front hall which led to the stairway.

They double-stepped up the stairs to Nona's room at the top. Elizabeth felt her youngest daughter's skin, usually hot and fever-ish, but now cold and damp. She propped the girl upright, tapped between her shoulder blades and raised her arms. By that time, Carol Jean was awake, blinking her eyes and standing in the doorway.

"Carol Jean, go into the bathroom and run the tub. Don't for-get to close the door." A warm, steamy bath often eased Nona's labored breathing.

"Mince, help me get Nona's pajamas off, and let's see if we can wake her up in the process." The two wriggled the tiny four-year old free of her clothing, tickling her and singing "Jesus Loves Me" over and over. Nona's lids fluttered, but her eyes remained closed. Elizabeth lifted her semi-conscious daughter and walked down the hall to where steam drifted out from around the bathroom door. With care, she placed Nona in the steamy tub, the water bubbling around her toes from the dribbling faucet.

They took turns scooping water over the little girl's shoulders, back and chest, and rubbing her arms and legs, the water-laden air enveloping them like fog. Other times, when this had happened to Nona, within moments she would begin to breathe with a normal cadence. This time, her chest rose and fell with hesitation, and she didn't wake up.

"Turn off the water, Carol Jean, so Nona can hear me better!"

Elizabeth pinched Nona's cheeks and placed her lips against her tiny ears.

"Wake up, Nona, and look at me, please!"

She jostled Nona's face between her hands, but the girl's pale, grey face remained serene and unresponsive. Her lips were purple, and the area around them was tinged with blue. A surge of pure, uncontrolled panic overtook Elizabeth.

"Mom, this isn't working! She looks worse than before," Mince yelled, her voice shaking her mother into action.

As if in slow motion, Elizabeth began to lift Nona from the tub, balancing the girl's slim frame against her own while she wrapped the tiny, limp body in a bath towel.

"Run downstairs for my purse, Mince. Be sure the car keys are there and help your sister lift the garage door. Carol Jean, put on some clothes and back the car out. I'll be right down."

"Are we taking Nona to the hospital again? Pops said not to." Mince's voice was small, like an echo in the distance.

"Yes, we're taking your sister to the hospital. Now, do as I said. Run!" Elizabeth walked with care down the hallway, Nona wrapped in her arms.

Mince edged past them, leapt down the stairwell, and hurried into her parents' room to retrieve her mother's worn purse with the keys in the side pocket. Carol Jean, shirt inside-out and hair uncombed, raced to join Mince, heading for the garage. Elizabeth pulled a nightgown over Nona, lifted her, and began to walk with slow, careful steps. The girls were outside and struggling to lift the heavy tilting garage door as Elizabeth, with Nona, arrived at the back door.

"Squat down and try using your legs. On the count of three, lift!" Carol Jean called out.

"One, two, three, lift!"

The wooden door, braced and hinged with rusty steel, resisted, its springs howling so Elizabeth could hear it inside the house. The screeching ceased, and Elizabeth knew they had succeeded in raising the relic door. She cradled Nona in her arms and was all the way to the bottom porch step when Eddie's hand gripped her shoulder from behind.

"Where ya going, Lizzie?"

"I'm taking Nona to the hospital this time, Ed. She's in a bad way." Elizabeth attempted to pull away from his grasp, but his hands were like shackles holding her.

"We've been through this before. It doesn't do a lick of good to take her to that place."

"It's different this time. Look at her, at her skin color. She's barely breathing."

Eddie slouched in closer to his young daughter, the smell of alcohol enveloping Elizabeth until she felt like gagging.

"Don't look no different than any other time we've wasted our money taking her to that useless dump."

"Eddie, let me do this. I'll pay for it from my paycheck, so it won't cost you a nickel."

"That is where you're wrong, Lizzie, because what's mine is mine and what's your's is mine. When your paycheck is spent on useless trips to the doctor, that's my money being thrown down the toilet."

"Eddie, it's our little girl . . ."

"Turn around and put Nona back upstairs. She'll be better in the morning, like always." He grabbed Elizabeth's shoulders and shoved her. Elizabeth pitched forward from the force of his push, but managed to stay upright, Nona still safe in her arms. This was a battle she would not win, at least not this way. Holding Nona close, Elizabeth started the long walk through the house to climb the mountain of stairs to her daughter's bedroom.

"What's taking so long?" Mince yelled through the back door. "You should have seen Carol Jean back that car out. I never thought she'd do it, but she did!"

"Tell her to drive it right back in, because no one's going anywhere," Eddie responded. "Then, get in here and get to bed." His words were slurred, and Elizabeth prayed Mince would stop talking.

Upstairs, Elizabeth placed Nona on her bed, rubbing her arms and legs to increase her circulation. Within moments, Mince was there, looking into the doorway, with Carol Jean slouching behind her.

"It took her three tries, but she got it in! Is Nona better? Is that why we're not going to the hospital?"

"We are going to the hospital."

"But, Pops said . . ."

"Never mind what he said. Go sit on the steps where you can see the living room and tell me when he's asleep. When he starts to snore, that's when we go to the hospital."

Mince and Carol Jean started toward the stairs, then returned. "Pops isn't in the living room. He's sitting at the bottom of the stairs. We'll never be able to get past him." Carol Jean looked as defeated as Mince.

"We'll wait for awhile. Maybe he'll get up and move. Then we'll take Nona. Now, come over here and help me keep your little sister company."

They waited in Nona's room, Elizabeth massaging her and whispering in the girl's ear. Carol Jean fell asleep across the end of the bed, and Mince leaned against her mother. An hour or more passed, and then Mince crawled off the bed, tiptoed to the hall, and peeked down the stairs.

It wasn't long until she returned. "He's gone from the step! I think he went to bed." Before Elizabeth could stop her, Mince began creeping down the stairs.

Soon she was back, her movements soundless, and her voice a whisper. "There's snoring coming from your bedroom."

Without hesitation, Elizabeth nudged Carol Jean awake and pulled Nona into her arms. They would not be stopped this time. "Don't make a sound, whatever you do," she warned the girls as they started down the steps ahead of her.

Carol Jean backed the car out of their narrow garage. Elizabeth placed Nona in the back seat with her head on Mince's lap and her feet resting on Carol Jean. Their car crawled, lights off, down the driveway and into the street. Elizabeth looked behind her at Mince and Carol Jean, sitting like tombstones, as the lights of their house disappeared behind them.

IF ONLY

THEY PULLED UP TO THE HOSPITAL, JERKING TO A HALT underneath a canopy shielding the emergency entrance. Elizabeth lifted Nona from the back seat and carried her through the thick glass doors held open by Mince and Carol Jean.

"Please, somebody, help us," Elizabeth yelled. Two nurses came running and soon the emergency team surrounded them, placing Nona on a gurney. Elizabeth hung on beside her, answering the nurses' rapid fire questions. When they entered a room labeled "E1" Elizabeth was told to wait with her family.

An hour later, Elizabeth, Carol Jean and Mince were sitting together on a crackling fake leather couch located in the hospital waiting room for families of very sick patients. It was up two floors from the general waiting area, and the room was empty except for the three of them.

Time passed at glacier pace. At the nearby nurses' station, a clock guarded the desk. Elizabeth stared at its hands, marching in slow motion and timed to the ticking of the passing minutes. After awhile, the plump lady in a pink uniform who had ushered them to the waiting room, stopped with a clipboard clamped with forms for Elizabeth to complete.

The woman patted Elizabeth's arm. "Take your time with these and bring them to the nurses' station when you've finished. Let me know if you need anything, and get some rest."

Watching the woman's broad, pink behind waddle away, Elizabeth wanted to scream that the last thing in the world she wanted to do was sleep, even though her eyes burned with fatigue and her whole body ached for Nona.

"Wait!" Elizabeth called to the pink figure. "Is there a pay phone somewhere nearby? I need to call my parents."

The phone rang several times before Elizabeth heard her father's deep, sleepy voice answer. They would be at the hospital as soon as possible he told her. Elizabeth hung up, relieved because her folks' presence would make everything seem better, even if it wasn't.

It was quiet on the third floor that night. A single nurse, uniformed in white, worked behind the desk at the station, a white nurses' cap perched atop her silvery hair like an angel's wings. From a distant hallway, the blur of voices could be heard, and an occasional call paging a doctor or nurse echoed through the restrained silence. A janitor swung a wide swath of pine-scented soapy water past the waiting area with a steady, determined rhythm. It was an ordinary night in the hospital. No reason to think otherwise, Elizabeth told herself.

An elevator dinged, and Marta and William stepped off, hurrying toward them. The gravity of what was happening was mirrored in their faces, her mother's twinkling eyes veiled in worry, and her father grim, his usual smile a thin, pink line. As soon as they saw the girls, however, their grandparents smiled and hurried to embrace them. On their grandmother's arm was the old wicker picnic basket, filled with sandwiches, fruit slices, and cookies, along with their old barn thermos containing pink lemonade.

"Have you heard any news?" William asked Elizabeth.

"No. The last thing they said, before they asked me to step out, was that they would do everything they could."

Elizabeth began pacing to the nurses' station and back, her tennis shoes squeaking on the spotless hospital tiles. The girls sat with their grandparents, as Marta read to them from her worn Bible in a calm, reassuring voice.

At the far, dark reaches of the hallway, Elizabeth turned. Someone was approaching from the opposite end of the corridor, the figure backlit by the glowing exit sign behind them. The person was tall and walked with long strides, their rubber-soled shoes whisper quiet. Elizabeth moved toward the person, her heart pounding in her chest and her breath on hold.

"Mrs. Dembrowski? I'm Dr. Hartman." He reached his cool, slender hands toward her. "I am sorry to tell you that we could not save your daughter. Her condition was so deteriorated, there was very little we could do."

Though he continued to talk, Elizabeth heard nothing, felt nothing. Her parents held her upright or she would have fallen onto the floor, and through it, and then through all the floors until she was in the ground . . . deep, deep in the ground.

"I want to see her, to let her know she's not alone." Elizabeth said, latching onto the doctor's coat sleeve. "I need to see my little girl."

He took her hand and began to walk her away toward the glow of the red exit sign.

"Please let us come along to say good-bye," Mince begged.

"Let me go first," Elizabeth said, disappearing down the hallway. "I'll come back to get you."

In the center of the dimly lit room was a narrow, metal gurney. Elizabeth extended a trembling hand to pull back a blue sheet, the color of new ice. There was Nona, eyes closed and mouth upturned in a slight smile. Elizabeth reached to hold her child, light as air, then pressed her lips to Nona's velvety cheek. She sobbed in silence at the loss of her beautiful girl, a loss caused by Eddie and Northland.

Elizabeth allowed Mince and Carol Jean to see Nona's covered body. The family joined hands, and William and Marta said the Lord's Prayer for Nona, while Elizabeth and her daughters wept.

They left the hospital, but did not go home. Instead, Elizabeth's parents took them to the farm, arriving there as the sun was sprinkling its orange haze over the eastern cornfields. Coffee was brewed and poured, including a cup for Mince and Carol Jean. They sat and sipped, and then the family began the chores of milking the cows and tending the hogs, feeding the calves and chickens, and cleaning the barn.

Hours later, Elizabeth noticed Art's car approaching on Sloan's Creek Road. She walked from the barn toward the farmhouse, meeting the vehicle as it pulled in the gravel driveway. Eddie jumped out of the car before it came to a stop.

"What are you doing here?" Elizabeth asked.

"Some nurse called Mrs. Dukane. Alice told me you and the girls were at the hospital, and that she was supposed to take care of Lucky. By the time we got to the hospital, you had already left with your folks, and nobody would tell me anything. I figured, since you weren't at home, that you would be here at the farm."

"You shouldn't have come, Eddie. There's nothing anyone can do. It's all over."

"What do you mean? What's wrong?"

"It's so like you not to remember what you've done. It doesn't matter anyway. She's gone . . . our little girl is gone. There's no bringing her back."

"Don't tell me Nona . . ." Eddie moved toward Elizabeth, but she stepped back further away from him. Her face was frozen in grief and betrayal.

"Yes, Nona. If only we could have made it to the hospital sooner, she might have had a chance. But, that's not the way it happened, was it, Eddie?"

"Wait. Are you saying it was my fault?"

"She needed to go to the hospital, Eddie, but you said no. You said we couldn't waste the money!" Elizabeth's voice was razor sharp and becoming louder with each word.

"Why would you say a lie like that? Why blame me, instead of yourself? It's not my fault you didn't get her help fast enough. If you had, our daughter would be alive."

Elizabeth lunged toward him, screaming unintelligible sounds, arms flailing. It was Art who stepped in and pushed the two apart before Eddie could retaliate.

"You see what I mean, Art? The woman is crazy, always attacking me when she should be accepting responsibility."

"I think you have said enough, Eddie." Art was ushering Eddie away from Elizabeth and toward car.

"Get out of here, Eddie," Elizabeth said, "and don't bother coming back."

Later, Elizabeth and her parents drove into town to make the funeral arrangements. In the afternoon, Eddie and Art arrived at the farm again, but William sent them away. After that, Elizabeth took some pills the doctor had given her, swallowing them without a drink of water. Upstairs in her old bedroom, the one with the blue flowered wallpaper, she laid across the faded chenille bedspread, her eyes closed, but her memories wide awake. She wondered how her life would have been different if she hadn't been named Homecoming Queen her senior year.

When Elizabeth was elected, no one was more dumbfounded than she was. She had no intention of attending the dance, since she'd never been to such an event in her first three years of high school and didn't see any reason to attend this year, especially since Eddie Dembrowski had been elected Homecoming King.

Eddie was the polar opposite of Elizabeth. While she was a quiet, reserved farm girl, Eddie was an outgoing and popular "townie." Everyone, including Elizabeth, knew Eddie didn't care who the Homecoming Queen was, as long as he was King. He already had his date for the dance, which came as no surprise, so his commitment to whomever was elected queen was strictly for show. At the start of the Homecoming parade, Eddie was sitting on the back of Clay Landers' green convertible, wearing his letterman's jacket crammed with medals and pins, joking and causing an uproar with his team-mates who were hanging around. Then, Elizabeth stepped into the car. Clay reached over to hold Elizabeth's hand, and the two of them were laughing over some private joke.

When she sat down and lifted her face to look at Eddie, he appeared to be speechless, a rare occurrence, Elizabeth guessed. She gave him one glance with her green eyes, fringed in long, dark lashes, then tossed her ebony hair, and looked away. Over her tall, slender figure, she wore a forest green wool coat loaned to her by Clay's mother. It was because of Clay's urging and encouragement that Elizabeth had accepted the Homecoming coronation.

Throughout the parade, Elizabeth and Eddie didn't talk much. They waved and smiled at the townsfolk lining Main Street and down onto Park Avenue. Elizabeth was relieved when it was over, although she had to admit it wasn't as bad as she had anticipated.

Eddie and the team won the football game, so the dance that night was both a Homecoming and a victory celebration. Elizabeth and Eddie were crowned and seated on a throne along the north end of the gym. Watching their court line up for the royal promenade, Eddie was talkative and amiable, but when it was time for the royal couple to waltz together, Eddie became rude and obnoxious. He made wisecracks and carried on with the crowd, ignoring his dance partner, and embarrassing and humiliating Elizabeth, who couldn't get off the dance floor, and away from Eddie, quickly enough. If only, in the months ahead, she had heeded the warning of that awful night.

BLAME

ELIZABETH WANDERED DOWNSTAIRS AGAIN, UNABLE
to sleep, consumed by grief and regret. She was met by the nicker-
ing sound of the treadle on her mother's old black sewing machine.
Marta's foot pumped nonstop as she maneuvered delicate pink
taffeta and white tulle, putting together a perfect dress for her little granddaughter.

"An angel's dress for an angel," Elizabeth said, wrapping her
slender arms around Marta's shoulders.

"Lots of people have stopped by," Mince told Elizabeth. "You
should see the kitchen. Food and stuff are piled all over."

"I saw Mince stick her finger into a pan of brownies. Disgusting."
Carol Jean had parked herself at the telephone table. "I've had to
answer the phone about a million times. It's lucky I have the perfect
voice for phone conversing."

"You have both been very helpful. Now, go out to the barn to
help your grandfather with the afternoon chores. There'll be some
lemonade for you when you're finished."

When the chores were done, the two girls ended up playing
checkers on the back porch. Elizabeth joined them, bringing along
the promised lemonade and a plate of the contaminated brownies.

"We have something to tell you," Mince said, arranging her black
pieces. She didn't look up at Carol Jean or Elizabeth.

"No, we don't. There's nothing to tell." Carol Jean spoke, her lips ventriloquist tight. She skipped a red checker across the board. "King me!"

Elizabeth could see tears puddling around Mince's eyes. "What is it?"

"You can't say there's nothing, Carol Jean! We did it! We killed Nona!" Her hand hovered above the game board, but didn't make a move.

Carol Jean grabbed her sister's wrist, squeezing. "You shut up and listen. We didn't do anything to hurt Nona. We wanted to help her." She released Mince and moved her red checker one space.

"Mom, you said never to take Nona into the river, but we did," Mince said. "You were at work. The house was hot like a furnace and so was Nona. We went in the water to cool off and took Nona with us. It's our fault she died."

"It's not our fault!" Carol Jean's words erupted with a volume that startled them all. The girl bolted forward, upending the checker board and scattering the playing pieces on the floor around them.

Elizabeth placed her hand on Carol Jean's shoulder and sat her down. "You are right. It wasn't your fault. Nona had a sick heart, and that made her lungs sick, too. The doctor thought she might improve and gain strength as she grew up, but she didn't."

"Whose fault is it, then?" Mince asked.

"It's no one's fault."

"Except for Pops," Carol Jean said, looking at no one in particular.

"What your Pops did was wrong. Getting Nona to the hospital sooner might have given her a better chance. Pops took away that chance."

Elizabeth blamed Eddie for what happened that day, but more than that, she felt Nona's deterioration was because of the air she was forced to breathe every day. Surrounded by toxic fumes from the mill,

Nona's heart and lungs were compromised far more quickly than she could survive. In a better environment, the girl would have had time to grow and strengthen, and not die from her disease. When she thought about what might have been, Elizabeth was overcome with sadness and a new-found determination to find justice for Nona. She blinked away her tears and focussed on Mince and Carol Jean.

"The bugs are getting bad here in the shade," Elizabeth said. "You two go sit out in front where there's a little sun, and I'll grab some cards. I'll bet we can talk Grams into a game of Canasta."

Elizabeth loved the front porch of the Sloan farmhouse. It stretched the distance across the south face of the two-story house, like a broad, welcoming smile. An ornate white railing surrounded the entire porch, its delicate, white spindles turned on an ancient lathe by Elizabeth's great-grandfather in the mid-1800s. The ornate oak front door had been handmade by her grandfather. All very necessary, William always said, but the porch swing he himself had designed, made, and hung, was there for enjoying.

The four of them played cards, but lacked enthusiasm for the game. Marta soon gave up, destined for the kitchen. "Somebody has to make sense of all that donated food."

The remaining three sat together on William's porch swing, its chains creaking a bit as they swayed. The sun was too high to peek under the porch roof, so they roosted, heads in the shade and feet in the sunlight. Elizabeth pushed the swing into motion, her bare feet nudging it with deliberation. Carol Jean's feet shuffled along the porch boards, but Mince's toes swung loose, her feet unable to reach. No one spoke for a long time.

"I've never known anyone who died before," Mince said.

"I did," Carol Jean said, "but I wasn't sad or anything, because it was Mr. Nettehoven, the school janitor. In class, all of us made a pretty card for his family. Our teacher, Miss Larson, put them together in a manila envelope and delivered it to the funeral home, with a bouquet of flowers. She said it was the gesture that counted."

"It's weird," Mince reflected out loud. "I mean, our sister is dead, and it doesn't seem like anything is different."

Elizabeth swallowed the lump in her throat. "When someone we love dies, it reminds me of the lull before a thunderstorm. We know bad weather is there; we can see it, hear it, even feel it, but it takes time for the storm to happen. Then, the wind picks up, and after a few scattered drops, a downpour begins. It might subside for a bit, and, then we're drenched in rain again."

"We're in the lull, before we really know how bad it's going to be?" Carol Jean sounded unconvinced.

"I think we're already in the storm, at the very beginning," Elizabeth answered.

"Our tears are the rain, right?" Mince asked. "We don't know how hard it's gonna rain or for how long."

"It's going to rain hard, Love, and for a long time, I'm afraid," Elizabeth said with broken-hearted certainty.

BLACK

"FOR THE LOVE OF . . ." ELIZABETH PAUSED, UNABLE TO conceal the exasperation creeping into her voice. "Put on the sundress, Mince! It doesn't matter that it's dark blue and not black."

"It does matter. People are supposed to wear black at a funeral, not blue." Mince's voice, sounding unfamiliar, was high-pitched and whining, as she stared into her sparse closet. On an ordinary day, Elizabeth was accustomed to Mince not giving a single thought about what clothes she wore, but today was not an ordinary day. It was Wednesday, the day of Nona's funeral. They had been back at home for less than twenty-four hours and both girls had been irritable and argumentative.

"I don't see why I can't have a new black dress to wear," Mince said.

"You can't have a new dress because I cannot afford to buy you one."

"You always say that," Mince grumped, arms crossed in front of her chest. "I'm not going."

"Of course, you're going. It's for your little sister."

"She won't know if I'm there or not. She's dead."

"But I will know if you're there, and I need you with me. We all need you," Elizabeth said.

"I don't want to go. You can't make me."

"Not another word about this. You are going. End of discussion."

"If you would stop being a grouch, Mince," Carol Jean said, "I have an idea for what you can wear." Carol Jean was skilled at putting together an outfit out of nothing but mismatched pieces, and Elizabeth gave her oldest daughter an appreciative glance.

Elizabeth watched as Mince stepped into the black cotton skirt her sister handed her, and then Carol Jean pulled up the zipper. The skirt was at least four inches too big around Mince's slender waist.

"This is huge. It will never fit me," Mince pouted. "I'm not wearing this."

"Give me a sec, will you?" Carol Jean mumbled through the safety pins she held in her mouth. One by one, she gathered even tucks around the waistline of the skirt, pinning from the inside, until the skirt hugged Mince's middle.

"Now, put on your white blouse, the sleeveless one, and tuck it into the skirt. I'll be right back."

"Come on Mince. I'll help you find that blouse." Elizabeth nudged Mince, who huffed out an exasperated sigh. Together, they located the white top, and Mince was finishing up the buttoning and tucking in when Carol Jean appeared, carrying a long, grey satin scarf.

"This looks stupid!" Mince complained, as Elizabeth adjusted the skirt's waistline.

"It won't, if you'd give me a chance to finish!" With nimble fingers, Carol Jean folded the scarf into even, tuxedo pleats. She centered the scarf around Mince's waist, covering the pinned, gathered fabric of the skirt, then tied the ends of the scarf into a tidy bow at the back.

"It's a cummerbund, all the rage with movie stars in Hollywood. Your blouse will stay tucked in, and it looks like a dress."

"It's bunched up around my stomach. I feel itchy," Mince said. She poked a finger inside her waistband, scratching and scowling.

"At least the skirt won't drop down around your ankles, and you are wearing black!" Elizabeth turned the frowning girl around to face the mirror. "See, proper funeral black."

Elizabeth pulled Mince into the bathroom and began brushing her hair into a smooth ponytail. Carol Jean perched on the toilet seat, applying a coat of polish to her fingernails.

"You did a wonderful job on Mince's outfit," Elizabeth told Carol Jean. "You have a little bit of the seamstress in you, like your grandmother."

"Thanks. Now, if she would leave it alone . . ."

"I would, if it didn't itch so much," Mince said, twisting and adjusting her waistband.

"Stop fidgeting and let me finish your hair." Elizabeth worked a white satin ribbon around Mince's thick ponytail. "There, was that so bad?"

"It's still not a black dress."

"You are impossible," Carol Jean said, pulling Mince's ponytail.

A horn sounded outside. Elizabeth accompanied the girls to William and Marta's car, walked Lucky over to Mrs. Dukane's house for the day, and joined the family to travel the short, sad distance to the church for Nona's funeral. Elizabeth wished they could drive forever and never arrive at their destination.

William drove into the parking lot behind the Trinity Lutheran Church on Madison Street, stopped, and turned off the car. No one moved. The silent family remained frozen in their seats. Elizabeth watched Mince lean her head out the window and blink upward into the blinding sunlight, straining to see the single bell in the church's steeple, the tallest in town.

"Will they ring the bell today for Nona?" Mince asked.

From the front seat, Marta said, "Yes, the bells always are rung for a. . . " Her voice trailed off, the word trapped and unspoken.

"That will be nice," Mince said. "Nona would have liked that."

"It's not nice, because someone has to be dead to get the funeral bells!" Carol Jean folded her arms across her chest, like armor protecting her body.

"I meant the sound would be nice. You don't have to yell!"

"Girls, this is not the time or the place for arguments," Elizabeth said. "Let's go inside the church."

Art and Eddie pulled in as Elizabeth and the others walked together toward the church. To Elizabeth, Eddie was invisible, and she hurried the girls along without giving him a glance.

The family started up the church's steep, wooden steps, stacked across the front of the building. Mince stumbled a bit on the hem of her skirt, and, from behind, Eddie's hand reached to steady her, but Elizabeth brushed it aside and assisted Mince, urging her forward.

"Mince, go catch up with your grandparents." She glared at her husband. "You'll only make things worse by being here. Are you drunk?"

"A few beers doesn't make me drunk," Eddie argued, "and I have as much right as you do to be here."

Since being turned away at the farm, Eddie had not come around. Art claimed Eddie remembered nothing of the night when Nona died or how he had stopped them from taking Nona to the hospital. It was classic Eddie: pretend you don't remember anything, and all will be forgiven. Not this time, Elizabeth promised herself.

Inside the church, the air was lifeless and still, like the coffin waiting at the unadorned altar. The closed casket, wearing a blanket of fresh pink flowers, was white and small as a window box. William had spent one day and night building it for Nona. Using pale oaken planks, he planed, dovetailed, and fitted the pieces together as if they had grown that way. Elizabeth's mother lined the box with pink satin, tufted with pearls, and trimmed in lace.

"It's all pink and perfect, like Nona would have wanted," Elizabeth whispered to her parents. They nodded and managed to smile at the thought of Nona.

Elizabeth looked behind her. Filling the church were damp-eyed ladies with handkerchiefs, men with sweating faces tucked in wet, worn collars, and fidgeting, whispering kids from school. Carol Jean turned to wave at her friends, but Elizabeth laid a finger against her daughter's cheek and faced her forward again. Elizabeth saw Mince grin as Carol Jean flushed a deep pink.

At that moment, Elizabeth spotted Eddie's father, Jasper, walking down the aisle. From the pew behind Elizabeth, Eddie rose and reached for Jasper's hand.

"Thank you for coming," she heard Eddie whisper in Jasper's large, sunburned ear.

"She was my granddaughter. Darn shame, that's all I gotta say." He nodded toward Elizabeth, then moved to sit at the back of the church, leaving a trail of fuel oil smell.

As friends and neighbors came forward to pay their respects, Elizabeth and her family accepted their condolences. When Madeira Prince, tall and stately, strode up to the family, she wrapped Elizabeth in an embrace that lasted longer than most. Without hesitation, Madeira hugged her way down the family, each individual rising to be enfolded in the woman's outstretched arms. Julian followed, shaking each person's hand.

High-heeled footsteps clicked their way up the aisle as Audrey Landers charged toward the front of the church. Pumping Elizabeth's hand, the woman's ample bosom bounced in a low-cut, transparent black blouse. Behind her, Clayton and Cynthia followed. Nodding first toward the family, Clayton embraced Elizabeth, holding her close and whispering words into her ear, and then Audrey pulled the two apart with a yank on her husband's arm.

As the last people settled in, feet and hymnal pages shuffling, the organist began a medley of children's hymns. Art, who had been ushering, approached the front of the church and held every member of the family, including Eddie. Elizabeth moved over and motioned for Art to sit with them in the first pew.

"Sit with us, please, Art. You are as much a part of our family as anyone."

Though he looked embarrassed, Art sat down on the far end of the bench in the first row.

The funeral lasted forty-five minutes, from beginning prayer to the closing hymn. Following the final note, the pallbearers, all men from the mill, stood in unison and came to the altar. They lifted the tiny casket with Nona's body inside and marched out of the church.

Elizabeth, Carol Jean, Mince, Marta, and William stood to follow the casket bearers. Stepping into the aisle, Elizabeth placed an arm around her daughters' shoulders. At first, Elizabeth felt unable to move, the endless path ahead thick with a cement swallowing her steps. After a time, Mince and Carol Jean began to walk, and Elizabeth found the strength to go with them.

Making the long journey out of the church, Elizabeth gazed at the crowd of heads nodding towards her family as they passed. At the end of one pew sat their neighbor, Mrs. Dukane, a widow since her husband, Tom, passed from a heart attack while unloading chemicals at the paper mill. Behind her was John Hohlfeld and his son and daughter. Their mother, a pulp boiler operator at the mill, had succumbed to a stroke three years earlier. To Elizabeth's left sat Arlene and Wayne Nelson, whose son had died in a car accident. Across the aisle, the Knapp family filled one entire pew, minus their oldest daughter, Margaret, who was a secretary at Northland. Behind the Knapps, Edith Martin was seated with Arlyss Wilson, both widows whose husbands, union mill men, died in the same year. In the last row, Rita Lindhom was sitting alone, having lost her husband, Frank, to cancer last year. Gathered together like this, Elizabeth was struck by the realization that so many other families had suffered losses, too.

Near the back of the church, Elizabeth spotted Clayton. He nodded toward her and her daughters, as did the two men seated beside him. Like Clay, the strangers were dressed in dark, tailored suits, with professional haircuts and somber, fleshy faces. Elizabeth thought she recognized the two from other funerals she'd attended, and she recalled when she had asked about them, someone said they were big shots from Northland. Their presence at Nona's funeral made Elizabeth burn with anger.

They buried Nona at Peace in the Valley Cemetery. Elizabeth tried to keep her eyes from looking at the soil piled aside, waiting to refill the hole and smother Nona's coffin, now dangling on satiny ropes above the abyss. During the Lord's Prayer, Elizabeth felt light-headed and wobbled a bit. When Eddie stepped in to steady her, she pulled away and stood strong.

After the funeral service, their family and friends gathered at the farm. Elizabeth watched as clouds of dust rolled in behind the cars rumbling down Sloan's Creek Road. It touched her that people who had been in the church plus many others had come to pay their respects to their family. In the room behind her, the church auxiliary ladies bustled about, tables laden with casseroles and hams, jello and homemade bread, pineapple upside-down cakes, done-up pickles and beets in jars. These last few days, food had been piling up in the pantry, dishes made with sympathy and the relief that comes with knowing the loss happened to someone else's family and not your own.

In various rooms, the talking and whispering of visitors drummed up an unintelligible rumble of conversations, and the entire house was wrapped in the aroma of percolated coffee and per-spiring people, as dishes, kettles, silverware, and ladies' voices rattled.

"There's more forks needed on the buffet."

"You'd think the least those men could do is change their shoes!"

"Somebody dropped a plate with red jello on the living room carpet."

"Elizabeth, you be sure to eat something, hon."

"Bring that poor girl a chair. She looks about ready to keel over."

Eddie had shown up at the farm uninvited, and Elizabeth refused to acknowledge him. She watched as folks shook his hand and offered their sympathies, but, for the most part, few words were spoken to him.

"Guess I'll be leaving," he said to no one in particular, as he passed through the guests. "If it does any good, I am sorry." Eddie directed his words toward Elizabeth, his voice loud enough for the others in the room to notice, but folks looked away and said nothing.

"I left Lucky at Mrs. Dukane's for the day," Elizabeth said, fol-lowing him to the door. "I would appreciate it if you would bring him home and sleep at the house tonight."

"Isn't that generous of you, Lizzie? I don't guess I need your invi-tation to be staying at my own home."

"You are not staying at home. This is only temporary."

"We'll see about that," Eddie said as he left, the door slamming behind him.

When the last car was two glowing embers disappearing down the road, the family began the task of carrying on with life. The church ladies had left the house spotless, dishes washed, the last food wrapped, sealed and stored. Elizabeth and her mother worked together, re-shelving the good china, a reminder of the funeral, stor-ing it away, high in the pantry.

Elizabeth's parents urged her to stay at the farm a little longer.

"You are exhausted," her mother said, "and one more day won't matter."

"I'll lose my job at Landers. For every one job, there are five people wanting it."

"Clay said to take your time," Marta reminded her. "No one will fault you for not being there, after what's happened. Besides, you and the girls need some rest."

In the end, Elizabeth decided the three of them would stay the night at the farm, knowing it was inevitable they would have to face their home without Nona, but not until tomorrow.

STAY AWAY

IT WAS MID-MORNING WHEN ELIZABETH AND THE GIRLS returned home. Dreading another confrontation with Eddie, Elizabeth was relieved to find the house empty, despite the fact that she had asked Eddie to stay there for the night with Lucky. Elizabeth sent Mince next door to Mrs. Dukane's, anticipating the dog was still with their neighbor.

"Give her our thanks," Elizabeth said as she filled a basket with leftovers from the funeral. "Take this food to her as a gift for how kind she has been."

Within a few minutes, Mince returned with Lucky, his tail wagging and nose exploring the kitchen.

"Mrs. Dukane said thanks for the food and that Lucky was a good boy," Mince said, stroking Lucky's head. "She said he's already been fed."

"Lucky, get out of the kitchen," Elizabeth said, giving him a hug, and a gentle push. "Did she mention your Pops being around?"

"Nope."

Elizabeth sent the girls upstairs and began working in the kitchen, storing and freezing the abundance of food her folks sent home with them after the funeral. She was missing another day of work, and that worried her, but she rationalized it was already too late to clock-in for the day. Being honest with herself, she had to admit all she wanted to do was be home with Mince and Carol Jean, instead of leaving the two to fend for themselves again.

"Hello! Anybody home?" called a voice from the back porch.

Elizabeth opened the screen and welcomed Art. "What brings you here?"

"It was another one of those nights, Liz. I couldn't get Eddie to leave the tavern. Then, he refused to come here, something about going where he's not wanted. Got over to my place and put him to bed there. Sorry about Lucky being left with the neighbor again."

"That's all right. How about we sit outside where it's a little cooler and have a lemonade together?" she said.

Elizabeth filled two glasses and walked outside to the old picnic table, where Art waited, moving his car keys in a figure eight pattern across the worn, bleached out boards.

She set the glasses on the table, tossed an ice cube to Lucky, and sat down across from Art. "Here I am again, thanking you for being a good friend to us," she said, reaching to touch his hand.

"Eddie's like a man out of control, Elizabeth. Losing Nona was hard on him."

Elizabeth pulled her hand away and stared down at her rough, raw fingers. "The only hard thing for Eddie was admitting it was his fault she didn't get to the hospital in time. I will never forgive him for that night."

"I can't believe Eddie would stop you from taking her to get medical help."

Elizabeth told him about what happened. "By the time she received treatment, it was too late. That's on Eddie."

"I'd say you're right in feeling that way."

"Being right doesn't make it any easier. I want him to stay away, but I don't know how we're going to make it on our own." Her eyes brimmed with hot, hesitant tears.

Art pulled a worn, leather-laced wallet from his back pocket. "I won't take 'No' for an answer. This will keep you going until your next paycheck." He forced several bills into her hands and turned around to leave, but she grabbed his arm and stopped him.

"I'll never forget this," Elizabeth said, as she reached up to kiss his cheek. "Thank you."

He left without another word and walked down the driveway to his car. Elizabeth watched his tall figure fold into the front seat and back away.

Exhausted, she dropped onto the bench of the old picnic table, her hand stroking Lucky.

Looking across the yard to the hazy river, Elizabeth wondered how her life would have turned out if she hadn't agreed to help Eddie.

She could still see him, back all those years ago, waiting in the school library's periodicals' section, slouched at a table near the center of the room, flipping through the pages of a sports' magazine hidden behind a propped up algebra textbook, pretending to be studying.

"You came. I figured you would," he said, smiling up at her with white, even teeth. "It's like old times."

"There were no old times. Don't hurt yourself patting your own back. I missed the bus, so I thought, at least I'd get a free ride home."

Earlier that day, Eddie had stopped her in the hall, his letterman's jacket jangling with medals. Already late for class, Elizabeth agreed to meet Eddie after school. She told herself the reason she showed up was because she missed the bus, but inside, Elizabeth was a little curious about what Eddie wanted.

With practiced sincerity, Eddie explained he had been offered a football scholarship and what he hoped to accomplish, with her help. He said he had not taken school seriously and had never studied, admitting he needed someone to show him how to raise his grades. Elizabeth was that someone, Eddie claimed.

"Why me?"

"I know you're excellent at studying and getting top grades. Plus, you were real nice during all the Homecoming stuff."

"Very flattering, but what's in it for me?"

"I'll pay you a dollar an hour, plus the ride home. We can study whenever it fits your schedule. I realize the person who can help me is somebody who doesn't care about me. That would be you. I'll behave, I promise." He laid his right hand over his heart, flashing a grin at Elizabeth.

She hesitated. An inner voice spoke volumes in her head about the hazards of such an arrangement, especially after the Homecoming experience with Eddie and knowing his reputation. Still, he seemed sincere, and she needed the money for college.

"A buck fifty an hour after school, two bucks if we meet weekends, plus the ride home. No excuses from you, Eddie. I don't have the time to do your work and mine, so it's all up to you."

"You drive a hard bargain, Miss Sloan." He paused for dramatic effect. "It's a deal!

"We'll see how much of a deal this is, especially for me. Now, about that ride home . . ."

If only she had listened to that voice in her head. If only she could go back in time to that moment when her instincts had warned her to stay away from Eddie Dembrowski.

THE FOURTH OF JULY

IT WAS THE FOURTH OF JULY, NONA'S FAVORITE HOLI-day. Elizabeth, Lucky, and the girls started out early, walking the two miles to Peace in the Valley Cemetery where Nona was buried. As they neared Nona's grave, the group slowed, their steps muffled in the dusty road leading to her burial place. Her gravestone was small and white, with an angel perched upon its arch, watching over the little girl forever asleep there. In the ground around the stone's base, Mince and Carol Jean planted sticks topped with glittery stars in red, white, and blue, so Nona would have her own fireworks. Elizabeth scattered red, white, and blue flowers across the grave, its mounded dirt still without a grassy cover. Lucky walked around the border of Nona's gravesite and then laid down beside it, resting his head near her stone. The girls and Elizabeth stood silent for the longest while, as the morning sun lifted higher, dappling its light across the cemetery.

"We should go. Your grandparents will be at the house soon," Elizabeth said.

"Bye, Nona," Mince said, patting the ground. "I miss you and so does Lucky."

"Good-bye, Little Sis. I wish you could come dance with me again," Carol Jean said, wiping away her tears.

"We love you, Nona, and think about you every moment of every day," Elizabeth said, allowing her tears to flow, something she tried to avoid doing in front of the girls when they were at home.

When they got back, William and Marta were already in the house, their vehicle and trailer parked in the driveway. Mince and Carol Jean hurried inside to greet their grandparents, with Elizabeth close behind.

"Who's ready for fried chicken?" Marta said, hugging her two granddaughters.

"Better yet, who's ready for dessert?" William asked, presenting the three pies he had carried in. "I think the person who brought the dessert deserves the biggest hug!"

The girls hugged their grandfather, admiring the apple, blueberry, and strawberry rhubarb pies topped with golden crusts.

Marta nudged him on the shoulder. "It seems to me that *carrying* three pies into the house does not qualify for hugs, when we all know who made the pies."

"Thank you, Grams, for the chicken and the pies!" Mince said as she reached around her grandmother's waist and squeezed.

"Sorry we were a little late. We were at the cemetery, visiting Nona."

"I figured as much. This will be another hard day for all of us," Marta said.

"Enough sadness! Let's eat lunch and head to the County Park before all the good selling spots are taken," William said. "We have a load of produce that needs to be sold."

"Did I hear lunch was ready? Talk about perfect timing," Eddie said, strolling in through the back door.

"What are you doing here, Eddie?" Elizabeth asked.

"I live here, or did you forget whose name is on the deed?" Eddie retrieved a cold beer from the refrigerator and pried off the cap. "Besides, July Fourth is a family celebration."

Eddie waved his brown beer bottle toward his father-in-law. "William, how about a beer?"

"Thanks, but I'll have to say no. If I'm going to sell at the park this afternoon, I'd better have my wits about me. Nobody trusts a drunken farmer," William said, "or any drunken man, I'd guess."

Elizabeth did not want a confrontation with Eddie in front of the girls, so she decided it was easier to allow him to stay. They ate lunch outside, sharing old blankets they spread in the coolest shady spots of the yard. Eddie sat alone.

After the meal, everyone wandered inside where Elizabeth served pie with vanilla ice cream melting atop each piece. Carol Jean and Mince took their dessert out to the back porch, and giving in to Lucky's whining, Elizabeth opened the back door to let him out. She smiled as Lucky parked himself at the foot of the porch steps, his head moving in syncopated swings with Mince's fork, back and forth from the plate to her mouth. That dog loved ice cream.

When she had finished the pie, Mince set her plate, with the remaining ice cream rolling around its perimeter, on the ground in front of Lucky. Their family had a rule about not giving him any sweets, but before Elizabeth could object, Lucky licked the plate clean and flashed a toothy grin up at Mince. Elizabeth backed away from the door so her daughters would not hear her laugh.

"Mom's going to be mad!" Carol Jean said with an accusing tone Elizabeth knew well.

"Not if she doesn't hear about it," Mince warned her, "so keep your big blabbermouth shut for once."

"I'm not a blabbermouth. You're the one who . . ." Carol Jean began, but stopped mid-sentence. She turned around toward the loud, angry voices hurtling from the kitchen, past Elizabeth and out the screen door to the girls' ears.

"Oh, great, here it goes!" Carol Jean grabbed their plates and piled them on the step.

"Let's get out of here," Mince said.

Elizabeth came out onto the porch and down the steps. "I'll take your plates to the kitchen for you. Stay outside, and I'll call you when it's time to leave for the park."

Mince and Carol Jean started off, with Lucky still licking his lips and following behind. Elizabeth watched the sisters meander away from the house, and in the distance ahead of them, the river looked uncharacteristically normal as it wandered past in shades of cerulean and aqua. Because of a slight breeze, the mists and fumes had blown off, and summer's fragrances filled the air. Her daughters patted the stump of their old apple tree, and then they continued on to approach the sandy drop to the river.

"Girls, don't go into the water!" she warned. They stopped and waved in acknowledgement. Elizabeth, with reluctance, stepped inside to face what she recognized as another argument between her parents and her husband. William and Eddie were standing nose to nose in the middle of the kitchen, broken plates scattered at their feet.

Marta was bent over, picking up pieces of glass. "Now look what you've done, Eddie. Throwing dishes in a tantrum will not solve anything."

"You have no idea what it's like to hold down a job and then lose it," Eddie said, his finger tapping William's chest, "when all you've ever done is work for yourself. You never had to answer to anybody."

"Running a farm is a job, Eddie, a twenty-four hours a day, seven days a week, three hundred sixty-five days a year job, where you answer to the bottom line."

"Spare me the lecture . . ." Eddie began. His eyes narrowed as he noticed Elizabeth, and he stomped out the door past her, his feet crushing what remained of the broken plates.

"I'm sorry, Liz," William said. "Talking to Eddie is like stamping out fires and never knowing where they're going to flare up next."

Marta worked a broom around the kitchen, sweeping up the last of the glass. "I am not certain how the argument started, but I'm sorry it did."

Elizabeth grabbed the wastebasket and held it as her mother emptied the dustpan into it. "Please, don't apologize, Mom. It doesn't matter how it began. Let's forget about Eddie and try to have a fun holiday."

Elizabeth called the girls to the house, and they piled into William's car, which was pulling his trailer loaded with garden produce for selling at the park.

"We'll stay until we get tired of staying," William promised. "Then, we'll all go for a swim and watch the fireworks."

The County Park was along the bay, with the river emptying into it. The area was dotted with trees providing a dappling of shade. Old elms spread like whisk brooms across their tops, and ancient oaks grew with gnarled, knobby arthritic limbs. Several flower gardens throughout the park's once-green lawns were struggling in the heat and drought. There were aging, grey, wooden pavilions for group affairs like family or class reunions, splintery picnic tables beside greasy grills, and a sandy playground with swings, monkey bars, tee-ter-totters, and a squeaky merry-go-round.

Inside the main entrance was the vendor area, where William found an acceptable place for setting up his trailer. Elizabeth and the girls unloaded several fold-out tables, wooden trays, and wicker baskets for displaying the vegetables and fruit, and a green and white striped awning Marta had made. It attached to the trailer and covered as much or as little of the produce as they wanted.

They began to work, Marta directing the set-up. Lucky knew to stay out of the way and out of the heat, resting in the shade underneath the produce tables.

"Mince, put out the beets, beans, and peas in the center baskets, closer to the front, because they're all right to be manhandled," Marta said. "Also, place a sample of our new summer potatoes in between."

"Carol Jean, arrange the loose-leaf, romaine, batavia, and mesclun lettuces in a thick ruffle to decorate the edges of the tables, and be sure to band them in bunches about eight inches around."

Elizabeth placed crisp stems of ruby-colored rhubarb, pint boxes of plump blueberries, and the final quarts of the end-of-season strawberries in rows along the backs of the tables. When all was ready, Marta made some final adjustments, turning a beet here and a potato there, until it satisfied her critical eye.

William nodded his approval as she used her one gallon copper sprinkling can to shower the entire display with cool, fresh water. "I don't know how you do it, dear wife, but you make every kind of vegetable look beautiful and delicious."

William had his own specialty, Elizabeth had learned over the years. He knew everybody, and everybody knew and respected him. Many people stopped to shop, and everyone expressed their condolences over Nona's death.

Through the crowd of shoppers, Elizabeth spotted Eddie approaching, and she could feel the tension constricting her insides.

"Thought I'd come to check out the ole bottom line, William. Looks like you're making lots of easy money." Eddie reached into a box of blueberries and grabbed a handful, tossing them into his mouth.

"Making money in farming is never easy, Eddie. It's made with back-breaking, never- ending work, and there are no guarantees." William kept his voice even, but Elizabeth could hear his annoyance and irritation.

"Looks like Lizzie and my girls deserve a part of the cash you're bringing in, seeing's how they're working for you."

Eddie had moved on to the strawberries, selecting the largest ones which he threw into his mouth whole, the berry juice collecting around his cracked lips. "Plus, it's a holiday, so that's double time. Ain't that how the pickle business does it, Lizzie?"

"Ed, you need to leave. Don't spoil this day for Carol Jean and Mince." Elizabeth tried to walk Eddie away from the stand, but he became immovable when a figure walked toward them.

It was Clayton Landers. William reached out to greet the man, and Elizabeth watched as her father held Clay captive with his vice-like handshake and steady gaze. Catching sight of Eddie, Clay smiled, his even teeth glistening white against his tanned, lean face.

"It's a pleasure seeing Elizabeth every day at my factory, Eddie. She's an inspiration to all of us, after what she's been through."

"We both lost a daughter, you know," Eddie said, walking closer to face Clay.

"Really? From what I heard, you were more worried about money than your little girl's life."

Eddie lunged at Clayton, but William intervened, his considerable size coming between the two, scrambling men.

"I will not allow fighting, not here, and not about Nona. Eddie, leave now, and don't come back."

"This ain't over, Landers," Eddie said as he huffed away, finger pointing at Clay.

Clayton smiled and began filling a paper bag, engaging Mince and Carol Jean in a conversation about what lettuce to buy.

"If I don't bring home produce from the Sloan farm, I'll be subject to Hurricane Audrey's wrath," Clayton joked.

While he was filling his paper sack full of vegetables, two men approached Clay, the two men Elizabeth had seen seated beside him at Nona's funeral. The men greeted one another in a friendly, familiar way, as though they knew each other well. Elizabeth didn't want to stare, so she stole glances as the three men conversed, laughing and slapping one another on the back. When Clay noticed her glancing in their direction, he urged the two men closer to where Elizabeth was working.

"Liz, I'd like you to meet Ted Landramen and Ellis Hendriks," Clay said. "Ted and I went to college together, and Ellis, he sticks around because he loves our company."

The three laughed, and Ted and Ellis reached out to shake Elizabeth's hand.

"Have we met before?" Elizabeth asked. "I believe I've seen you somewhere."

"Ted and Ellis were at Nona's funeral."

"Our deepest sympathies," Ted said, "from us personally and also from Northland as well."

"Liz, these two are a couple of the good guys who helped run the mill," Clay explained.

"Northland cares about what happens to our employees, and we consider them to be part of the company family," Ellis said, with what felt like forced sincerity to Elizabeth, who thought his eyes were empty and cold.

She turned her attention to the line of customers waiting for her help, and Clayton and his two friends left. Elizabeth thought about Clay being close with men like that, men who claimed the mill cared about the employees and their families. It didn't mean anything, she told herself, because the men had been friends for years. Still, it nagged at Elizabeth.

When the produce was sold and the cash box was filled with bills tied in bundles, the family packed up the trailer. They drove over to the beach area, ran to the changing rooms, swimming suits in hand, and made their way to the water. Elizabeth and Marta lagged behind the others while Carol Jean found the perfect blade of beach sedge.

"What are you going to do with that?" Marta asked.

"It itches," Carol Jean said with a sigh, sliding the reed into her battered cast.

The languid bay stretched out before them, but Elizabeth was aware there would be no convincing Marta to join them in a swim, no matter how calm the water. Marta's respect for water was only surpassed by her fear of it.

"Appreciation for a body of water of this magnitude requires a large sailing vessel and life jackets!" Marta told Elizabeth.

By that time of the day, most of the beach had been vacated, though the sun was still shimmering and hot in the western sky. Grabbing hands, Elizabeth, William, and Mince ran galloping in stumbling steps through the sand, then in high prancing leaps into the still cold waters of the bay, with Lucky leaping in alongside. Once one of them succumbed to the water, the three-person chain tumbled in, shrieking and laughing in watery garbles. Then a splash and dunk frenzy ensued, until everyone was exhausted and too chilled to continue.

Sullen and grumpy, Carol Jean stood at the waters' edge with Marta, whose forehead was furrowed in worry. She held a pile of old towels, which she used to wrap the shivering swimmers, mummy style, as they raced out of the water. Into the wooden dressing rooms they ran to change, laughing and searching for lost socks and missing tennis shoes.

"Don't dawdle. The mosquitoes are fierce and swarming," Marta called in to them.

Elizabeth and Marta rubbed catmint leaves on faces, hands and legs, necks and ears, urging the others to pull down their sleeves and pull up their socks.

"Stand still, Mince, before you are eaten alive!" Elizabeth worked her over, the strong mint fragrance permeating the air.

"Come, sit." William motioned towards the fire he had built of bleached driftwood. He reined them in close to sit on scratchy, worn-thin horse blankets from the farm. From a frayed wicker picnic basket, Marta produced leftover chicken, jars of pickles, and pieces of the day's pies, all of which they ate with sandy fingers. Mince snuck bits of chicken and pie to Lucky, perched beside her and wrapped in a soft, old towel.

Later, the family laid back on the blankets, wiggling down into the sand underneath.

"I wish Nona was here," Mince said. "She loved stars and fireworks."

"She loved everything about the Fourth of July," Elizabeth said.

"I'm glad Pops isn't here," Carol Jean said, scratching into her cast with a stick.

"Me, too. Things are better when he's not around," Mince said.

"Girls, forget about your Pops. Let's enjoy the fireworks," Elizabeth said, although she agreed with both of her daughters.

Elizabeth and her family stared overhead as the velvet darkness seeped across the sky.

The western sun, in a reluctant retreat, clung to the horizon in shades of purple, gold, and magenta, the colors swimming in Elizabeth's teary eyes as she envisioned Nona sitting there with them. Waiting for that exact moment when the last sliver would disappear, the family applauded as the setting sun slipped away, leaving a golden glow dwindling in its absence. The blackening sky, on cue, became a tapestry studded with stars.

"Nona would have loved the sky tonight," Marta said, her voice quiet and sad.

"She would have clapped the loudest of all," Mince added.

A barrage of fireworks exploded overhead, with plumes of glittering sparkles showering the darkness with color and sound. Lucky ducked his head beneath the blankets as the sky entertained and awed them. With the cannon blast of the grand finale, the summer night's quiet returned, except for a loud snort coming from William, who had fallen asleep.

Mince and Carol Jean giggled, and Elizabeth jostled his shoulder to waken him.

"What a show! I don't know how, but every year it gets better and better!" William said, swatting a swarm of insects hovering around them.

"What do you say, Marta? Let's get our ladies home before the mosquitoes drink them down a quart."

ANOTHER BAD DAY

THE FOLLOWING AFTERNOON, ELIZABETH PEERED OUT her front door as a caravan of dusty cars and trucks pulled into the driveway and parked along the street in front of her house. They were vehicles she recognized, belonging to the union men from the mill. The gathering was news to her, but it had been many weeks since the mayor had mentioned the governor might take interest in the layoff at the mill, and she thought the meeting could have something to do with that. She hurried through the house to the back door, arriving as Eddie sat himself down, enthroned at the picnic table, opening and passing around bottles of beer.

From the sound of things, Elizabeth was certain most of the men were half-drunk and all of them looked defeated. She was more than curious about what was going on, so she took the chance of moving in closer. The guys were either too involved in the discussion or too drunk to pay any attention to her as she sat in an old lawn chair behind the men.

Things hadn't turned out the way Eddie expected, which, Elizabeth figured, was to be expected.

"I can't believe he sent that worthless, good-for-nothing in his place," Eddie said.

"Who was the guy?" asked someone seated behind Eddie.

"The governor's Labor Secretary, a paper-pushing, powerless nobody." Eddie swallowed long until his bottle was empty.

"The governor's too important to take time for a bunch of factory bums," Art added.

"Didn't he say he was going to help us?"

"I thought he was supposed to get the mill open again."

"And what about our unemployment comp?"

"The governor was too busy, so he sends this useless schmuck. The schmuck spent the day getting his picture taken with the mayor and the other bigwigs in town, like big shot, Clay Landers," Art said.

"This guy strutted through the plant and the warehouse, everyone hovering around him, like flies circling cow dung." Eddie and the men around the table laughed.

"Then, he made a fancy speech to us outside," Art said, "pretty much saying it's too bad what happened, but unemployment is a federal law and out of the state's jurisdiction. No mention of reopening the mill."

"He smiles, waves, and sits his fat behind in a fancy black car. Drives off into the sunset. Problem solved!" Eddie said.

The discussion stalled while the drinking continued. From behind them, Elizabeth's voice broke the silence.

"What about the condition of the river and the air we can hardly breathe? Did you ask about that?" As she said the words, Elizabeth understood that speaking out was an enormous risk. First, she was a woman, second, she was not a union member, and, third, Eddie was there.

The men looked from Elizabeth to Eddie, no one saying a word. They waited, drinking their beer, watching Eddie for a reaction.

"Not that it's any of your business, but we're worried about jobs. Those unimportant issues never came up. Guess we're supposed to feel lucky the guy showed up at all," Eddie said.

"What are you going to do about this?" Elizabeth asked.

"If we knew that, we wouldn't be sitting here. We'd be doing it, Lizzie, so butt out. This is a man's fight, and we'll handle it."

There wasn't much else to say. The men sat, hunched over their beers, sweat seeping through their shirts, eyes staring into the hopeless future. Then, Eddie stood up.

"I say it's not over, not by a long shot. What this mill did isn't going to go away because they say so. Maybe, for now, they can sleep at night without a care in the world. I think it's time we give them something to worry about!"

"Ed's right, as usual," Art added. Everyone laughed, including Elizabeth, because Eddie was a hothead whose tirades were tolerated, but often ignored.

"No, really, this time he is right. Following the proper channels has gotten us nowhere. We have to figure out something that will get their attention, but this time, we'll do it our way. What do you say? Are you guys in it for the long haul, no matter how ugly it gets?"

A cheer and the clanking of bottles being raised together followed Elizabeth into the house. Everyone, including her, realized they had nothing more to lose. The mill's closing was a scab over a wound that was festering below the surface, a trauma that was oozing, infectious, and toxic. Elizabeth recognized that despite everything, the mill had provided jobs, and, so far, not one person was courageous enough to say or do anything that might jeopardize their livelihood any further. Would the men truly be willing to take on the mill, now that they were unemployed, perhaps permanently? If they wouldn't, who would, Elizabeth wondered.

The men said Clayton Landers was there at that meeting with the Labor Secretary. Clay was associated with influential people, so Elizabeth reasoned it might be worth it to talk to him, to find out his thoughts on what the governor's representative had said. The last thing she wanted to do was involve Clay in Eddie's problems, but the situation was about much more than lost jobs. For her daughters and the whole town, she needed to talk to Clay and ask for his help.

Elizabeth left the house, walking at a fast clip toward the Landers Pickle Factory.

For now, weekends at the pickle factory were slow, with a skeleton crew to handle any late deliveries and to clean the vats. Elizabeth was aware that Clay worked six, sometimes seven, days a week during pickle season, and with so few personnel around, it would be the ideal time to speak to him.

Spread out along the river, Clay's factory could be smelled well before it could be seen, its briny odors combining with the caustic fumes from the paper mill. Elizabeth cut across the parking lot close to the main doors, which she found were unlocked. Catching her reflection in the window, she raked her fingers through her thick hair and chewed her lips to pinkness, then hurried into the building.

The air inside was thick with the vinegar smell of the pickle business, and only the bloody glow of the blinking exit signs lighted the hall leading to the office. Elizabeth's shoes were silent on the concrete floors, with only the sounds from the factory echoing in the empty corridor. The first door on the left was the location of the main office.

She tapped her knuckles on the frosted window and turned the knob without waiting for an offer to enter. All the employee desks were vacant, as Elizabeth had hoped. Through the reception area, around the corner and past the executive secretary's desk, Elizabeth saw Clay's office door, propped open. He was seated behind a mammoth desk spread with tidy stacks of files and papers, phone in hand. Glancing up, a surprised expression on his face gave way to a smile when he saw Elizabeth. Motioning her into the office, Clay continued his phone conversation.

She did not sit, but wandered around the office, skimming the book titles on the shelves and studying diplomas, certificates, trophies, and memorabilia. Family photos of ski vacations, holidays, and birthdays were framed and arranged on one wall. There was Audrey, bikini-clad and tanned, on a white beach, and another of Audrey and Clay holding a plump baby Cynthia in front of their newly finished home. Elizabeth envied the life Clay had made for himself.

"You really ought to give a guy a little notice, Liz. I would have picked up the place a bit and put on the coffee pot." He had finished his phone call and stepped around the desk to give her a welcome hug. "To what do I owe the honor, Miss Sloan?"

"First, most folks know me as Mrs. Dembrowski, but you can call me Elizabeth."

"My apologies." He bent into a gallant bow, and then sat on the edge of his desk, and waited for Elizabeth to speak.

"I need information and advice and was hoping you could help me."

"I'm nothing if not informational and advisory."

"That's Clayton." A husky voice filled the room, as Clayton's wife, Audrey, sashayed in from the adjoining office. "Always full of words, telling people what to do and how to do it."

"Doesn't sound very flattering, when you put it like that, Audrey," Clay said.

"Do go on, Lizzie. Clayton and I are a team. We share everything, isn't that right, darling?"

She hoisted herself onto her husband's desk, skirt sliding up to expose tanned, muscular legs, which she crossed at the knees. From her pocket, she pulled an engraved silver case. Audrey slid it open and removed a slim, hand rolled cigarette, placing it between her tangerine- colored lips.

"Light me, darling." She leaned in close to her husband, eyes never leaving Elizabeth's face.

A lighter in Clayton's hands snapped open, its flame lifting towards the outstretched cigarette. Audrey inhaled and turned to blow the smoke in Elizabeth's direction.

"Go ahead, Liz. You can speak in front of Audrey," Clay said.

Hesitant, Elizabeth coughed to clear the smoke from her throat. "The men from the mill were gathered at our house this afternoon, furious the governor himself failed to show up as promised. You can imagine how angry and disappointed they were learning that not much of anything can be done by state officials about the unemployment compensation, because it is a federal law." She paused, Clay's eyes locked onto hers, his arms crossed over his smooth, crisp shirt.

"They said you were there, so I thought you could give me a more enlightened perspective on what happened. If you want to know the truth, the guys were already half drunk when I began listening to their discussion, so I'm not sure I have the information correct."

"You have the information straight. The unemployment issue has to be prosecuted at the federal level, even though local and state officials are investigating what happened. It's a long shot that any money will be recovered. I would not recommend the union guys, or anyone else for that matter, get involved in that mess."

"Do you think the Labor Secretary was sympathetic to what the mill's operations have done to the river, not to mention the air and the soil?"

Clay's smile was half-hearted. "It didn't come up, Liz. Secretary Stewart grew up north of here, so it's not like he would be unaware of the decline of fish, wildlife, and growing conditions. It's a sticky situation. The mill has paid a great deal in taxes over the years, and, up until the layoffs, has been the main provider of jobs around here."

"Including a job for that husband of yours." Audrey dropped her cigarette with a sputter into Clayton's half-filled coffee cup.

Elizabeth nodded her head, sick to death of the rhetoric about jobs and taxes she and every person in town had heard many times from their mayor, the city council, the county board chairman, county supervisors, and other politicians. She couldn't hide her frustration.

"I suppose somewhere, in all the stickiness, are contributions by the paper company to anyone who would support their business, and to hell with the public good!"

"You're not wrong. Secretary Stewart is a good guy, but this is a gargantuan, long-lived monster that no one wants to battle. It's not right, but that's the way it is."

"The thing is, it won't matter that the jobs are gone and families have no money, because we're all going to be dead from breathing the air and using the water."

Audrey pushed herself off the desk and stood at her husband's side, resting her hand on his shoulder.

"Aren't you being a bit dramatic, Lizzie? This town and the people in it are doing fine, and as far as I can tell, there is plenty of air and water. If people lose their jobs at the mill, they will find new ones. Simple as that."

Elizabeth struggled to control her anger at the arrogance and lack of compassion Audrey displayed, her life being so far removed from that of ordinary people. However, Elizabeth did recognize, as her father used to say, it would do no good to get into a pissing match with a skunk.

"What can we do to help, Liz?" Clayton asked.

"I wish I knew. It isn't only the loss of jobs. As Nona's health worsened, I was helpless to do anything about it, and that makes me crazy. My little girl died, and lots of other people are suffering with lung and heart problems and who knows what else? Nobody seems to care."

"I think people care, but they feel powerless to do anything. Northland has a great deal of clout and is not shy about using it."

"So we wait until more people are dying?"

"Really, Lizzie, dying? Where's the proof that people are dying because of the mill?" Audrey said.

"Audrey, this isn't the time nor the place for getting into all of that."

"I believe your friend has already opened up the topic, and I think it is the perfect opportunity for her to back up her accusations with facts, if they exist."

Elizabeth's cheeks were flushed, her heart pounding, palms sweaty. It was her theory there were more people who had suffered and died because of the mill. Proving that theory with facts was not something she could do.

"Let's agree that some damage has occurred," Clayton said. "Right now we need to focus on getting financial help for the men who are out of work."

"Of course, you are right." Elizabeth was grateful Clayton had defused Audrey's confrontation and deflected her demand for facts from Elizabeth.

"As usual, Clay, you are the voice of reason and the ambassador of good will," Audrey said, "not to mention the champion of the poor and downtrodden."

"Accolades undeserved, dear wife. Liz, give me some time to talk to people I know at the capital, and see if there is anything we can do besides wait for the feds to straighten this out. There might be someone with connections who can move this along or at least get some money released to the employees who should be receiving unemployment compensation. I'll contact Secretary Stewart, but, I have to tell you, if there was anything he could have done, I think he would have seized the opportunity to reveal that in front of the press. Above all, we have to take care that we don't make the situation worse."

"I doubt that is possible, Clayton."

Elizabeth walked toward the office door. "Let me know if you learn anything that might help."

"I will do that, but I'm not making any promises."

"He never makes a promise he cannot keep." Audrey laughed and threw her arms around her husband's neck.

INVITATIONS

ONE SULTRY MONDAY IN JULY, ELIZABETH RETURNED home from work with an envelope for each of her daughters. Inside was an invitation, printed in script on a creamy, translucent vellum.

You are cordially invited to a Summer

Pool Party

Hosted by Cynthia Alexis Landers

On Saturday, July 25

2:00 P.M. - 7:00 P.M.

Bring your swimsuit & please stay for

a pool-side picnic to follow.

"Isn't that a wonderful gesture?" Elizabeth stretched a pickle-scented arm around each of her daughters. "It's about time you girls have some fun. You need to laugh and swim and be with your friends." She smiled, but it was a pasted-on, sad smile.

Carol Jean squealed and hugged the invitation to her chest, but Mince was worried.

"Pops won't let us," Mince said. "He hates the whole Landers' family."

Elizabeth turned Mince and Carol Jean to face her. "Your father doesn't have anything to say about this. I will see to it that you go to this pool party, no matter what."

Eddie had moved back home one day while Elizabeth was at work. She was furious and wanted him gone, but the girls were there, and Elizabeth was too exhausted to argue with him, especially in front of Mince and Carol Jean. For the time being, Eddie would live there with them, as Elizabeth did her best to avoid him and to keep the girls out of the line of fire.

The day before the swimming party, Mince and Carol Jean were laying out in the backyard, working on their suntans and practicing holding their breath, as Elizabeth returned from work. She joined them on their blanket, removing her damp work shoes and wriggling her bare toes.

"I could make it all the way across the Landers' pool on one breath," Mince huffed at Carol Jean.

"You could not, because your body's not tall enough. You have to be long and have lung strength." Carol Jean stretched her gangly limbs from the top of the blanket to its frayed bottom edge, demonstrating the necessary length. She turned her mended arm for more sun exposure.

Mince leaned over to inspect it. "It's so white, like the milky-white belly of a fish. You'll never get it tan by tomorrow."

"Shut up, Mince! You don't know anything," Carol Jean snapped, rubbing baby oil across her pale arm.

"Carol Jean, that's no way to talk to your sister."

"It doesn't matter if we're tan or not. Pops isn't going to let us go." Mince rolled over onto her back, eyes squinting.

"Mom, didn't you say we would go, no matter what? If Pops stops us, I'll never forgive him. Everybody who's somebody is invited."

"Then why are we invited? We're nobody and nobody's sister."

Carol Jean's face fell, but only for a moment. "That is absolutely not true. Mom, you're an old friend of the Landers' family, and Mince, you're a good friend of Cynthia. Everyone knows I'm one of the most popular girls in middle school. Why shouldn't we be invited?"

"Okay, so we got invited. A thousand invitations will not convince Pops to let us go to a party at the Landers' house. Period."

"It doesn't take a thousand invitations, it only takes one, and you have that. Leave the rest up to me," Elizabeth reassured the girls.

The back screen door slammed. Eddie was home early, standing on the porch.

"Well, well, the old ball and chain is home. You two girls finished with your chores?"

"Yes, Pops!" Both girls answered in unison.

Then Carol Jean added, "We even have Saturday's chores done, so we're all ready for the party."

In that moment, Elizabeth felt the hot, summery air turn frigid under her husband's glare.

"What party?" He was down the porch steps, walking towards them.

"It's a little party for the kids to have some fun," Elizabeth said.

Before Elizabeth could stop her, Carol Jean chimed in. "It's the Landers' pool party. The one we were invited to last week. All the kids are going. Plus, there's a big picnic afterward, so it's a free meal. We were lucky to be invited." Like a mouse stuck in a muck hole, Carol Jean was sinking deeper and deeper with every damning word.

Mince was attempting to stop Carol Jean by shoving a boney elbow into her sister's rib cage, but it was too late.

"You're lucky? It's not luck that got you invited. It's pity, and this family doesn't need any more pity." Eddie leaned over, hands big as frying pans resting on his knees, his sour beer breath spewing as he spit out the words.

"You can forget about going to any pool party given by Clayton Landers or anyone else. Do you hear me?"

"It's not your decision, Eddie. I've already told the girls they will be going to the party, and that's the end of it."

"Everything in this family is my decision, Lizzie. Don't ever doubt that."

They sat in silence, watching him strut to the house and stomp up the back steps. Throwing open the screen door, Eddie turned and glared in their direction, then went inside. Lucky ambled from his shady spot under the porch, dropped down beside Carol Jean, and placed his head in her lap. Hot, angry tears rolled down her face.

"I hate him so much," she said through clenched teeth. "He should have died, not Nona."

Elizabeth couldn't blame Carol Jean for feeling the way she did. Leave it to Eddie to ruin a simple party invitation.

After the argument with Eddie about the pool party, Elizabeth invited the girls to walk downtown for a sandwich at the Peterson's Corner Cafe. It was a luxury they could not afford, but Elizabeth hoped it would help to get their minds off Pops. Besides, last week the cafe had installed air conditioning, so the promise of a meal in a cool place away from home was too hard to resist. Elizabeth kept her true motive for the outing to herself.

When they had finished their food, sipped the last of the cherry Coke, and crunched the final ice cube, Elizabeth suggested the three stop at the public library, a few blocks down the street.

"It's open on Friday nights until 8:00, and you know the library is cool and quiet. Besides, you both could check out some books."

"I would't be caught dead in the library on a Friday night," Carol Jean said.

"Because you have so many other things to do, right?" Mince smirked.

"Never mind the arguing, you two. I have some things I want to do at the library, so you are coming with me. Carol Jean, you can sit out on the steps and wait if you think entering a library will somehow damage your image."

Carol Jean resisted going into the air conditioned building for less than five minutes before she gave in, and Elizabeth saw her hurry into the coolness of the library. As Elizabeth wandered about, she watched Carol Jean gathering a pile of magazines like Modern Stars, Screen Stars, and Teen Magazine. Nearby, Mince located the action and adventure books, all she needed to keep her occupied.

Elizabeth found herself in the Periodicals Section, as Audrey's challenging question reverberated through her head. "Where's the proof that people are dying because of the mill?" Audrey had asked. Elizabeth began pulling newspapers, thumbing through to the Obituaries' section of each. There were the usual deaths of persons who had lived and died as expected, natural causes taking them late in their sixties and seventies, some into their eighties, even nineties, as well as additional deaths every month not fitting into the usual expectation. For the sake of thoroughness, she copied every deceased person's name, address, and the date and cause of their death, not knowing how or if these deaths were linked to the mill or each other. When she had finished with the papers of the last two weeks that were hanging in the newspaper rack, Elizabeth asked the librarian for assistance with the microfilm system. She was told it was housed in a small room off the main library, where papers from past months and years were stored on microfilm.

It wasn't difficult to use, but many years had passed since Elizabeth had researched in a library, so it was fortunate when Carol Jean sauntered into the room where her mother was working.

"What are you looking at?" Carol Jean asked.

"I was curious about something someone mentioned to me at the plant, so I thought I'd check it out. It's been a long time since I've looked at microfilm, though. Would you be able to help me with it?"

"Sure. That's one thing I liked about my English class this year, doing research for a term paper." Carol Jean pulled a chair up next to Elizabeth. "What section do you want to read?"

Together, the mother and daughter began scanning the obituaries, starting with the most recent papers and working their way back in time. Carol Jean read the information out loud as Elizabeth added it to her growing list of names and deaths.

When Carol Jean said, "Nona Evangeline Dembrowski," neither of them moved or said anything for a moment.

"You don't have to read me the information. This one I know by heart," Elizabeth said as she wrote the details of her own daughter's death with a trembling hand.

"What are you doing?" Mince joined them, dropping down a stack of books on the table.

"We're doing some digging. Would you like to help?" Elizabeth asked.

Mince leaned over Carol Jean's shoulder as they continued to search through the films of past papers. By the time the librarian announced the library would be closing in ten minutes, the three of them had collected a good deal of data.

In the hot summer night, they walked home through the darkened streets. Carol Jean asked, "What are you going to do with all that stuff you wrote down?"

Elizabeth hugged her notebook to her chest. "I'm not sure yet. It's something that we might need to know some day, that's all."

A MEETING AND A POOL PARTY

ON SATURDAY, THE POOL PARTY DAY, CARS AND PICKUP
trucks began arriving at the Dembrowski house around noon. It was
a union meeting with their lawyer, Eddie had informed Elizabeth,
one to which she was not invited. Elizabeth recognized most of the
same men from the mill, clothed in grey work pants and shirts worn
thin from too many years of wearing. The group assembled in the
dining room, so Elizabeth sat at her desk in the adjoining den, clip-
ping and sorting coupons, close enough to see the room and hear
what was being said, without being noticed.

New to the usual gathering was Attorney Julian R. Prince.
Elizabeth could see him standing at the end of the long, oval table,
the light streaming in through the windows behind him, his presence
aglow like a biblical vision. She had always admired Julian's quiet,
composed voice, and when he began to speak, the men listened.

"I offer my deepest condolences to Eddie and his family. There is
no greater tragedy than losing a child like Nona." He paused, searching to locate Eddie, awarding him with a solemn, sympathetic nod.
Elizabeth felt a familiar lump form in her throat hearing Nona's name.

The attorney's eyes, framed in glistening, thick glasses, scanned
the entire room. "You all have suffered, perhaps not to the degree
of the Dembrowski family, but it has been suffering all the same.
For what it's worth, you have my deepest regret over the mill's treatment of you, its dedicated employees, and of the residents in this

community. Managements' actions have been, and continue to be, abhorrent, repugnant, an absolute abomination, not to mention unethical, as well as, we believe, illegal." He paused, nudging his glasses with a well-manicured pointer finger. "Having said that, we must keep in mind that what we view as right and just is in direct opposition to how those in power think and operate."

Elizabeth could hear mumbles of agreement ripple through the room, along with a few uneasy, saddened chuckles.

"Legally, the Northland Paper Company, Inc., had a responsibility to report the amounts of wages paid their employees and then to pay employer contributions to the unemployment compensation system. These proceeds should have been deposited in the Federal Unemployment Trust Fund, from which withdrawals can be made during times of layoff, termination, or economic recession."

"If that's the law, where's our money?" Eddie asked.

"Approximately fifteen years ago, someone, or more than one person, with access to those funds, began a premeditated, systematic misappropriation of said assets."

"You mean someone embezzled our money," Art said.

"That appears to be the case," Julian replied.

"If there's a law, then there's a record of everything somewhere, and we should be able to find our money," Art declared.

"It's not that simple. I know records were falsified to conceal under-reporting of wages paid. Small amounts of money, too small to be red-flagged, were secreted over long periods of time. Then, during the last two years, it looks like very large sums were converted for unintended and unsanctioned use."

"It sounds like you have already seen the company records."

"The judge granted me a preliminary look at Northland's books," Julian said. "At a glance, I'd say the proof is in those records."

"Sounds like we've got 'em by the balls," Eddie said.

"What we suspect and what we find as verifiable evidence will take time."

"Let's get what we need! There's nothing can stop us if we go in and take it, right boys?" Eddie said.

"Not necessary, Eddie. The good news is that all financial records have been subpoenaed as of this morning, to be turned over no later than Monday at 5:00 P.M."

The men's voices murmured, their conversations subdued, and Elizabeth could not discern what was being said.

Julian continued. "None of this guarantees recovery of anything. Even with concrete proof of embezzlement, we have no idea where the missing funds are, or if they even exist any longer."

"We have to wait, while the bank takes away our homes and our kids ain't got any food to eat?"

"With regard to the embezzlement case, the short answer is yes."

A honking car horn interrupted Julian Prince and startled Elizabeth, who was dreading the confrontation she anticipated would be happening soon. She heard her father enter the house as Mince was hurrying to greet him.

"Gramps is here," Mince said as she passed through the den.

"Go meet him. I'm right behind you," Elizabeth said.

Earlier in the week, when Eddie told her about the union meeting scheduled for that day, Elizabeth and her father worked out a plan so William would pick them up as the meeting was being conducted. Elizabeth hoped that in front of the men, Eddie would not want to embarrass himself by appearing jealous and mean denying his daughters this experience. That might be enough to discourage him from making a scene.

Striding past the men meeting around the dining room table, Mince entered the kitchen to greet her grandfather with a hug. As William walked Mince back into the dining room, his hands resting protectively on the girl's shoulders, Elizabeth came in the room and stood beside them.

"Don't get up fellas," William smiled, acknowledging those he knew, which was nearly everyone.

"Sorry for the interruption, but I'm here to escort my grand-daughters to a very important pool party." He placed Mince's hand on the crook of his arm and pivoted around to escort her to the car. Carol Jean scurried in, following close behind and carrying bags Elizabeth had prepared for the sisters. On her way out, Elizabeth stopped to fill Lucky's water bowl, stalling and straining to hear if Eddie would react in front of his buddies.

"Lucky kids," Julian commented. "I notice none of you gents were invited!"

"The last thing we need to see is Art's hairy, white legs sticking out of a pair of swim trunks!" Eddie laughed when he said it, but Elizabeth could tell he was furious because he had no choice but to allow the girls to leave.

Relieved, Elizabeth was walking out the door when she felt a hand grab her arm from behind.

"You haven't heard the last of this, Lizzie," Eddie said. Twisting her arm, he shoved her forward, causing her to stumble down the steps.

Elizabeth was grateful William and the girls were busy getting organized in the car and didn't see her wobble and nearly fall. Rubbing a scuffed elbow, she climbed into the front seat. Mince reached over the seat and hugged her mother from behind, and as the car backed down the driveway, Mince and Carol Jean cheered.

"What lucky girls you are to be able to attend Cynthia's party," Elizabeth said. "We want you to have a wonderful time and not worry about anything. Gramps and I will square things with your dad, so you enjoy yourselves. Remember, if you would like to be invited back again, make them glad they invited you this time."

Carol Jean dug into the bags she had carried out for her mother. "I can't believe you got us new swimsuits to wear!"

"Prince's had a great sale on summer things, so I thought, what the heck? Besides, you had both grown out of your old suits. I couldn't resist the swimsuit coverups and sandals, too. You are going to look so terrific!"

The girls hurried to change their clothes in the back seat.

"No peeking, anybody," Carol Jean said, struggling to stay covered while undressing.

"Does everything fit all right?" Elizabeth asked.

"It's perfect," Carol Jean beamed, smoothing her swimsuit around her slender waist.

"What if Pops wouldn't have let us go? How could you be sure we'd get to wear this stuff?" Mince worried.

"Because," William answered, "your dad cannot say no to me, that's how! Now, we're here, so are you ready?" He stepped out and reached to open the car door for them, letting loose a long, appreciative whistle as they exited from the vehicle.

"As pretty as Esther Williams. My gorgeous ladies, your party awaits!" he said.

Mince hesitated, and Elizabeth sensed the girl's apprehension. This was her first real party with an actual invitation, music, food, and a swimming pool. Elizabeth stepped out of the car and helped the girls gather their things to take inside. Together, the three walked up the long winding sidewalk to the Landers' impressive home. Carol Jean must have had been feeling some butterflies herself, Elizabeth thought, because she reached for her younger sister's hand and held on to it all the way to the front door. Elizabeth felt the tears in her eyes, as she thought of Nona, who would never know the love and joy of growing up with these two sisters.

Carol Jean and Mince turned to wave at their grandfather's car as Clay opened the door, music blaring from inside.

"If it isn't the beautiful Dembrowski girls." His words were directed at the two sisters, but his eyes were focussed on Elizabeth.

"Welcome to the craziness!" He gestured toward the open front door, as Cynthia bounded out past him.

"Hi, Mince and Carol Jean! I'm so glad you could come to my party. Come on, the fun is this way, as if you couldn't tell!" She laughed and grabbed both their hands, pulling them into the house.

Clay stepped outside, closing the door behind him. "It was good of you to allow your daughters to come to the party. Cynthia was afraid they might not be here, with all that has happened."

He stood facing Elizabeth, taller than she remembered him to be. She liked the way the years had matured Clayton, lines fanning out from his eyes as he smiled at her.

"I am so glad you came along to drop them off," Clay said.

"I couldn't let them miss the party of the summer, could I?" Elizabeth felt herself smiling, an unusual occurrence since Nona died. "Thank you for thinking of them. Carol Jean and Mince both needed this."

"I am always thinking of you, and the girls, of course." Clay leaned in toward Elizabeth, their faces so close she could see the curl of his eyelashes. His face was smooth and tanned, like the hand he reached out to enfold her own. She should have pulled away and stepped back, but she didn't.

"I wanted to tell you this in private," Clayton said. "I had a chance to meet with Labor Secretary Stewart in Madison. We discussed the alleged embezzlement of the millworkers' unemployment, which the Secretary feels is a true injustice for the workmen involved. However, not much will happen until the company records are confiscated and reviewed. Stewart feels terrible about the situation, but his hands are tied."

"Everything was subpoenaed by the judge this morning, to be handed over by Monday," Elizabeth said. "Who's to say someone didn't falsify their files already? What's to stop them from deleting or destroying information altogether?"

"Nothing. For all we know, that could be happening as we speak, or perhaps the mill has been doing that all along. Anything is possible, Liz."

"What if the files obtained by the subpoena aren't the real records of the company, but something they cooked up to satisfy the courts? That could mean the actual files are being kept hidden somewhere."

"Are we still talking about the alleged unemployment compensation embezzlement, or is there something else you're looking for?"

"I don't know. Maybe. I mean, if I could find something to prove Northland's culpability in the water and air quality, then I could link it to Nona's death."

"Now you're reaching," Clay said. "I guess we'll have to wait until the attorneys analyze everything and go from there."

"I have do something now. If there are company records being withheld, we need to find them before something happens to them," Elizabeth said.

"How do we do that?"

"I wish I knew."

"Hello, Clay!" a voice called out from the street.

Elizabeth and Clay turned to see William leaning out the window of his car, and Elizabeth withdrew her hand from Clay's grasp.

"Good to see you, William." Clayton waved back.

Elizabeth felt the heat rise to her cheeks. Had her father seen Clay leaning close to her and holding her hand?

"Hotter than blazes in this car, Liz, but Marta will be hotter still, under the collar, if we don't get to the Farmers' Market soon."

"I'd better go," Elizabeth said.

"Good to see you," Clay said, his hand holding her arm for a brief time.

Elizabeth kept her eyes averted as she hurried down the sidewalk to the street, hoping William wouldn't make a big deal about what he saw. Though he gave her a sideways glance when she slid into the car, no mention was made of her encounter with Clay. At the park, cars were bumper to bumper along the road, because the parking lots and grassy places not occupied with farmers' booths were full. Elizabeth and William hurried from the stifling car into the shady coolness beneath the trees. When they reached their booth, a dozen people were lined up for ice cream, while others admired and examined the produce.

"Thank goodness you are here!" Marta waved, then continued her ice cream scooping without missing a beat. "The ice cream supply is holding up better than the ice cream server!" Her flushed face glowed underneath a checkered floppy hat.

"Thanks so much, Mom, for holding down the fort for us." Elizabeth slipped on a red apron and gathered her thick hair within the confines of a finely stitched hair net.

"How did it all go?" Marta asked.

"Our two granddaughters are, at this very moment, enjoying a fine afternoon at the Landers' pool," William replied.

"And Eddie?"

Elizabeth stopped bagging carrots for a moment. "We made it out of the house, and that's all that matters."

Things stayed busy for the next several hours, the three working like a well-coached team. It was almost six thirty before business slowed, as families left for home or wandered to their picnic spots, grills spewing flames and silvery smoke. Elizabeth poured them each a glass of lemonade and leaned against the vegetable bins.

"It was a good day, I'd say." William was counting bills and change from their coffee can. "I think the ice cream added an additional thirty dollars, Marta, thanks to you." He leaned over and kissed his wife's rosy, damp cheek.

The couple began to inventory the sales and remaining produce, working together like a hand and its glove. Elizabeth watched her parents, always amazed at how their marriage worked without seeming like work at all. Her thoughts drifted back to when she and Eddie had first begun together. It hadn't seemed like work then, either.

THE STUDYING BEGINS AND THE PARTY ENDS

ELIZABETH AND EDDIE STUDIED TWICE A WEEK AT FIRST. As semester finals approached, Eddie worried he needed more help, so Elizabeth's parents allowed them to study at the Sloan house on Saturday afternoons, books spread out over the kitchen table. Elizabeth thought Eddie was unbelievably uneducated for someone completing his senior year.

"Quit worrying about the SAT and admissions' exam. If you can't raise the grades of your regular classes, taking those tests won't matter."

"Thanks for those words of encouragement, Miss Mary Sunshine! Don't worry, I'll make it work. I always do."

"Study, okay, Eddie? Seriously, it will make a difference, and there's only so much I can do. You need to open the books and study!"

"Yes, sir, Captain, sir!" Eddie smirked, saluting her in mock submission.

Elizabeth couldn't help but smile. Despite the fact that Eddie was crude and didn't care about school, she was attracted to him.

"Trouble," her father had called Eddie, but that didn't change the butterflies she felt every time she was with him.

They spent the next week focussed on Eddie's semester exams and the upcoming SAT. He called her after finals were completed.

"I want to thank you," he began. "I think I did okay, and that's because of your help."

"No need to thank me. I was doing the job you paid me to do."

"I'd like it if you'd let me buy you a burger for doing such a good job," he offered over the phone.

"Don't start celebrating yet, Eddie. Let's wait until exam results are posted before we begin the applause. Look, I gotta go. I'll see you Tuesday at the library." She hung up, needing to get Eddie out of her head. What she couldn't risk was more time spent with Eddie Dembrowski.

All those years ago, that younger version of herself had recognized Eddie was a trap. Why she hadn't listened to that warning, Elizabeth still couldn't say.

"Did you hear me Elizabeth?" Marta asked.

"What? Sorry, Mom, guess I was daydreaming. What did you say?"

"I asked you what time we're supposed to get the girls from their party."

"It ends at seven o'clock, and I want to be there on time. It's embarrassing to be the last one waiting for a ride home."

They were finishing up the packing, and in their haste, not one of the three noticed Eddie strolling towards them.

"Seems like you are all in a pretty big hurry to close up shop," he snarled, "and that's a disappointment for an ice cream lover like me."

"Ice cream's been sold out for hours, Eddie," Marta offered, her smile a thin line on her face. "Too bad you didn't get here earlier. My newest flavor, raspberry sugar, was a big hit with the customers."

"Busy man like me can't always get away. Next time, maybe you'll save me a couple of scoops." Eddie sauntered towards them and leaned his frame against the produce trailer.

"Whoever is the last paying customer gets the final scoop," William said without looking up. "That's business, Eddie. Now, if you'll excuse me, we're hoping to get out of the park before seven." He moved beyond his son-in-law, stacking crates and produce baskets and hauling them for storage.

Eddie grabbed several boxes from Elizabeth's arms, following William to the trailer.

"Let me give you a hand, Lizzie," he said with sarcasm dripping from every word. "We're a team, in this together, isn't that what you said?"

Stowing the boxes, Eddie slammed the trailer panel shut. He glanced toward his in-laws, who were busy loading boxes and crates on the other side, unable to see him over the packed trailer. With the ferocity and swiftness of a predatory animal, Eddie grabbed Elizabeth by the shoulders, squeezing until she wanted to scream, knowing she wouldn't.

"Get one thing into that thick head of yours, Lizzie. My girls are to be kept away from the likes of Clayton Landers."

His hand released her shoulder and squeezed her chin in a vice-like grip. "While you're at it, keep your pretty self away from him, too. If you ever do anything again without my say-so, things will be a hell of a lot sorrier than they already are. Understand?"

He left, but not before dismissing her with a stinging slap. For a moment, Elizabeth didn't breathe. Shaking her head to clear it, she forced herself into action.

"We need to leave," she yelled at her folks. "I don't want Eddie to show up at Clayton's house, making a scene in front of all the girls' friends."

"All finished. Let's go!" her father responded, coming around the trailer after closing the last panel.

"What happened?" William asked, examining Elizabeth's crimson cheek.

"Never mind, Dad. We don't have time for any trouble right now," Elizabeth said, turning her face away.

"Time or not, with Eddie, there will always be trouble," William said.

William drove fast, and they arrived before Eddie, who pulled up behind them, nearly rear ending their trailer as he slammed on his brakes. With an unplanned synchronization, the doors of both cars flew open. Eddie was quick, rounding the front of his vehicle in a blink, but it was Elizabeth who first reached the girls as they waited on the front walk.

"It looks like you two have been at a swimming party!" Elizabeth fingered Mince's tangled ponytail, then placed her arms around both girls' shoulders. "Did you behave like young ladies, and did you remember to thank Cynthia and her parents?"

Before either girl could answer, Eddie took charge. "Isn't this a pretty picture? Not many times do we get to visit the other side of the tracks. Smells good up here."

Mince looked at her mother. "Yes, we thanked everybody, and I think we were the best behaved kids there, right Carol Jean?"

"Oh, definitely, and look at the cool party gifts they gave everyone!" She began rummaging in her beach bag for the gift.

Eddie's face was flushed with anger. "A little charity gift to the poor folk. That's just great!"

"Eddie, don't make a scene here in front of the other kids and their parents. We can discuss this at home, all right?" Elizabeth was ushering the girls past their father towards William who had opened the back door of his car.

"That's right, Eddie," William said. "It was an afternoon for your two girls to enjoy, so let it be."

"Sure, I'll let it be," Eddie sneered, tapping his temple with a rugged finger. "It'll be right up here, waiting for our private discussion, Lizzie." He got into his car, slamming the beat-up door, the engine struggling to a feeble start.

"Get in, girls," Elizabeth directed, not giving Eddie a glance as he drove away, their old car coughing at the effort.

"Tell us all about this big, splashy pool party," Marta requested. She looked over the seat at her granddaughters sitting beside Elizabeth.

Catching the expression on Marta's face, Elizabeth thought the three of them, lined up in the backseat, must look like sitting ducks, waiting for hunting season to begin.

REMEMBERING

THOUGH THEIR EXCITEMENT WAS DEFLATED, BETWEEN them, Mince and Carol Jean told all about the party. If she hadn't known better, Elizabeth would have sworn the two sisters were at different parties. Carol Jean saw life with stars in her eyes, and they were all revolving around her. Mince was the realist, and Elizabeth appreciated that this time Mince decided not to burst her sister's bubble.

"The pool was the best," Mince decided, "and the french fries and the real bakery cake. I had two pieces, but only because Cynthia offered."

"You had two of everything," Carol Jean said. "The pool was beautiful, and they played really good music. All my friends were there, plus some boys from my class. Janice had a new haircut that looked cute, sort of Audrey Hepburn style. Everybody was wearing mascara and eye shadow. We all decided blue definitely is the best color."

"You didn't even go in the pool, except for your feet," Mince said. "We played Marco Polo and tag and had a cannonball contest."

"You should have seen the cute swimming suits! Mary Ann wore a bright yellow two-piece suit. Very Hollywood. Everyone loved my suit! They said it was identical to one featured in Teen Magazine, and that it flattered my figure."

"Cynthia's parents were so nice, too," Mince added. "Mr. Landers cooked the burgers himself, right on this fancy grill they had outside. Oh, and I tried shrimp, which looked kind of creepy, with this red sauce that was spicy."

"Inside they had an actual cook who made everything else, including making homemade french fries. I have to admit those were delicious," Carol Jean said.

The banter continued until every detail of the afternoon had been discussed. Elizabeth loved the fact that both her daughters had enjoyed the party, though in different ways.

That night, after the girls were in bed, Elizabeth checked on them and then wandered down the hall to peer into Nona's bedroom. It remained, frozen in time, as Nona had left it that final day. There wasn't enough strength in Elizabeth to push herself over the threshold and enter the room. Instead, she clicked off the light switch and struggled for the courage to back away.

The kitchen, still missing the lace curtains she had once thought so important, was the coolest room in the house, with a crossbreeze between the back door and the open dining room windows. Exhausted, but unwilling to sleep, Elizabeth stood in the faint breeze, leaning into the old enamel sink. Methodically, she began to scrub the latest batch of pickling cucumbers. Canning came naturally to her after all these years, and her movements fell into a practiced rhythm. As she worked, jars rattling in unison inside the boiling canning kettle, Elizabeth's thoughts drifted to a time imprinted in her memory, in the Sloan farmhouse kitchen, and her own mother standing over a steaming stove.

Elizabeth had been tutoring Eddie for over seven months. In part, their time together had been successful. Eddie's GPA had risen to 2.56, and he felt confident the SAT he had completed the week before had gone well. By the time his university entrance exam was administered, the SAT results would be mailed. It would all come together before graduation, in time for Eddie to receive confirmation of his acceptance at the University and on the football squad. By July, he would be on campus for early training sessions.

Their time together had changed. Studying was still the impetus, but later, after they were almost numb from memorization and recitation, the magnetism between the two was undeniable. In the beginning, Eddie was almost hesitant about being physically close to someone as different as Elizabeth. He would lean close to her at the end of their evenings, pressing his lips against hers. Soon, the kisses lingered, their fingers entwined.

Elizabeth told herself each time that she would resist. Then, Eddie's arms would be enveloping her, and she found herself unable to think. Before long, their trip home took more and more time. Eddie often parked the car along Dahlia Road, not far from Sloan's Creek Road, but much less traveled and very dark. Elizabeth found herself looking forward to being alone with Eddie, and despite everything around her pushing him away, everything within her pulled Eddie closer and closer.

That Monday, in early May, Elizabeth sat watching her mother preparing supper, steam rolling upward from several kettles.

"Is there something wrong?" her mother asked. "Never once in the last school year have I seen you sit down at that table without having your head buried in textbooks and class notes." She reached to lower the gas flames under each of the pots and wiped her hands on the embroidered apron tied around her middle.

Sitting across the table from Elizabeth, she took her daughter's hands into her rough, weathered ones. "Tell me, my darling daughter, what is on your mind?"

"I'm pregnant, Mom." Elizabeth took a deep breath and closed her eyes. "Say you don't hate me, okay?"

SMASHED

THE SLAMMING OF A CAR DOOR REGISTERED SOME-
where in her brain, pulling Elizabeth to the present. Without knocking, Art came in through the tattered screen door, the muggy night
air following him inside. Elizabeth wiped her hands on her worn
embroidered apron as she turned to greet Art, who looked haggard.

"What's happened?" She stepped toward Art, allowing her husband's best friend to place his hands on her shoulders, steadying her.

"It's not too bad, Elizabeth," Art reassured her, "but Eddie has
been in a slight car accident." She drew in a labored breath and
exhaled a deep sigh.

"He's okay, a little banged up, is all. You need to come with me to
the police station. They'll only release him to a family member, given
his inebriated condition. Guess they don't trust him in the hands of
his drinking buddy, hey?"

"What was he thinking, Art? If he was so drunk, he shouldn't
have been driving at all. Why did you let him drive?"

He released his hold on her shoulders and stepped back.
"Nobody tells Eddie anything, especially when he's been drinking all
day. I was doing the best I could by being in the car with him, which,
I might add, was a considerable sacrifice seeing's how I could have
been killed as easy as not."

Elizabeth shook her head in dismay. "I'm sorry, Art. It's not your fault. Of course, I'll come with you to the station. Give me a minute to check on the girls. I'll meet you outside."

Elizabeth turned off the stove, tossed the remainder of cucumbers into the refrigerator, and ran upstairs.

In Carol Jean's room, she shook her oldest daughter awake. "I'll be gone for a little while," she told the girl, who sat blinking away the sleep from her eyes. "It shouldn't be long, and the doors will all be locked. All right?"

"Okay. When will you be back?" Without waiting for her mother's answer, Carol Jean rolled over and closed her eyes again.

The Police Department was located within the downtown Municipal Building, not far from Prince's store. Elizabeth couldn't remember the last time she'd been inside the ancient, yellow brick building. Not since her drivers' test, she guessed, a long time ago.

As they entered the set of heavy, glass doors criss-crossed with wobbly wire mesh, Elizabeth and Art were met by Officer Jim McDougal, one of Eddie's football teammates from high school. Though somewhat heavier now, Jim still resembled the young fullback of past years, with a neck thick as a marble pillar, set on shoulders expansive and bullish, but lacking the fleshy, round beer belly Eddie had gained over time.

"Elizabeth, I have Eddie in holding right now," McDougal stated in a professional voice, walking them towards a bench in the hallway. "He was pretty drunk, and that prevented him from serious injury. I've taped up a nasty gash on his face, which is about the worst of it. The car, I hate to tell you, was not so lucky. It's a total loss."

Elizabeth dropped onto the bench, and to her surprise, the officer sat down next to her and took her hands in his.

"I've known Eddie since we were kids, and I understand things have been real bad for him and all of you," Jim said.

"I'm not saying it's protocol, but I'm only citing Eddie for a traffic violation, rather than arresting him for drunken driving and assaulting an officer." Elizabeth noticed the angry swelling around Jim's eye. She shook her head in useless remorse for what had happened.

"Anyway, he'll have to pay a fine within the next week, but for right now, you can take him home. Jacobson's towed what was left of your vehicle over to their salvage yard on County O, in case you'd like to look it over. Since the car is totaled, I suspect there's little chance of Eddie driving drunk any time soon."

"Thank you, Jim. It is more than kind of you to do this. I'll see to it the fine is paid, and he won't be driving again at all, rest assured."

At that moment, accompanied by another officer, Eddie strolled out with an insouciance, released from his cell, his grin belying the anger Elizabeth could detect in his eyes.

"The troops are here to save the day! Imagine that," he sneered, all the while the officer was unlocking his handcuffs. "Thank you kindly, Officer McDougal, for the warm and friendly accommodations. It's been a pleasure seeing you again, Jimmie Boy!"

With that, Eddie swaggered down the hallway, then struggled to open the heavy doors. He cursed and demanded someone open the door, pounding on the glass, then realized he had been pushing when pulling was what would open it. Elizabeth and Art followed Eddie outside and found him swaying with uncertainty.

"Car's in the back lot," Art directed. Eddie grunted in response, not looking at either of them as his unsteady legs took him toward the parking lot behind the station.

The three rode home in silence. Elizabeth stared ahead, occasionally glancing over her shoulder at Eddie, lolling in the back seat, his mouth open. The car smelled of taverns and cigarettes.

Pulling into the driveway, Art stopped in front of the garage. Eddie tumbled from the vehicle and staggered toward the house.

"Get some sleep, buddy," Art offered. "Things will look a whole lot different in the morning."

"Yeah, peachy. You know, Art, ole pal, you and my cock-eyed optimist wife are two peas in a pod!"

Elizabeth exited the car and looked at her sorry excuse for a husband. "For goodness sake, Art's the only reason you are not sitting in jail right now. Don't say something you can't take back."

"Lizzie, my whole life is one big "something I can't take back." With that, he walked inside, the screen door slapping against its ragged frame.

"I am sorry, Art. Eddie doesn't appreciate what a good friend you are to him."

"Not another word," Art said. "If I listened to everything Eddie said, I'd have jumped off that cliff down at the quarry back fifteen years ago, and I would have been drowned dead."

He laughed an embarrassed laugh, easing the car door closed. "Stay out of his line of fire, Elizabeth, for your own good. I'll see ya."

As she opened the back screen, Lucky squeezed past, headed for the yard. Elizabeth decided to spend some time sitting outside, while the dog snuffled in the nighttime shadows. Maybe Eddie would be passed out by the time she went in.

Elizabeth waited a good fifteen minutes before determining it was safe to enter the house. She scooted Lucky up the steps and opened the door, its hinges creaking in slow motion. Eddie startled her as he waited in the dark kitchen, backlit with a faint glow from a light somewhere in the house.

In the dark, he reached for her, and Elizabeth thought he was going to embrace her for coming to his rescue. When his hands closed around her throat instead, the absurdity of expecting an embrace, under different circumstances, would have been humorous.

"You and my old buddy, Art, hey? Aren't you two cozy as a couple of rats in hole." His grip tightened as Elizabeth struggled to stay conscious, and then he let go.

Elizabeth rubbed her neck and coughed. "Art was with you, Eddie, not me, remember? He is now, and has always been, your best friend, not mine. He's trying to help you, and sometimes that means helping me. That's all there is to it."

"He's too conveniently close whenever you need something."

"Like tonight, Eddie? When he helped me get you out of jail? Or how about when you almost killed the both of you, driving drunk?"

"Shut the hell up, Lizzie!"

This time she couldn't shut up. "What about our car, Eddie? How am I supposed to get to work or get groceries or drive out to the farm? Any ideas, Eddie? Oh, I know! I'll ask 'our' best friend, Art. I'm pretty sure he'd be happy to help!"

It was the shattering sound that made her think he had hit her with the beer bottle. The side of her face seemed to explode, and the flares from that explosion filled her vision. Then Elizabeth blacked out, crumbling to the linoleum floor like a ragged dishtowel.

She awoke in semi-darkness, stretched out on the living room couch. Lucky's warm breath brushed her with shallow puffs, his nose resting next to her face. The pain in Elizabeth's head was excruciating, and she touched her face tentatively, grimacing. Everything was swollen, her left eye squeezed shut. At least it didn't feel cut open, so Eddie must have used his fist and not the bottle, Elizabeth decided. Through her right eye, she could see Lucky, his worried gaze fixed on her injured face, and his long pink tongue lapping her hands with care. It was almost morning before Elizabeth felt steady enough to sit up.

THE LIE

EDDIE PLACED A STEAMING CUP OF COFFEE ON THE low table in front of Elizabeth. With shaking hands, she lifted the drink and sipped. Staring straight ahead, she was able to see through her right eye only, the left swollen to a narrow slit. She felt submerged in deep water, the patterns of morning sun dappling the room like bubbles rising from deep beneath her. Eddie sat down on the couch next to her, shifting his weight and clasping and unclasping his hands. When Elizabeth did not move or speak, Eddie started talking.

"I don't guess sorry is going to fix much," he began, "but there is plenty of blame to go around." He paused. Elizabeth was silent.

"You do things on purpose to make me crazy mad. Nothin' I said about the girls going to the pool party mattered," Eddie said. "It's no secret how I feel about Clayton Landers, but that didn't make one bit of difference to you. Then William showed up, and I knew you two had schemed against me all along." He reached to place his hands around hers, but she pulled back, sloshing coffee.

"You don't have to look at me or anything like that, but would you say something, so I know I'm not talking to entertain myself?"

"We'll say we were in a car accident," Elizabeth managed through her cracked lips. "Both of us were in the car, and that's how it happened."

Before Eddie could respond, Mince shuffled into the living room, hair on end and sleep etched on her face. "Morning, Mom. Aren't we going to chur. . ."

She stopped as her eyes settled on her mother's swollen, discolored face. "What happened to your face?" Mince reached to touch Elizabeth, who took hold of her daughter's hand.

"It looks much worse than it is, Love," she reassured Mince. "I hardly know it is there, except for a little headache."

Eddie rose to get Elizabeth some aspirin, and Mince sat down in his place. "What happened? How did you hurt your face?"

"Your dad and I were driving home with Art from the Blue Moon. We had gone there after you went to bed, to play cards. Anyway, I remembered something Gramps had left at the County Park that afternoon, so we were heading out on County Park Road to go retrieve it."

Elizabeth paused and the pounding in her head eased. When Mince opened her mouth to begin asking questions, Elizabeth continued her tale.

"Without warning, this enormous white-tailed deer leapt from the ditch, almost in front of the car. Your father veered in time to avoid hitting the deer, which was so lucky. Unfortunately, as the car swerved, it caught the gravel on the other side of the road, and we lost control and ended up hitting a tree. It was okay, though, because we couldn't hit that deer, could we?" Elizabeth had amazed herself with how little effort it took to fabricate such a lie.

"You're not really hurt? What about Art? And the deer?" Mince was close to tears, and her mother pulled the child over to sit close to her on the couch.

"Everybody, including the deer, is fine. In a couple of days, you won't even know the accident happened, so please don't worry about it, sweet girl."

Mince placed her arms around Elizabeth, resting her head against her mother's shoulder. Elizabeth understood that no matter how hard her daughter tried, the image of her mother's damaged face was there, scratched into the girl's memory. No amount of explaining was going to erase it away.

Later that morning, Elizabeth heard her daughters' angry voices exploding out of the living room.

"It's a lie. It wasn't Pops she left with. It was Art, in Art's car," Carol Jean said.

"Maybe they were going to meet Pops at the Blue Moon. Maybe Art was giving her a ride."

"Grow up, Mince! Mom was with Art, and that's called cheating, and Pops hit her for it."

"I don't believe you. I believe our parents, and you should, too."

"Why would I believe our cheating mother and the drunken father who beats her for it?"

"Shut up, Carol Jean. Shut your ugly mouth!"

Elizabeth arrived in time to see Mince jump with such force onto the couch she sent both girls tumbling onto the floor. Carol Jean shrieked and grabbed a handful of Mince's hair, with Mince thrashing hard to escape. Before either could do any real damage, Elizabeth was pushing them apart, with Lucky at her side, frantic and barking at the girls screaming at one another and entangled on the floor.

"This is what you've decided you would become? Common hooligans, yelling and brawling? My goodness, what will become of us?"

Elizabeth yanked Mince off the floor and sat her onto the couch. "Calm down."

"It's not any different than you and Pops, is it?" Carol Jean asked, her defiant chin thrust in the air, her back against the couch.

"That's enough, young lady. There will be no more fighting in this house, with words or otherwise! We are a family and the only way we can survive in this world is to be there for each other, no matter what."

Mince looked into Elizabeth's swollen, contorted face. "I'm sorry for fighting and everything." She looked at her sister. "I'm sorry, Carol Jean, for telling you to shut up and for whomping you off the couch."

"Yeah, I'm sorry, Mom. Mince, I accept your apology."

Elizabeth cleared her throat, her face softening as best it could, considering her injuries. "Cherish each other, for we all have experienced how quickly things change and how we lose those we love. Now, go outside and take Lucky with you."

She glanced out the narrow window at the end of the room. "I think your grandparents are here. They'll want to know why we didn't make it to church this morning."

"What should we say about the accident?" Mince asked.

"Tell them the truth, about the deer and hitting the tree. Offer them some fresh lemonade. I need to lie down for awhile to get rid of this headache."

Carol Jean and Mince went outside to greet their grandparents, and Elizabeth waited, hoping to escape the deluge of questions her folks would have if they saw the injuries on her face.

"I brought you some leftover blueberry muffins from the church brunch. Thought we'd see you there," Marta said.

"Yes, you missed a good sermon, short and to the point," William added. "That Pastor Whitaker knows the value of a grand summer morning!"

Before the girls could stop them, Elizabeth heard William and Marta making their way into the house.

"Grams, wait! Let's sit at the picnic table in the shade and have lemonade and muffins together," Carol Jean said.

"You two go ahead, but we've already had our fill this morning," William said, opening the screen door. "Hello, anybody?"

They were inside, so Elizabeth had no choice but to face them.

"Mom, Dad, happy Sunday," Elizabeth said, forcing her swollen face into what she hoped was a smile.

"My good lord! What happened?" Marta rushed to Elizabeth.

"It was a slight accident. You should see the other guy!" Elizabeth's attempt at a joke fell flat.

"Doesn't look like a little accident. Have you been to see a doctor?"

Carol Jean and Mince had come in, and Elizabeth understood she needed to downplay her injuries.

"Yes and nothing's broken. A few bruises and contusions."

"Mom said it looks a lot worse than it feels," Mince added.

"Explain how this accident happened," William said, "in detail."

"We were driving home when a deer appeared right in front of the car. It was unavoidable."

"Who was driving?" William asked. "Where did it happen?"

"What about the deer?" Marta said.

"The deer was okay," Mince answered.

"We all were lucky, including the deer. We swerved to avoid hitting it, but in swerving, we ended up crashing into a tree." Elizabeth's head was pounding, a painful pulse punctuated with every word she said.

"I suppose Eddie was driving. Was he drunk?" William asked.

"Eddie was driving. He has a nasty gash on his forehead, and that's all."

"He was drunk," her father said, answering his own question. "Why do you get in the car with that drunk? He is a menace, trouble following him like rubble after a tornado."

"Pops was drunk again," Carol Jean said.

"It doesn't change anything. We're both okay." Elizabeth wanted to reassure everyone.

"What about the car? How badly was it damaged?" Marta said.

"At the salvage yard, but not salvageable," Elizabeth said.

"What will you do without a car? How will you get to work?" Marta asked.

"Mom, I'm not sure. I'll figure it out."

"Where's Eddie? I want to talk to him," William said.

"I don't know where he is, but he's not here."

"William, let it go." Marta turned William towards the door. "We should leave so Elizabeth can rest. She looks exhausted."

"I'll let it go, for now, as long as you don't need us to stay. Elizabeth, you call us from the pay phone at the plant tomorrow, so we know you are all right."

"Go on home, and I'll call you on my lunch hour. I'll be fine."

"Girls, promise to take good care of your mother," Marta said, placing a gentle hand on Elizabeth's shoulder.

"We promise, Grams. Thanks for the muffins."

"Come on, dear wife," William said, "I've hay to cut and animals to tend, and nobody, not even the Lord on the Sabbath, will fault me for taking care of his crops and his creatures."

William added, "Don't forget this Wednesday is our day to sell sweet corn downtown. We'll pick you girls up at around 9:00, give or take. If it rains, though it seems unlikely, we'll come on Friday instead, same time, okay?"

At the car, Marta handed Elizabeth an extra box of blueberries left over from the day's batches of muffins. "Play your cards right, and you might get a blueberry cobbler today," she told the girls.

Elizabeth, Mince, and Carol Jean stood at the end of the driveway, waving good-bye. "Thanks for being here for me," Elizabeth told her daughters as the car disappeared into the distance. Elizabeth felt sick inside as she stared down at the box of plump, ripe, purple-blue berries, the color of bruises. She had lied to her daughters and her parents to protect them from the painful truth, and, in doing so, she had protected Eddie and covered up his drunken attack against her. That fact pained Elizabeth more than her battered face.

PEOPLE MIGHT STARE

WITH THEIR DEMOLISHED CAR DUMPED AT THE SALVAGE yard, Elizabeth had no choice but to walk to the pickle plant on Monday morning. The hazy streets were hot and stifling, despite the fact that the day's light had not yet winked over the horizon. Her bloody left eye was now open, its swelling deflated, but the facial bruising had blossomed into startling shades of reddish purple and blue. Despite layers of makeup, there was no hiding it, so Elizabeth had given up and tied her kerchief as usual over her hair and behind her ears, tucking in the stray dark curls. She was glad for the empty, early day and moved along, head down, metal lunch box rattling at her side, her lengthy stride slower than usual. If she kept a steady pace, she'd make it to work in less than an hour.

While walking, Elizabeth skimmed through their fabricated story, in case someone at work took the time to notice her. She and Eddie had decided to stick with the car accident tale, and Art agreed to go along. Thanks to Eddie's old teammate, Officer McDougal, the police were not releasing the details of the accident, so Eddie was off the hook. Off the hook, like what she had tried to do for Eddie thirteen years ago, Elizabeth remembered.

She had waited, numb and terrified, for her parents to return from the barn. Her father stopped to scrape the bottoms of his barn boots, scratching them across the metal blade until they were clean. Then he removed each boot, placing them inside the back door on the old, faded welcome mat. On rusted metal hooks along the pine paneled wall, he hung his weathered barn coat. William, wrapped in the earthy smell of cows, manure, hay, and soil, entered the kitchen and walked to the sink, not looking at Elizabeth as he worked the orange Lava soap around his leathery hands.

"Your father and I have an idea about what to do next." Elizabeth's mother was looking at William, rather than at her daughter. "First, we need to know if you have told Eddie, and, if so, whether the two of you have any plans?"

Elizabeth's voice was almost a whisper. "No, I haven't told him, but it doesn't matter."

"Do you think there is any chance for you and Eddie to have a life together?"

"No, no chance, for sure. He has his future all set, and this would definitely mess everything up for him."

Her father turned from the sink and spoke. "I don't suppose he could have thought of that before . . ." His voice broke and he turned to go into the living room.

"We think your Aunt Helen would be willing to have you live with her on their farm in Illinois until you are able to come back home," he said. "I'll go make the call."

It broke Elizabeth's heart to think about that evening in May, so many years ago, when her parents laid out their plans for her future, of which Eddie had no part. They would send Elizabeth away, and when it was all over, she would return to the life they had wanted for her.

Elizabeth forced those painful memories to fade away like the dwindling darkness as she crossed the pickle plant's vacant parking lot. It was still early, and she was grateful to enter the building alone. Feeding her time card into the slot, she glanced down the still empty hall, waiting for the machine to work. It clattered and rang out like a freight train at a road crossing.

"If I didn't know better, I'd say you were working for a promotion!" Clay's office door was down the hall from his receptionist's desk. Elizabeth thought he would already be at work, but had hoped to whisk past unseen. Nothing much went unnoticed where Clay was concerned.

"I'd accept one, if you're offering!" she responded, keeping her voice light-hearted. She didn't stop, didn't turn around, didn't do anything but pray he would stay inside his office. Instead, he emerged, a pair of coffee mugs in hand. "How about letting me buy you a cup. There's not much to do until the next truck gets here."

"You know, Mr. Landers, it doesn't look good when you fraternize with the help." Elizabeth hesitated in the darkest part of the hall, looking over her shoulder to answer him.

"You do have an image to maintain, being the boss and owner." She managed a laugh and started to leave, but he wouldn't let it go.

"It's a cup of coffee, Liz. I thought we could talk about the latest developments at the mill." Clay walked toward her, the coffee cup extended.

Elizabeth had no choice but to turn around. Unable to meet his gaze, she kept her eyes downcast, noticing his immaculate white shirt cuffs, undone and rolled over twice. Her eyes traced his shirt buttons upward, to the imported silk tie loosened from his collar, as though he'd been working for a time.

"Thank you. Coffee sounds wonderful."

Taking the cup, Elizabeth stepped past Clay and walked the hallway to his office. It surprised her when she released a deep sigh of relief as she entered his personal workspace.

"What happened to your face, Liz?" His soft Italian shoes made no stepping sounds, and he was there beside her before she could sit down. Reaching for her chin, he turned her face toward him with featherlike gentleness. "Did Eddie do this to you?"

"Nothing like that, Clay. We had a car accident, Saturday night. On our way out to the County Park, Eddie swerved to avoid hitting a deer and hit a tree instead. The deer is fine. The tree and the car didn't fare so well." Realizing she was talking too fast, explaining too much, she stopped. Do not cry, she warned herself.

"You must have hit something pretty squarely and very hard."

"I'll be all right. Eddie got the worst of it, with a really deep cut over his eye, and, of course, the car is done for." Her hand wobbled as she raised the steaming cup to her lips. "It looks much worse than it feels."

Clay didn't seem convinced, that familiar v-shaped wrinkle drawn up between his brows.

"Why don't you take the day off, to recover a bit more. I know a guy with some pull who could give you the okay to go home."

"That's not necessary, but thank you for the offer."

Elizabeth handed the coffee cup to Clayton, turned to leave, and then stopped. "On second thought, maybe taking the afternoon off would be good. I'm pretty sure I can make it for a half day, but going home at noon and resting might help."

"The afternoon is yours," Clay said. "I'll give you a ride."

"No, thank you." The last thing she needed was Eddie or anyone else seeing her with Clay. "The walk will do me good."

"It's called a sick day, that's time off with pay, Liz." He walked to her and put his arms around her in a gentle embrace. "I am so sorry this happened to you."

How Elizabeth made it through that morning, she wasn't sure. After the first few inquiries, people stopped asking what had happened to her, although their unavoidable, curious stares continued. The dull, aching hum in her head gave way to a pulsating throb, causing her to feel faint and nauseous. When the buzzer signaled the noon hour break, Elizabeth picked up her lunch box and left through the east door of the plant, still wearing her hair net and name tag.

Despite the midday heat, the outside air provided relief from the pounding in her head. To avoid any passing traffic, Elizabeth turned onto the first side street intersecting Main, where the factory was located. Overhead, elm trees touched leafy fingertips across the narrow pavement, their shadows cool and dark, and she slowed her pace, enjoying the escape from the heat and clamoring noise of Landers. Instead of turning to take her street home, Elizabeth walked the ten blocks in the opposite direction to the public library, determined to continue her research, despite the pain pulsing in her head. She entered through the little-used side door, hoping to proceed unnoticed.

She removed her hair net, pulling her hair around her face, hoping it would conceal the damage. At the front desk, a woman was almost hidden behind an enormous pile of books.

"I'd like to look something up on the microfilm," Elizabeth said.

Looking over the top of her glasses, the librarian stared at Elizabeth's face with disapproval. Elizabeth watched the woman glance around the empty room, seeking protection from a possible attack by someone who appeared to be a street-fighting ruffian.

"Have you used a microfilm before? It can be tricky."

"Yes, my daughter and I used it a few days ago. I know what to do."

"Be careful and don't break anything. Those devices are expensive."

Elizabeth hurried to the microfilm room, set apart from the main library, and was relieved to find it unoccupied. Withdrawing the notes she had stashed in her lunchbox, she struggled a bit with the machine, and then managed to load the film. Elizabeth located

PLANS AND A PISTOL

ELIZABETH WAS WELCOMED ONTO HER BLOCK BY A neighbor's sputtering lawnmower and the sweetness of newly mown grass, sparse as it was, mixed with the gas and oil odors spewing from his machine. Close to home, on both sides of the street, cars and pick-up trucks belonging to Eddie's union friends were parked, each more dusty and dilapidated than the last. The one exception was a newly waxed silver Cadillac parked in front, the vehicle owned by Julian Prince.

Away from the noise inside the house, Carol Jean, Mince, and Lucky were slumped on the front porch, battling mosquitoes and watching brown bats flutter falling through the darkening sky.

It was Mince who spotted Elizabeth first. "You're home!"

Mince jumped past all three steps to hug her mother. "I've been waiting for hours for you!"

"Hello, my darling daughters!" While Elizabeth held Mince's slender body, her gaze was focused on Carol Jean, who kept her distance, her face unsmiling and eyes stone cold.

"I'm sorry it is so late. The shift went overtime, and then I missed my ride home. Come, let's sit together."

Mince and Carol Jean nudged over on the step, Elizabeth squeezing between them. She threaded her arms around both girls, as Lucky dropped at their feet.

"Your face looks horrible," Carol Jean said, a slight quiver in her voice betraying her true concern for her mother.

"As bruises go, this one is progressing at the usual pace. In a few days, I will turn a lovely shade of pea green and for a grand finale, a sickening yellow."

Elizabeth recognized that her bruised face and bloody red eye worried her daughters, so she smiled, attempting to lighten the mood.

"As I told you, it looks much worse than it feels, as long as I don't bump into anything else with my face!"

They laughed a little, even Carol Jean, but were silenced when ramming through the screen door came the rumbling of the men's voices, like boulders avalanching down a concrete street.

"They've been here since before supper," Carol Jean offered.

"I think they're really mad about something," Mince concluded. "At least it sounds that way."

"Lots of things to be mad about, I guess," Elizabeth responded, "but it's grownup stuff, and I don't want you to worry about it. Instead, I'd love to hear all about your summer day."

After awhile, Elizabeth left the girls outside so they could join the neighbor kids in a game of Kick the Can, while she went inside, hoping to learn what was happening with the mill workers. On the pretense of watching television, she turned on the old set with the volume down low. She stared at the screen, but her focus was on the voices coming from the next room.

"Based on the subpoenaed files, it appears the person in charge of unemployment payments from 1950–1960 was Robert Whiting."

"Ain Bob dead?" Joe Clark asked of no one in particular.

"Died in an automobile accident about six months ago. At that time, he was worth about $3000. It appears as though any funds he may have embezzled were either spent, hidden, or confiscated by someone else." There was a long pause before Julian continued. "One other person may have been involved, a payroll clerk, Nadine Dahl."

"We all knew Nadine. Can't believe she'd have been involved in embezzling, even from the petty cash drawer," Eddie said.

"It's a moot point, anyway. Mrs. Dahl has been in the County Home for the last nine months. Dementia. Memory's gone."

"What about some of the big shots?" Eddie said.

"I believe someone much higher up is involved, but I think Northland is confident they have neutralized the situation by the implication of Robert and Nadine. What we need to find is written proof that the managers of the company, willfully and with malice, conducted illegal business practices."

"You mean there's more proof? Where do you think it is?" Art said.

"I can't be sure, but I suspect what was turned over by Northland was the tip of the iceberg. There were people in charge, and they need to be held responsible. This company has more paperwork, and we'll have to figure out a way to get it."

"If a subpoena didn't get it, how are we supposed to force them to turn over the hidden records? Maybe we should say please," Eddie said.

Elizabeth struggled to hear a raspy, tobacco-ravaged voice coming from what must have been the back of the room. She stood in the doorway and strained to discern who was speaking.

"I know where stuff is. Hell, I guess I know where the skeletons are buried."

Now she recognized the voice. It was Jasper, her father-in-law, who had worked at the mill all of his life.

Julian Prince addressed the group again. "It's one thing to know storage locations and a different thing to be able to access them."

"I've got access," Jasper said, "because I've got keys."

"Jasper, I thought on that last day, all the company keys were turned in to management, no exceptions," Art said.

"I did turn in the company's keys, as per the order. I didn't happen to give them MY personal set of keys to the kingdom. Any janitor worth his weight in mops has his own set, in case the kingdom goes to hell."

Julian Prince didn't speak until the uproar quelled a bit. "Men, as your legal counsel and an officer of the court, I must, at this point, take my leave. Whatever commences from this new information cannot be discussed in my presence, for obvious reasons. My advice to you is to take careful actions and do them within the law."

The sound of moving chairs and muffled voices followed Julian as he left the men and walked past the living room, where Elizabeth had rushed to sit in front of the television again.

"How did it go?" she said as Julian leaned into the room.

"It is hard to say. Hopefully, things will improve as we work the case."

"I hope so." Elizabeth turned toward Julian, and the pale light from the television washed across her bloody eye and bruised face.

Julian, an experienced and imperturbable lawyer, showed no reaction to her battered condition.

"I do, too." He had turned to leave, then faced her again. "If you ever need anything, Elizabeth, please do not hesitate to contact Madeira or me."

The men proceeded to converse in low tones that Elizabeth strained to hear, and most left within ten minutes of Julian's departure. Elizabeth moved closer to the dining room where Art, Eddie, and Jasper remained, hunched around the table, empty beer bottles standing sentry at the table's center.

"Two trucks is all we need," Eddie asserted. "Any more, and we'll draw too much attention."

"I can bring the old Chevy, used to be my dad's. Got no license plates and the VIN is filed off. Can't be traced back to me," Art offered.

"Good man," Eddie said, slapping Art's back. "Jasper, do you think your old Ford, the one behind your garage, could make it?"

"That old beauty runs like a top. Needs some oil, and maybe a shove to get started."

"It's settled. We'll use Art's old Chevy and that rattletrap Jasper keeps parked back by his garage. Art, put some gas in that old clunker," Eddie said.

The men chuckled, and Elizabeth smiled, too. Art was notorious for running out of gas on a regular basis.

"Bring boxes, gunny sacks, and flashlights. Don't forget flashlights," Art said.

"I'll walk over to Jasper's tomorrow at midnight. We'll meet up with Art at Peace in the Valley Cemetery."

Jasper cleared his throat. "Might be better to meet at 2:00 A.M. The night watchman takes his lunch break at 2:30. I know where he'll be for at least thirty minutes, so we could work our way around him."

"Old man, I was doubtful about your coming along, but you're starting to convince me otherwise," Eddie said.

"You wouldn't get anywhere without me," Jasper replied.

"Tomorrow night, 2:00 A.M. Come sober, and shut your big mouths about the particulars," Art said.

"Get outta here!" Eddie said, closing and hooking the back door behind them.

Eddie was in the back hall, where Elizabeth found him standing on the step stool. His head brushed the ceiling as he dug into the far corner of the uppermost shelf.

"What're you doing, Eddie?"

"Lizzie, you scared the heck out of me! You shouldn't sneak up on a guy like that."

"Walking into the hall isn't sneaking, Eddie, except if you're trying to hide something."

"I'm not, so cut the detective routine and butt out." He worked his way down using only one hand for support. In his other hand he held a pistol.

"What are you doing with that? Don't tell me you're going to use a gun for something!"

Eddie nestled the pistol in both hands, testing its weight and balance. "This isn't just any gun, Gloomy Gladys. It's a genuine World War I German Luger. Other than shrapnel in his back, it's the only thing my dad brought home after the war."

"Jasper meant it as a souvenir, not a weapon, Eddie. Put it back."

"You are one royal pain, Lizzie. I'm holding the thing, that's all. It's not loaded." He stared down the barrel of the pistol, closing one eye as he focused it at Elizabeth's right eyeball.

"Tell me you are not going to take that gun out of the house, Eddie!"

"Who said I was taking it anywhere?"

"I'm guessing you wouldn't carry it around here. You must be planning to do something with it."

"You're not guessing, Lizzie. I think you were sneaking around, listening in on my private conversation with the guys."

"It's my house, too, Eddie. Sometimes things get overheard."

"You'd better forget you overheard anything, because it's none of your business."

"Don't bring the gun with you tomorrow night, Eddie."

"What if I need it, as protection, in case something happens?"

"Then, you will probably be arrested for threatening someone, or worse yet, for shooting someone. "

"All I was going to do was bring it along, unloaded, in case I needed to get a person's attention."

"You don't need that kind of attention, Eddie."

"All right, I'll put it back. You'd better hope somebody doesn't start something with me, because you've left me defenseless." Eddie struggled back up to the top shelf, grunting with the effort.

Elizabeth shook her aching head in disgust and began to walk away, as Eddie returned the pistol to its storage spot. Jumping to the floor, he caught her by the wrist and spun her around to face him.

"What happens around here with these men is my business. You stay out of it, and keep your mouth shut about anything you've overheard. Got it?"

CAUGHT

AFTER ELIZABETH HEARD EDDIE LEAVE THE HOUSE THE
following night, she stayed up, pacing the floor and waiting to learn
how things turned out for the three men. Perhaps Eddie, Art, and
Jasper would get lucky and find what they needed to retrieve their
unemployment benefits. Perhaps they would find nothing and come
home empty-handed. Maybe they would be caught and arrested, or
worse, maybe some innocent person would get hurt. Though she
wanted to choke Eddie for being a drunk, for being a terrible person,
and for throwing their lives into chaos, tonight she wanted him to be
successful and find what they were looking for.

By early morning, Elizabeth was on her fourth cup of coffee.
She perched with Lucky on the front porch, waiting for word about
Eddie, and watching the brightening sky. She was exhausted and had
to work a long shift that day, so, with reluctance, they went inside.
Against the toaster, Elizabeth propped a note to Carol Jean and
Mince, listing their chores for the day. Having no idea where Eddie
was or what had happened to him, she simply wrote that the girls
should take care of Lucky and themselves, and that she would be
home from work as soon as possible.

The street that stretched out ahead of her was a long, empty
tunnel, illuminated by the occasional street light. Before Elizabeth
reached the end of her block, a silver car stopped beside her, and
Julian Prince stepped out.

"Elizabeth, glad I caught you." He walked toward her, files in his hand.

"What are you doing here at this hour, Julian?"

"I'm afraid I have some bad news. Eddie and Jasper were arrested last night."

"Arrested for what?" Elizabeth asked, although she already knew the answer. What she didn't know was what had happened to Art, their third partner in crime.

"Breaking and entering." Julian opened a file and started scanning official-looking papers. "If that gets bumped up to burglary, which is likely, since Eddie was carrying a firearm, then it's a different ballgame. Plus, there's a possible assault charge because Eddie roughed up the security guard."

"Don't tell me they broke into Northland." Elizabeth worked to sound surprised.

"I'm afraid so. Would you be willing to come with me to the police station? We could find out what the exact charges are, when they will be be arraigned, and the bail amount."

"Julian, there is no way we have the money for bail."

"Worry about that later. Let's drive over there and begin the process of getting these two guys out of jail."

On the way to the Municipal Building, Elizabeth had Julian detour to Landers where she reported to Clay what was happening.

"By all means, take whatever time necessary, Liz. If you need help with Eddie's bail, let me know," Clay said, his hand on her shoulder.

"Thank you, Clay. I'll try to get back to work as soon as possible."

"Don't worry about work, Liz. Take the day to get your family situation figured out. Your job will be here when you return. That's what friends are for."

Elizabeth and Julian arrived at the Police Department shortly after 5:30 A.M. and an officer directed them toward a cluttered and paper-strewn desk. A middle-aged man dressed in a rumpled, worn suit stood and gestured for the two to be seated.

"Detective Anderson, thanks for meeting with us. This is Elizabeth Dembrowski, Eddie's wife."

The detective stared at Elizabeth's damaged face, then nodded a greeting in her direction. "As Mr. Prince has probably told you, your husband and his father were arrested in the offices of the Northland Paper Company last night. The two have been informed of the possible charges, including burglary, robbery, and possessing a firearm. Additional assault charges could be filed depending on the willingness of the guard to press charges."

"Detective, you know these two men are harmless and had no intention of committing a crime," Julian said, "and they would never have used that old souvenir gun Jasper saved from the war."

"That is not my call. The D.A. will decide today what the exact charges will be. When an arraignment is scheduled, your office will be contacted. For your information, Eddie did use that old souvenir gun."

"I'd like to meet with the arresting officer, if he's available," Julian said, "and I'll need to meet with Eddie and Jasper, of course."

"Follow me." The detective lead Elizabeth and Julian down a narrow hallway to a small, windowless room.

"I'll send over the officer, but only the attorney is allowed," Detective Anderson said.

Before entering the meeting room, Julian paused to greet a tall, slender, distinguished man, with silvery hair and a trim beard to match.

"Richard, you're up early!" Julian said.

"Criminals have no respect for my sleep requirements, Julian."

"Elizabeth, this is Richard Jordan, Northland's lawyer. Richard, Elizabeth Dembrowski."

"The burglar's wife," Richard said.

"A bit premature, Richard," Julian said. "No formal charged have been filed against my client."

"Depends on your point of view," the attorney responded. "I'm meeting with the D.A this afternoon to discuss how we will proceed."

After Northland's attorney left, Elizabeth sat outside the room where Julian interviewed the arresting officer. When he emerged, Julian said he would meet with Eddie and Jasper next.

"Do you want me to drive you back to the plant? This might take awhile."

"Thanks, but I'll wait."

"Should I tell Eddie you are here?"

"No, don't mention me."

Julian was gone for almost two hours. Elizabeth went back to the main lobby, and sat in the far corner, hoping no one would catch sight of her swollen, bruised face. The last thing she needed was for someone to notice and start asking questions. Luckily, it was a slow day for law enforcement, and Elizabeth was simply another citizen at the police station.

When Julian and Elizabeth left the Municipal Building, Art was outside, waiting near Julian's car. "What the hell are you doing here? You realize that Eddie and Jasper were arrested while loading your old truck?" Julian asked. He grabbed Art by the arm, and pushed him into the vehicle, and Julian and Elizabeth got in.

"You shouldn't be here," Elizabeth told Art.

"Elizabeth, I am sorry about all of this," Art said.

"Don't be. Eddie is a grown man. He knew what he was getting into."

"I feel guilty that he and Jasper were caught, and I wasn't. We were working to load the trucks and got separated. Eddie and Jasper were in the wrong place at the wrong time."

"Is there any way that truck can be traced back to you?" Julian asked.

"No."

"Good. Keep it that way. Stay out of this, Art. Two men being arrested is enough for me to worry about."

"Agreed. Elizabeth, I ended up with Jasper's truck. It's parked over there." Art handed her a large ring of keys. "I don't need it, but you do. I doubt Jasper will mind if you use it."

Julian dropped Elizabeth at the far end of the parking lot and drove off with Art. Jasper's truck was a bucket of rust, but a working vehicle nonetheless. Inside, it smelled of fuel oil, like Jasper.

Elizabeth worked the clutch and ground the gears, but managed to ease the old truck out of the lot onto the street. Though it was only a little past eight in the morning, the heat was already radiating off the blacktop and sidewalks, and the sun burned in a sky filled with vaporous, ivory ribbons. She should have driven straight to work at Landers, but the obituary notes in her lunch box kept nagging and nudging her. When she drove past the County Court House, Elizabeth made that her destination.

The receptionist in the Court House lobby directed Elizabeth to the Register of Deeds, where all County death certificates were filed. At the counter, a young high school student's facial expression reminded Elizabeth how alarming her bruised face still was.

"Car accident a couple of days ago," she explained to the girl. "I am looking for the death records for some of my long, lost relatives and was wondering how I would do that."

"I'm only a summer intern. It's vacation week for two of our secretaries and the other one is sick," she said, gesturing to the empty desks behind the counter. "Plus the Register of Deeds is in meetings all day."

"Does that mean you can't help me?"

The girl hesitated for a moment, analyzing Elizabeth and said, "I guess I could show you where to find that information."

Elizabeth followed her to a windowless room, its walls lined with volumes of labeled binders. "The death records are in the black binders, years indicated on the spine. Please be sure to return them to the correct place."

"Thank you so much. I will be very careful."

The girl was walking toward the door, when she stopped. "Also, deaths are categorized according to the selected causes of death in the green books over there, the ones listed as Wisconsin Deaths Categorized by the ICD (International Statistical Classification of Diseases, Injuries and Causes of Death) Seventh Edition. It's pretty interesting and summarizes in charts the stuff that is in all the other volumes."

Alone in the room, Elizabeth used her library notes to search for the death certificates of the persons' names she had taken from the obituaries. Because she had recorded dates of death, matching the newspaper information to the official statistics was not difficult. Using a red pencil, she checked off each fact that was identical between the two sources and circled any discrepancies. It was tedious and time-consuming, and Elizabeth was so involved she did not realize hours had passed, and that the lights were being shut off around the outer office. Then heels clicked their way toward Elizabeth in the back room.

"You're not supposed to be in here unattended." The woman's hand was on the switch. "This room is for approved personnel only." She moved to see what was on the table, but Elizabeth had already stacked her papers into a neat pile and shoved them inside her lunch box.

"The young lady said I could stay for a few minutes to finish copying the information from my daughter's death certificate. My little girl died this summer."

Before the woman could question her further, Elizabeth rushed out of the office and left the Court House. Jasper's old truck was one of only two vehicles left in the parking lot. The other was a silver Cadillac.

"Elizabeth, I didn't expect to see you here at the Court House," Julian said. He was standing beside his car door, briefcase in one hand and keys in the other.

"I had to drop off some records for my folks' about their farm. William hates to drive into town if he doesn't have to." Elizabeth wasn't sure why she lied to Julian, but it didn't feel wrong.

"You're a good daughter, a good mother," Julian said "and a good wife."

"Thank you, Julian." Elizabeth felt Julian was stalling, wanting to engage her in a conversation for which she did not have the time. "I really need to get home to the girls."

"Of course. How was work today?"

"Hot and pickly, like every other day." Elizabeth's face flushed, and she hoped it did not betray the fact that she had lied about being at work.

Julian laughed. "How could it be anything else? I'll let you know when I learn specifics about Eddie and Jasper."

Elizabeth climbed into the truck, waved to Julian and drove away, watching him in her rearview mirror. He stood like a post, a hard, wooden expression on his pale face.

FIRE!

THAT NIGHT, AFTER THE GIRLS HAD RETREATED upstairs, Elizabeth spread her notes across the kitchen table. At the Court House, she had been able to match death certificates with obituaries back to 1956, and though she had not reached her goal to go back at least fifteen years, the notes in front of her were glaring with red-pencil revelations. Certain discrepancies were at once noticeable because Elizabeth knew the deceased, like Mrs. Dukane's husband, Tom. While his family and the obituary stated his death was due to a heart attack, the official death certificate listed Cause of Death as "pneumonoconioses and chemical effects." It was similar to Edith Martin's husband, Robert, whose obituary listed a heart episode as the COD, while his death certificate showed "pneumonoconioses due to kaolin exposure." The Nelson's son, Patrick, listed as being a victim of an automobile accident in his obituary, in fact died of "unspecified acute lower respiratory infection" according to the death certificate.

By 2:00 A.M. Elizabeth had charted over one hundred discrepancies between the public notice and the official record for deaths in their area. Although she had not finished charting the years of facts she collected, Elizabeth put down her pencil and rubbed her burning eyes. Tomorrow, she would somehow find the time to visit the library and continue going back in the obituaries. Then, she would need at least another eight or ten hours in the Register of Deeds office matching death certificates with the obituaries. After completing that task, Elizabeth reasoned the ICD might provide some explanation about whether what she had discovered was erroneous reporting, or if it was something more.

She was exhausted, but after too many cups of coffee, sleep was an impossibility. The house was hot and stifling, so, despite the lateness of the hour, Elizabeth took Lucky and walked outside. Even in the dark, the mountain of dead tree limbs and plant debris was unavoidable. What a waste, Elizabeth thought, kicking at the pile. Picking up a broken branch, she flung it as far as she could into the thick, dark river, its fumes rising into the dead air.

"You can't take my daughter and get away with it," she yelled at the river, her voice like steel.

At that instant, Elizabeth decided she wanted the pile to be gone. In the garage, she found a box of stick matches and a shovel. Dragging an extra hose from the garage, she linked it to the hose attached to the house water faucet. Both hoses were pulled up close to the debris pile, and as an extra precaution, she trenched the cracked, dry soil surrounding the pile, not an easy task.

With the scratch of the match head, Elizabeth ignited some dry grass underneath the enormous mound. At first, nothing happened. Then, thin tendrils of metal-colored smoke began drifting upward, soon joined by flames, pointed like arrowheads. Elizabeth stepped back to admire her efforts, leaning against the shovel, drawing in the sweet, smoky smell.

When the fire seemed to stall, she worried the weight of the dead plants, layered on top of the tree limbs, would smother the flames altogether. Lighting another match, she knelt down to start the grass burning once again. For a moment, the fire hung in limbo, and then the entire pile exploded into an inferno, the heat so intense it caused Elizabeth to stumble backwards onto the ground, hands burning as she scrambled to distance herself from the searing air. Stunned, she watched the flames shoot higher, as the ground encircling the pile ignited and fiery debris rained down. Her eyes were stinging from the thick smoke, and she struggled to breathe. In desperation, she began to search for the hose, feeling blindly until she located it. Though it burned and blistered her hands, Elizabeth grabbed the melted, bubbling rubber, and held on. Turning the hose towards the rising flames, she opened the nozzle, but only a dribble of water wobbled out. Elizabeth ran for the faucet, hoping she had simply failed to turn it on all the way, but that wasn't so. It was cranked as far as it could go, wide open, with little water being drawn. The drought had lasted a long time, and the water pressure was diminished to a trickle.

In a panic, Elizabeth realized Lucky was not with her. She began screaming for him, but all she could see was the billowing, thick smoke. She called for him until her voice was a whisper, her throat singed from the smoke and heat.

The blaze continued to throw towering flames which engulfed the massive pile and began to creep through the tall reed canary grass, its dry blades as sharp as daggers. At first, she attempted to slow the fire by digging another trench, but the fire could not be contained. Although it was futile, she started hurling shovel after shovel of dirt and gravel onto the fingers of the fire as they grasped everything within reach. Elizabeth watched as the blaze crackled through the thorny raspberry canes, not far from the blueberry patch. Within ten feet of the patch stood their garage, its paint beginning to peel like burned skin.

How much time had passed, Elizabeth couldn't say. Somewhere, fire sirens wailed, and the yard was overtaken by heavy-coated firemen, hoses and tools slung over their shoulders. Because of the low water pressure, the fire hydrants could not extract enough stream, so a tanker truck had been called, one fireman told her. Meanwhile, the fire continued to burn out of control.

By that time, Carol Jean and Mince had been awakened by the commotion. They found Elizabeth slumped on the ground, watching as their garage caught fire and burned. Hugging her close, the girls helped her struggle to her feet as a young fireman approached.

"Is this your house?" he asked Elizabeth.

"Yes, it is. I'm sorry . . . I was trying to take care of the burn pile, and it exploded. Then, there was no water, only fire everywhere!" Elizabeth had begun to feel faint.

He studied Elizabeth, then directed her and the girls to sit at the picnic table. "Keep your mother here," he told Mince and Carol Jean. "She needs medical treatment."

"I couldn't find Lucky during the fire. We need to look for him." Elizabeth coughed and attempted to stand, but the girls begged her to stay put until she received help.

"I'll find him," Mince said. Before Elizabeth could stop her, the girl took off running, calling Lucky's name.

To Elizabeth, it felt as though the girl was gone for hours. When Mince returned at last, Lucky was with her, covered in soot and limping on scorched feet. Mince brought him straight to her mother, who was being treated by the fireman.

"He was hiding under Mrs. Dukane's front porch," Mince said.

Elizabeth yanked the oxygen mask from her face and pulled Lucky to her, whispering in his ear, telling him how sorry she was for scaring him and putting him in danger.

"I am fine, or I will be, once you check over my dog and tell me he's all right," Elizabeth told the young man.

Using picks and shovels, the firemen attempted to stall the fire, but by the time the water tanker arrived, the garage was fully engulfed. Water was directed onto what remained, until it was a smoldering pile of burned rubble and concrete block. Concerned for Elizabeth's house as well as the neighbors' homes, the firemen shot streams of water onto roofs and surrounding trees and shrubs.

"This is all my fault. I should never have started a fire in this hot, dry . . ." Elizabeth stopped mid-sentence and stared off beyond the backyard, which was a blackened carpet of smoke and ash. The smoldering grass wandered away from their property like a black snake, slithering its way down to the river.

One of the fireman was pointing over the burned terrain, toward the moving water.

"Will you look at that! If I wasn't seeing it myself, I wouldn't believe it."

The river behind the Dembrowski's house was on fire. Elizabeth was horrified as she watched flames rising and curling out of the water, lifting upward to form a cloud of smoke the color of old blood.

The sun was high in the sky when the last fire truck backed out of the driveway. There was nothing to be done about the burning river, the firemen claiming it would fizzle out in a few hours. It took over two days for the river to stop burning.

ALONE

IT WAS THE DAY AFTER ELIZABETH STARTED THE FIRE, and the river continued to burn. Small flames, like devilish tongues, darted out of the water, now a sludge-filled cesspool of ash and burned chemicals. When William and Marta turned into the drive-way at Elizabeth's house, the garage ahead of them had been reduced to a pile of smoldering boards and blackened concrete blocks. Surrounding it was a coal-black landscape reaching down to the river.

"When you told us there was a fire, you weren't kidding," William said. He scanned the devastation and shook his head. "You're lucky you didn't burn down the entire neighborhood."

"As long as you're not hurt, that's all that matters," Marta added. "We want the girls to be all right, too, so we think they should come home with us for a day or two."

"The fire's bad enough, but with Eddie's arrest, there are too many things going on here that our granddaughters should not have to deal with," William said. "They need to be in a place where they are safe."

"It is safe here, Dad," Elizabeth said. "I want them to be home with me."

"I disagree. They're better off with us out at the farm and away from this chaos. You know I'm right about this."

William and Marta had already decided, and Elizabeth did not have the will to take on her parents. At first, Carol Jean and Mince were reluctant to leave Elizabeth. They argued to stay at home, but their grandparents convinced the girls it was for the best. They would be safer under their grandparents' supervision and would be kept busy working at the farm.

Elizabeth stood in the driveway, waving good-bye to her family, Lucky following their vehicle to the street with a half-hearted bark. As the two walked together toward the pile that was the garage, Mrs. Dukane approached from her yard.

"I'd say it's done for," her neighbor said, pointing at what was left of Elizabeth's garage. "Heat's still coming off these piles."

"I'm sorry about the smoke and everything."

"It's okay, and nobody was hurt. I kind of wished my old garage had caught, too!"

They laughed, and Lucky nudged Mrs. Dukane's hand, begging to be petted.

"Lucky likes you," Elizabeth said. "I don't suppose you could take care of him for me today. The girls are gone to the farm, and my work hours are long. No telling what time I'll be home."

"I'd love to have the old boy over for a visit. How about a sleepover, too? Then, you don't have to worry none about getting home at any particular time, and I'd have some company."

Elizabeth left for the plant, relieved the girls and Lucky were safe, and feeling fortunate to have Jasper's old truck. Her shift had clocked in hours ago, but she hoped no one would pay attention to her tardiness. As Elizabeth was rushing down the corridor toward the intake room, Clayton called out to her from his office.

"Liz, I heard about the fire. Are you all right?"

"Yes, only a couple of blisters and scratches. Also, I burned down the garage, and don't forget the river I set on fire."

"You never could do things halfway. Always went for the extravaganza version. Are you sure you're good to work today?"

"Work would be a pleasure after the kind of night I've had."

It was a hot, busy day on the line, but Elizabeth appreciated the routine and being with the others on her shift. Linda, standing across the trough from Elizabeth, waved and yelled over the clatter, "Heard you had a barbecue yesterday." The entire crew, right down the line, broke up.

"Very funny," Elizabeth said.

"Hey, Liz," Rita from clean-up hollered, "if you'd invited me, I would've brought the marshmallows and weenies."

"It was sort of a spontaneous event," Elizabeth said. "Next time, you're all invited."

Applause spattered around the room, but the levity ended when their supervisor yelled, "Back to work, comedians."

When her shift ended, Elizabeth drove to the library, almost empty that late summer afternoon. In the microfilm room, she felt entombed in her own world, the cool, bookish air surrounding her like a fog. As she finished analyzing another year of obituaries, she realized the lights around the building were being switched off, and the clock on the wall indicated it was closing time. Putting away the microfilm and gathering her papers, Elizabeth walked back to the main room. Though not completely dark outside, the library, without lights, was shadowy. She waved to the librarian who followed her to the heavy front doors, locking them behind Elizabeth as she exited.

The night was still and the streets were empty. Elizabeth was deep in thought as she walked to her car many blocks away, when the muffled sound of footsteps nearby caused her to stop, listen, and scan the growing darkness around her.

"Is someone there?" she called out. Was there movement in the murky twilight? Elizabeth told herself she was being foolish, that this was not some scary movie plot.

Picking up her pace, Elizabeth hurried toward Jasper's old truck, parked several blocks ahead, deep in the shadows. She wished she had left the vehicle under a streetlight closer to the stores downtown, instead of on a dark side street, but, in the daylight, she had not wanted to be noticed by anyone, so she chose to avoid the areas with more pedestrians and traffic.

Without warning, Elizabeth was tackled from behind, causing her to tumble face down on the sidewalk. Sprawled out on the concrete, she struggled to get up, but the person grabbed her arm, twisting it behind her back. Her head was forced down, and a heavy foot crushed her already damaged face to the pavement, the twisting of her arm so severe she felt faint.

"Quit nosing around in what is none of your business," the voice above her growled. "We know where you and those two pretty daughters live."

A swift kick to her left side made her gasp for air. When she was at last able to sit upright, Elizabeth was alone on the dark street.

QUESTIONS

WITH HER RIGHT ARM ACHING AND HER BRUISED FACE
now scraped raw, Elizabeth drove home. When she knocked on Mrs.
Dukane's door, Elizabeth could hear her dog's familiar bark. The lock
clicked, the door swung open, and Lucky greeted her with a wagging
tail and sloppy licks.

"Elizabeth," Mrs. Dukane said, "I thought Lucky was sleeping
over here tonight. What the heck happened to you? Not another car
accident, I hope."

"This time I slipped at work and landed face first. It's like an ice
rink around those vats sometimes."

"You look terrible, no offense. You sure you don't want Lucky to
stay here?"

"Thanks for the offer and for keeping him today, but I think I'll
take him home. The girls will be back early tomorrow morning, and
I want Lucky there for them." Elizabeth and Lucky started down the
steps, and then she stopped.

"Is there something else?" Mrs. Dukane said, walking out onto
the porch.

"I realize this is coming out of the blue, but sometimes when
I'm alone in the house, I begin wondering how you have managed all
these years, living by yourself."

"It's been seven years. A person can get used to anything, I guess,
although I'll never stop missing my Tom."

"I can't imagine how hard it must be. He died of a heart attack rather suddenly, right?"

"Yes. He had a cold and a cough for awhile, was kind of tired and congested. Never any heart trouble as far as we knew, and then it gave out one day at the mill when he was lifting some heavy chemical containers."

"Did he have bronchitis or asthma?"

"No, never. The doctor never mentioned Tom's coughing and congestion at all. Why?"

"Do you remember who the doctor was?"

"Some specialist Northland was generous enough to bring in for Tom when he was hospitalized. What's with all the questions?"

"I'm trying to make sense of what happened to Nona, maybe find some common thread linking how folks are dying around here."

"That's crazy, Elizabeth. If I were you, I'd drop this. Northland was good to me when Tom died, and even though he wasn't old enough to qualify for a pension, they allowed me to have Tom's monthly stipend from the company. I can't afford to lose it."

"I'm not trying to make trouble, Alice, but I want to find the truth."

"The truth is Tom's dead, and I'm alive. That's not gonna change no matter what killed him. Leave it be." The woman returned to the house and slammed the door.

The following morning, Elizabeth's parents, along with Mince and Carol Jean, drove in early from the farm. The two girls were in a rush and flew out of the truck.

"I need to change into something cute," Carol Jean said, hurrying inside.

"I just need to change," Mince added, tagging along behind her sister.

"We'd like the girls to come along to sell corn downtown in front of Prince's store," Marta said. "Saturday's a good day for sweetcorn."

"If that's what they want to do, but it's a little early to sell corn. Sun's just come up."

"I promised them breakfast up at the Country Cafe if they got up early. Plenty of time to eat breakfast and sell sweet corn, too, if we get going." Marta was checking her watch.

"You spoil those girls, Mom. Did things go all right last night?"

"They were upset over the fire, but when we talked about how fortunate you were losing only that old garage, they seemed okay. We didn't talk about Eddie."

William gestured towards the river. "Looks like it has stopped percolating here. Downriver, it's still in flames, I hear. Burned for three miles, all the way to the Pensaukee Dam."

"Have you ever known of such a thing, Dad?"

"Lived a long time, but never have come across a phenomenon like a burning river," he replied. "Any news about Eddie and Jasper?"

"Not yet. I'm guessing the longer it takes, the more serious the charges will be. Julian Prince will contact me as soon as possible."

Carol Jean and Mince bounded out of the house and down the steps. Seeing them enjoying a bit of normalcy stabbed Elizabeth with guilt and sadness. She hugged them and held on until the girls wriggled free.

"Is everything all right? Your face still looks awful," Carol Jean said. "Are you going to get into trouble for the fire?"

"No, it was an accident. Nobody's in trouble."

"Better get a move on, girls. I need my coffee and sweet corn's only fresh for so long, " William said. "If it's alright with you, Elizabeth, the girls will stay at the farm one more night, and we'll bring them back to town for church in the morning," Marta said.

With her daughters safe in the hands of their grandparents, and Lucky guarding the house, Elizabeth left for the plant feeling less worried. She tried to put the attack on the street out of her mind, but her sore arm and bruised ribs kept reminding her of what happened. Recalling the attacker's voice made her stomach queasy.

Their shift at the pickle factory lasted only until noon that day, after a semi, loaded with cucumbers coming in from up north, flipped over on Highway 41. The crew clocked out, and Elizabeth fell into step with Sally Wilson, the two walking together to the parking lot.

"Wish we would have worked a full shift today," Sally said. "I could use the extra money."

"Yeah, me, too. Even so, time and a half made it worth the drive in today," Elizabeth said. "How's everything going, Sally?"

"It's been a struggle. I sure wish Doug was here."

"How long has it been?"

"Six years, and I miss him every day."

"I can't imagine what a shock that must have been, losing him at his young age and so quick, too."

"If you want to know the truth, Doug was sick off and on for awhile. He coughed an awful lot and couldn't catch his breath sometimes. He would feel nauseated and dizzy from the terrible headaches he had most days, but he never let on that he was sick. Had to keep the job, and we had no way to pay for doctors or anything like that."

The two women arrived at their vehicles, and both opened the doors to cool the interiors. Standing together in the only patch of shade in the lot, Elizabeth felt compelled to ask the woman one more question.

"Sally, if you don't mind me asking, what caused Doug's death?"

"I don't mind you asking, because I'm not sure. Dr. Cortland thought it might have had something to do with his lungs, but then the other doctor said his lungs had nothing to do with it, but that it was an aneurysm."

"Who was the other doctor?"

"Some specialist doctor Northland sent over when they heard Doug was in the hospital. Real kind of them, don't you think?"

"Real kind," Elizabeth said.

"Northland was good to me after Doug passed. Gave me a nice check to help with the medical and funeral expenses, plus a little extra to last me for a month or more. They helped me when nobody else would."

"Was there time for additional tests before Doug died? Did they perform an autopsy afterward?"

"Tests are expensive and the doctor said they wouldn't have helped anyway. Within hours, Doug was gone. Nothing was going to bring him back." Sally's face hardened. "Kinda sounds like you think I don't care what took Doug's life."

"No, I'm not saying that at all. Since my Nona died, I've been searching for why my little girl and so many others around here had lung and similar problems. Something is going on, has been for a long time. I want to know the reason why so many people, too many people, die."

"The reason is that people die, Elizabeth. Happens all the time." Sally pointed a boney finger in Elizabeth's direction. "The mill's been good to lots of folks when they've lost loved ones. Alice Dukane receives Tom's pension. Robert Martin's wife gets most of his, too. The list is a long one. Asking questions won't bring any of those people back, but it might stop Northland from helping their families."

Sitting in her sweltering truck, Elizabeth felt a shiver ripple up her spine. Every day there were more questions, and she wasn't certain she had the courage to uncover the answers.

DIGGING DEEPER

ELIZABETH DROVE HOME TO TAKE CARE OF LUCKY, avoiding the downtown where her family was selling corn. In the dining room, she spread her papers out across the old table, records arranged by year, with obituaries and death certificates matched back to 1956. In her last library visit, she had found obituaries going back five more years to 1951. These would require another visit to the Register of Deeds to reconcile them with the death certificates of the individuals.

Elizabeth stared with sadness at the list of names, lost lives reduced to handwritten notes scribbled across the paper. As Lucky rested his nose on her lap, she rubbed his silky ears, her eyes scanning what had been collected. One two-year period, stretching between 1956 and 1957, stood out, with over forty-nine deaths, a number surpassing other years by almost thirty percent. The causes of death, based on the official death certificates, were not identical, but could be related.

Elizabeth searched the house for their old dictionary and found it in a pile of books propping up a three-legged end table in the living room. One by one, she copied the definition for the cause of each person's death during that two-year period, causes such as acute lower respiratory infection, immunoproliferative neoplasm, chronic rheumatic heart disease, malignant neoplasms of the trachea, bronchus and lung, and various pneumoconioses caused by chemical exposure. When she closed the dictionary and looked at the list she had compiled, it was clear to her that, with rare exception, lung problems were involved in these victims' deaths.

Were they victims, or were the deaths medical coincidences? Elizabeth thought the families might be able to shed some light on that question, despite the reactions she received from Alice Dukane and Sally Wilson. She wondered if Sally would be willing to talk to her about Doug again, or if there would be a different response from any of the other families, although she wouldn't blame them if they shut her down, too. For some, the possible financial threat was too great a risk. In addition, dredging up those memories and feelings was gut-wrenching for them and for her, as well.

Elizabeth felt she needed additional time at the Court House to check death certificates, but she wasn't certain when it would be possible. Even with Eddie temporarily out of her way, the long shifts at Landers extended past the Court House hours, and she wanted to be home as much as possible with the girls. If she did find the time to go to the Court House, Elizabeth could also study the ICD to establish frequencies of the particular causes of death. Also, there was the chance the doctors involved might have a simple explanation for the discrepancies Elizabeth had found, and those doctors' signatures were on the death certificates. What she had now were the family names of each deceased person, so she began there.

Robert Martin's name stood out on the list. Elizabeth knew the family lived on the river not far from her house. According to his obituary, he had died of natural causes, but the death certificate listed "pneumonoconioses due to kaolin exposure." Elizabeth had read somewhere that the paper industry was the leading consumer of kaolin.

She leashed Lucky and walked the few blocks to the Martin's address. A blistering sun scorched the air, and the dry, papery leaves of trees lining the streets provided little relief.

At the Martins, the shades were drawn but the front door was open to the screen. Before Elizabeth could knock, Edith Martin was there.

"Hi, Edith. It's me, Elizabeth, from down the street."

"I know who you are. Ain't you the one started the big fire?"

"That was me. My apologies for all the smoke and commotion."

"Didn't bother me none. You can come in if your dog don't mind cats. I got several."

"I'll stay outside. I was hoping to talk to you about your husband."

"You knew Robert?"

"He worked with my husband, Eddie, at the mill. They were in the union together."

"That's right. You're married to the hothead, Eddie. No wonder you set the neighborhood on fire." The woman laughed, then coughed hard into a red kerchief.

"Yes, that's my Eddie." Elizabeth leaned in towards Edith. "Is there anything you could tell me about Robert's death?"

"Not much to tell. Been dead five years now."

"What caused Robert's death? Was he sick before he died?"

"Robert was not a sickly person, but he had been feeling poorly for a few months before he died. Always seemed to have a cough, lots of stuff rattling around in his chest. We couldn't afford a doctor for what seemed like nothing."

"Was this prior illness why Robert died?"

"At first they said he had a lung infection, but the special doctor said it was his heart that caused the chest problems. Called it a heart episode."

"That specialist, was it a doctor sent by Northland?"

"Yeah, that's right. How'd you know that?" Edith's eyes narrowed. "What's all this about?"

"As you know, my daughter Nona passed away this summer. I'd like to thank you for attending the funeral." Elizabeth smiled. "I thought I would return the kindness by finding out why Nona and others, like Robert, died."

"I already know why he died. Nothin' more to say about that. I recommend you mind your own business. Now, if you'll excuse me, I gotta feed my cats."

Elizabeth stood staring at the closed door until Lucky tugged hard on the leash, straining to go home. Instead of going left toward their house, Elizabeth walked in the opposite direction toward an address located a few blocks away. Lucky's tongue hung from his panting mouth, as he lagged behind.

"Only a couple more houses, old friend. You can make it." Elizabeth urged the dog onward, crossing the street to the sidewalk sprinkled with shade. The neighborhood was still and silent in the heavy, afternoon heat.

The Knapp family home sat toward the back of its withered yard. It was a large, two- story structure that, from the street, resembled a face, its white, wooden railings stretched along the broad, front porch like a toothy grin. Two upstairs windows had their shades pulled halfway down like drowsy eyes peering down over the porch's roof, a shingled mustache adorning the mouth-like entrance to the house.

Elizabeth hesitated. She knew of the Knapp family, but there was an unwelcoming feeling that enveloped her as she and Lucky stood before the home. Then Lucky began barking. Faces had appeared at the window which was tucked near the front door. When they disappeared, Lucky's barking quieted, and Elizabeth urged him forward.

The porch was worn, its cracked planks creaking underfoot. Dirty fingerprints of varying sizes smudged the once-white storm door, its screen punctuated with holes and tears. Elizabeth rang the door bell several times, then knocked.

"I hear you and pounding ain't gonna get me there any quicker."

"Hello, Mrs. Knapp. I'm Elizabeth Dembrowski."

The woman, shaded behind the tattered screen, wore a faded housedress, her hair pulled back in a tight knot at the nape of her neck.

"We were in the church at your girl's funeral," the woman said.

"Yes, and your being there was most appreciated. I know it must have been hard since you lost a daughter not that long ago."

"Margaret. That was her name." The woman's voice faltered.

"I'm sorry you lost Margaret."

"You're sorry. We're sorry. Enough said." She backed away from the screen and shut the heavy wooden door behind it.

"Mrs. Knapp, if I could have a minute more of your time . . ." Elizabeth said to the closed doors.

She and Lucky waited. It was apparent the discussion with Margaret's mother was over, so they descended the steps and walked away from the house.

"My mother's not been good since Margie died." The girl walking toward them was tall, perhaps eleven or twelve years old, with thick braids the color of cinnamon falling to her waist.

Elizabeth and Lucky waited for her to approach. "Was Margie your big sister?"

"Yes. We were like two peas in a pod." The girl had slate-grey eyes and freckles sprinkled over her face. "We looked the same, everyone said."

"What was Margie like?"

"She was funny and so smart. Graduated with honors from high school."

"I heard she worked at Northland."

"They offered her a job right out of school. It was in shipping and receiving. A real important job. She loved it."

"How long was she there?"

"Almost two years. Then she got sick."

"What happened?"

"She got weaker and weaker. Something to do with her heart and lungs. Even with all the doctors, nobody could help her."

"Did Northland hire those doctors by any chance?"

"I don't know."

"Linda, get in the house, now," a muffled voice called through the doors.

"I'd better go. Sorry about Nona."

Elizabeth wanted to ask more questions, but the girl was gone. Walking home with Lucky, thoughts were spinning in Elizabeth's head. Was her prying doing more harm than good? Were Northland's actions caring and generous, or were their motives sinister and self-serving? Who would want to stop Elizabeth's inquiries so much that they would threaten and attack her?

Parked in front of her house was the silver Cadillac owned by Julian Prince. On the front porch he waited, cool and stylish in beige slacks and a checked shirt open at the neck, expensive silk tie loosened, but not undone. Sunglasses shielded his eyes.

"You are one hard lady to locate," he said, removing the glasses, his eyes icy blue. "You need to get your phone service reconnected."

"Sorry," Elizabeth said. "I can't afford that right now."

"May I come inside so we can talk?" He patted Lucky and followed Elizabeth into the house.

Elizabeth poured two glasses of ice water and motioned for Julian to sit down. "I guess you're here about Eddie."

"The D.A. has decided to charge Jasper with trespassing, a misdemeanor. Because of the gun Eddie had in his possession, he is being charged with aggravated burglary, a Class E felony."

"What does all of that mean?"

"Jasper, due to his age and no prior arrests, will be released with time served, charged with a fine of $100, and no probation."

"Thank goodness. Jail would have been hard on Jasper. And Eddie?"

"Eddie could face a fine of up to $25,000 and twenty years in jail. Bail is set at $5000."

"He could go to jail for twenty years?"

"Those are the maximums. By pleading guilty, the judge could go easy on him, especially since Eddie only has a couple of drunk driving charges on his record."

"We don't have any money to pay for the bail. What will happen to Eddie?"

"He will stay in the County jail until sentencing, which should be in about three weeks. It's up to the judge, but Northland will most likely seek the maximum sentence for Eddie, choosing to make an example of him. The company has some hefty reasons for wanting their privacy protected. They won't tolerate meddling or having their company practices called into question."

Julian reached across the table and took Elizabeth's hand in his. "I know this sounds harsh, but maybe some time in jail will straighten Eddie out."

All Elizabeth could focus on was that Eddie might be in jail for twenty years.

"One more thing," Julian said. "It would look good for Eddie if you visited him, to reinforce that he is a family man. There are visiting hours tomorrow from 1:00 until 4:00 P.M."

"I can do that, but I'm not bringing the girls."

"That is up to you, Elizabeth."

After the man departed, Elizabeth recalled what Julian had said about Northland. Was his comment about protecting Northland's privacy and not tolerating meddling a warning for her? She believed Julian was on the side of the men at the mill, representing the union in their case against Northland, and he was Eddie's defense attorney. Elizabeth told herself Julian's words were meant to protect Eddie and the others. They had nothing to do with her.

With most of the afternoon still ahead of her, Elizabeth and Lucky climbed into Jasper's truck and drove north, out of town. The Nelsons and Hohlfelds lived off the highway near Copper Creek, a mile past the high school, and Elizabeth hoped they would be willing to talk to her. Wayne Nelson had been a classmate of hers and had played football with Eddie. That might count for something.

The Nelson's farm consisted of sixty acres of land, including some parcels rented out to the neighboring farmers. There was a large barn, several outbuildings, and a sprawling farm house. Elizabeth recalled that before their son, Patrick, passed away, the Nelson's place had been well-maintained and prosperous-looking. Now, a few years later, tall weeds grew up through the shrubbery, a downed tree littered the front yard, a gutter had come loose and hung across the picture window, and the once white siding hung, cracked and greying, against the house. A heavy chain straddled the driveway between two iron posts, and a hand painted sign warned strangers to stay away.

Elizabeth stopped short of the chain and stooped under it, striding toward the house. The place looked deserted. From inside a small shed, Wayne Nelson emerged, and Elizabeth was startled at the stranger he had become. Though a young man, Nelson had aged decades, his hair gray and face lined and creased. As he approached Elizabeth, he put up his hand to halt her progress.

"That chain's there for a reason. Turn yourself around and drive away."

"Wayne, it's me, Elizabeth Sloan, Eddie Dembrowski's wife."

"What do you want?"

"This summer, you know Eddie and I lost our young daughter, Nona. I'd like to ask you about your son, Patrick."

"It's a hard thing, losing a child." The man's face softened for a moment. "What's this got to do with my boy, Patrick?"

"I read in the newspaper your son was in a fatal car accident, but his death certificate stated he died from an acute lower respiratory infection."

"Yeah, that's right. When he was in the hospital recovering from the accident, some damned lung infection took him."

"He wasn't ill before the accident, with a cold or anything?"

"Nope, nothin' like that. My boy was healthy and then he was dead." Wayne stared at Elizabeth. "What's this all about? Why were you looking at Patrick's death certificate?"

"Since Nona passed, I've needed some closure and have begun searching records, trying to find some reason why she and so many others have died in this community. When I saw Patrick's name, knowing he was your son, I thought perhaps you might want to find the causes for these deaths, too."

"Folks die for all sorts of reasons. It's hard to accept, no matter what."

"It seems to me that around here there are numerous deaths with too many similarities in why they happened."

"It seems to me this is none of your business. It doesn't do any good to open up old wounds."

"I'm sorry if I have done that. My apologies for any intrusion on your privacy." She turned to leave. "I do have one more question, if you don't mind. Was there any specialist called in to consult in Patrick's case?"

"Not that it's any of your business, but there was this fellow from the city called in. It didn't help none. I'm done talking, and you should leave."

"I will, and thanks for speaking to me. I'm sorry for your loss, Wayne."

"Me, too."

She watched his stooped figure disappear into the old lean-to. Back at the truck, Lucky waited for her, head hanging out the window. They drove along Copper Creek until they reached the Hohlfeld's place, set far back from the road. Elizabeth turned down the gravel driveway, narrow and shaded by tall trees arching overhead, until the Hohlfeld's house came into view. Without warning, a figure stepped out of the woods. Elizabeth slammed her foot down hard onto the brake to avoid hitting the person.

He was a burly man, broad-shouldered, wearing soiled overalls and a faded shirt. A shock of white hair stood up on his head, like he'd removed a long-worn cap, and his skin was brown and cracked, like the ground beneath him. He walked to her truck window as Lucky barked a warning.

"You lost?"

"I'm looking for John Hohlfeld's place." Elizabeth held Lucky's collar and forced him to sit, but his low growl continued.

"You found it. Who are you?"

"Elizabeth Dembrowski, William Sloan's daughter." She offered her hand through the window. He ignored it.

"What do ya want?"

Elizabeth explained what she was doing. "Would you be willing to answer a few questions?"

"Like what?"

"I understand your wife, Connie, passed a few months ago. Was that unexpected?"

"If you call having a stroke unexpected, then, yes."

"Was Connie ill previous to having the stroke? Did she have any unusual physical symptoms?"

"Connie was a workhorse, never sick a day in her life."

"Did she spend a lot of time outdoors?"

"Like I said, she worked hard. Had a half acre garden, loved to fish, anything outside."

"But no symptoms out of the ordinary?"

"I got work to do. Get your truck and barking dog off my property."

For the remainder of the day, Elizabeth continued contacting persons who lost someone during the years she had researched. By that night, she had located and talked with nine families, none of whom offered any promising new information. Discouraged and exhausted, Elizabeth and Lucky returned home.

WARNING

LATER THAT NIGHT, LUCKY WAS SPRAWLED OUT BELOW the dining room windows where a slight breeze drifted in. With the girls staying at the farm, Elizabeth was again studying her notes spread across the table. Though there was nothing conclusive from today's encounters, a pattern was forming. First, of the nine families she visited, seven admitted their loved one had been ill in some way prior to their deaths. Second, most recalled a physician or specialist linked to Northland being involved in the case, whether it was in the hospital or in their home. Third, in the earlier years, six of the families received some sort of financial assistance from Northland, but that stopped after 1963.

What didn't connect was the fact that some of the deaths were people who had worked at the mill and some, like Nona and Patrick Nelson, were not. The ages of the deceased persons ranged from four years to sixty-four years. Elizabeth struggled to pinpoint what the missing link might be. There had to be a commonality among the people who died.

A thought flashed across her mind. All the deaths she had recorded lived in her community, that fact was obvious, but perhaps where they lived in the area connected them. Elizabeth searched through the desk and junk drawer, looking for a map, but found nothing. Their road maps had disappeared with the junked car. She hurried outside to Jasper's truck and began rummaging in the glove box for a map of their county.

Without warning, a force grabbed Elizabeth from behind and pushed her forward onto the floor of the vehicle. Hands like a noose encircled her neck and tightened.

"Stop snooping around, or you'll be sorry," the steel-handed person snarled. "We're watching your family and can get to them anytime."

Elizabeth had no chance to struggle or scream, but gasped once and lost consciousness.

When she came to, Elizabeth was face down on the floor of Jasper's truck. It smelled of fuel oil and dirt, and she welcomed being able to breathe it in. She sat up, coughed, and placed her hands on her neck. A panic gripped her with an intensity much greater than the hands that had held her throat, as she realized her attacker must have located Carol Jean, Mince, and her parents at the farm.

Waking Lucky and snatching her keys, Elizabeth hurried back to the truck. She drove through the hot summer night, pressing the old vehicle to its limits. Whatever she was doing, it was getting too close to the truth, and someone did not want that truth to be known. Was revealing the facts worth endangering her family? Despite the threat, Elizabeth vowed she would not stop, not until she held someone accountable for what happened to Nona and others like her.

As she approached the turnoff to the Sloan farm, the smell of burning wood filled the cab, its windshield sprinkled with flakes of ash and ember. The sky above her folks' place was lit in shades of fiery red and orange, but only when she crossed Sloan's Creek did she realize it was their barn that was ablaze.

Out of her mind with fear, Elizabeth rushed to the scene, searching for any sign of her parents and her daughters. One firefighter recalled seeing her father when the trucks first arrived at the farm, but had no idea of his whereabouts in the confusion now surrounding the enormous fire. She began running toward the farmhouse, and then, in the pasture east of the burning barn, she spotted a figure standing among the uneasy dairy cows.

It was difficult to know if her father was real or an apparition, his figure was so blackened by soot and smoke. Dark smudges encircled the whites of his eyes, and his hair was burned in patches atop his scalp. Elizabeth hurried inside the fence to her father's side and embraced him.

"Dad, are you all right?"

"I guess so. Might have a few burns on my hands, but nothing serious. Think my hair has seen better days." He began to laugh, but it turned into a coughing spell.

"Mom and the girls? Where are they?"

"In the house. I wouldn't let them come out. Too dangerous."

"Thank goodness everyone is okay. Any idea what happened?"

"I'm not sure. I was up getting a drink of water when I saw the smoke and flames coming from the barn. I called the fire department, woke the family, and ran outside. Went to open the door and the flames shot me backwards. I saved most of my herd, lost a few good ones, though." Her father's lip trembled, tears gathering in his eyes. "Lost Auntie Em and Berta, and one calf at least. We'll see how many others pass from all the smoke they took in."

Elizabeth ran her hand along the flank of Wilma, the nearest cow, her black and white coat now a sooty gray. "Poor old girl," Elizabeth said, looking into the cow's frightened face, the barn's flames reflected in the animal's dark eyes.

She placed her arm around her father's shoulder as they stood, watching the collapse of the barn that had belonged to their family for three generations. There was little the firefighters could do to save the barn building itself, but they managed to salvage the milk house, chicken coops, and machine shed nearby, and they prevented the fire from igniting the surrounding dry grasses and crops.

The firemen thought the fire was due to faulty wiring that had ignited hay stored in the haymow, but Elizabeth knew the real reason. Whoever attacked her and threatened her family had made good on that threat. Burning her parents' barn was an example of how far they would go to stop her, and it made her terrified and furious.

The following morning, Elizabeth told her family the legal situation concerning Jasper and Eddie. After losing the Sloan barn, Elizabeth hated to add to her family's worries, but they needed to hear the bad new from her and not someone else.

"The good thing is, Jasper has been released. I realize it sounds very bad for your Pops, but Mr. Prince has done everything he could to help him."

"Will Pops be able to come home before he goes to prison?" Mince asked.

"No, I don't think so. Immediately after his sentencing, he will be sent away. I will take care of you, and our family will be together, even if your Pops is gone."

"Don't forget, you always have Grams and me. We will be there for you, no matter what," William said. "Liz, your mother and I think it would be good for the girls to stay here for a few more days, if that's all right with you."

Elizabeth was out of options for her daughters' safety, but at least at the farm they would be in the care of their grandparents, rather than alone at home while she was working. It was Sunday, so it was decided Carol Jean and Mince would go home with their mother until the following morning, when Elizabeth had to work. Her folks agreed to pick them up then.

Elizabeth hugged her mother and dad, working her way out the door. "Mr. Prince advised me to visit Eddie this afternoon, so I need to get home." She waved from the truck window at her parents on the front porch, then remembered the maps she needed.

"Dad, do you have an extra city map, a township map, and maybe a county map I could use?" Elizabeth called out.

With maps from her dad, Elizabeth drove away. Glancing in the rearview mirror, she felt sick seeing the blackened bones of the Sloan barn reaching out of the smoldering rubble.

"I'm sad about the barn," Mince said, peering out the back window. "Where will the cows stay when it's cold?"

"Don't worry. Your Gramps will figure everything out. He has good neighbors who will help him build a new barn before the cold weather comes."

When they arrived back in town, instead of going home, Elizabeth drove the girls and Lucky to stay with Madeira and Julian while she visited Eddie in jail. The Princes were more than happy to have the company and agreed that Mince, Carol Jean, and Lucky were safer with them.

"I won't be gone long," Elizabeth said. "I'll put in an appearance and come back for the girls right away."

"Your visit should help Eddie's case," Julian said. "I appreciate your doing this."

At the jail, Elizabeth relinquished her purse and keys to the officer in charge and was accompanied to the visitor section. Despite the heat, the building was cool and damp, and its moldy smell made Elizabeth's stomach lurch. The tapping of her shoes on the concrete floor echoed behind her as she walked, and she pushed her shaking hands deep into her dress pockets.

Eddie was seated on the other side of the cubicle, where a wire mesh separated the visitors from the inmates.

"I didn't think I'd see you here," he said, his voice flat and emotionless.

"Mr. Prince said you weren't allowed any visitors until today. He told me it would help your case if it was on record that your family visited you, so here I am." Elizabeth realized she felt devoid of any emotion, with the exception of relief, seeing her husband in jail.

"Guess I'll need all the help I can get. You can say "I told you so" about the gun. If it wasn't for that, I'd have been released like Jasper."

"You never were one to listen to anything I said, so I won't bother saying "I told you so."

"Heard you burned down my garage and set the river on fire. What the hell were you thinking?"

"I was thinking I would get rid of the tree you cut down, the one your girls loved. As far as the river starting on fire, I blame that on the mill and whatever it is they are dumping into the water around here."

"Are you still harping about that crap? Mills and factories have been using rivers forever to help run their businesses, and by the way, give us jobs. I'm telling you to forget it."

It was the same old argument, and one she could never win, so she rose to leave.

"Word is you were at the Court House a couple of times. What were you doing there?"

"Nothing that should interest anyone else. I had to file some papers for my father, and I wanted a copy of Nona's death certificate. That's all."

"It had better be nothing, because if you do anything to anger the D.A. or Northland's lawyer, I could be in trouble."

"You're already in trouble, Eddie, and nothing I did caused that."

Before Eddie could retaliate, the officer tapped his shoulder with a baton, indicating their time was up. Eddie pushed back in his chair and pointed at Elizabeth.

"I'm warning you, butt out. You're always trying to fix things, and it never works. I promise, you'll be sorry if you make any trouble."

Eddie shuffled out. Elizabeth remained for a time staring through the barrier that had separated her from her husband, not unlike the plan her parents had attempted to implement to separate her from Eddie all those years ago. They had arranged for her to live with her aunt, and after the baby was born, she would return home to start over, attending college as planned.

When Eddie arrived at the farm that night thirteen years ago, Elizabeth stopped him before he could get out of the vehicle.

"You are not staying, Eddie, so listen. I found out I'm pregnant. Your future is set, and I care enough about you to want that for you. My parents have made arrangements for me. It's all settled."

The expression on Eddie's face was not one Elizabeth expected. Instead of being angry or upset, he looked relieved. He got out of the car and strode past her, starting toward the house.

"I want to talk to your parents," Eddie said, reaching to grab her hand. "I need you to come with me."

"My parents don't want to see you. Get out of here, Eddie, and go live your life."

"We can make this work, I promise. Come along and let me do the talking."

With reluctance, she accompanied him inside. Eddie turned on the charm and worked to convince her parents he and Elizabeth should marry. Appealing to their sense of family, he talked about the child they would be giving up, their grandchild.

"I know it seems like it wouldn't be true, but I've always hoped I would have a real family one day. I didn't grow up in one, but being here in your home has shown me what a good family is all about. Lizzie and I do love each other, and we will love this baby, given the chance."

Elizabeth's parents were not convinced, warning Elizabeth about all the pitfalls of Eddie's idea.

"Married life is hard enough, but starting out this way is the sure way to failure," William told them.

They argued for hours. In the end, William and Marta acquiesced, although they continued to voice their strong misgivings and objections. Elizabeth and Eddie were married, with the assurance that, because they would be living on campus, Elizabeth would begin classes as soon as possible. Their lives would be challenging and difficult, but Elizabeth was certain it would be worth the effort. Together, she and Eddie would make their situation work.

"Don't say we didn't warn you," William told Elizabeth.

UPENDED

AFTER VISITING EDDIE IN JAIL, ELIZABETH NEEDED A physical release for her feelings of helplessness and frustration. She decided she and the girls would spend the afternoon working on what was left of the burned garage. They stacked what remained of the concrete wall blocks, pulled nails, and raked debris into piles. It was grimy, smoky, depressing work, but Elizabeth had to admit it felt energizing to take charge of something of which she had lost control only a few days ago.

"That's enough for today," Elizabeth said, pulling off her work gloves. "Go inside and take a bath, and I'll make you some sandwiches for supper."

"You said we could go to the movies with Kathy and her sister, right?" Carol Jean asked.

"Yes, for the third time, you can go to the movies. You earned that money working hard this summer, and there is no crime in spending a little of it."

"You are so cool!" Carol Jean called over her shoulder, already halfway up the stairs. "I get the tub first."

That evening, Elizabeth drove her daughters to the movies and made them promise to wait for her to pick them up. "Stand in front so you can see me when I get there," she told them.

Later, when Elizabeth and Lucky were alone in the house, she opened the maps from her father, spreading the creases flat against the desk. Using the addresses she had collected, Elizabeth began marking an "X" on the location of each, using a different colored pencil for different years. Within a short time, the marks were intersecting and overlapping, a pattern appearing like images on developing photo paper. With her fingertip, Elizabeth traced the marks, most accumulating along the winding path of the river, with the greatest concentration of deaths nearest to the mill and upriver from it. Over a dozen marks indicated deaths along Copper Creek and adjoining waterways, and at least twenty marks were scattered throughout the area in no particular pattern. Were those marks far outside the river vicinity unrelated to the others, and why were so many deaths located upstream from the mill?

Elizabeth admitted she had very little knowledge about how the mill operated. If Northland had been discharging toxic effluence into the river, she would need to find an official record of that. Another visit to the Court House was in order to allow completion of her research at the Register of Deeds and to locate a record of the mill's violations, if there were any.

Deep in thought, Elizabeth studied the moon's glow, diffused by the dismal sky. Then she noticed the clock. The movie had ended ten minutes ago. Elizabeth steadied her hands and reassured herself Mince and Carol Jean would wait at the theatre as she had told them to do. Though in a panic, she took the time to collect her research papers in an old gunnysack. After choosing and then rejecting several hiding places for the bag, she ended up tossing it down the laundry chute and heard it tumble down to the basement.

Yelling for Lucky, the two ran out the back, jumped into the truck and sped down the driveway, throwing aside gravel and dust. The streets were deserted, illuminated by streetlights casting a dull glow in the sweltering night, as Elizabeth drove the distance to the theatre in record time.

When she pulled up in front of the Showtime Cinema, Elizabeth's stomach tightened because, instead of the usual groups of kids milling around after the movie, the sidewalk was empty, and the theatre marquee lights were off. Carol Jean and Mince were not there. Realizing she must stay calm, Elizabeth drove around the block, in case the girls had waited at the rear of the building. The area was deserted, so she turned right, driving up one block and down the next, increasing the area she was covering, block by block, east to west, north then south. The quiet, empty town offered no sign of her daughters. Elizabeth, sick with fear, was almost home when she noticed a car parked in front of the house. It was a Cadillac.

Carol Jean and Mince were stepping out of the vehicle as Elizabeth slammed to a halt. She and Lucky got out of the truck and hurried to the girls, who were standing with Julian Prince, all three staring at the her.

"You were supposed to wait for me to pick you up. I've been driving all over town looking for you." Elizabeth was hugging her daughters, who looked embarrassed.

"The movie was kind of short. We waited and waited, and then Mr. Prince stopped and asked if we'd like a ride," Carol Jean explained.

"We figured we'd get home so you wouldn't have to come get us," Mince said. "I'm sorry we made you worried."

"I'm afraid this is all my fault, Elizabeth," Julian said. "I didn't want the girls standing alone in front of the dark movie theatre, and then I thought they might like an ice cream, so we took a little side trip to the Dairy Queen. I should have brought them directly home."

"You scared me half to death," Elizabeth said, looking at her daughters.

"Again," Julian said, "I take full responsibility for the mixup."

Hearing the apologies and seeing the expressions on the faces watching her, Elizabeth was beginning to feel like a crazy person.

"It's all right," Elizabeth said. "I might have overreacted a bit. Thank you for giving them a ride home and for treating them to ice cream."

When Julian left, Mince, Carol Jean, and Lucky climbed into the bed of the truck, and Elizabeth pulled the vehicle to the back entrance of the house.

"The doors are locked," Elizabeth said, stepping ahead of them with her house key in hand. "Wait outside with Lucky until I am inside and turn on some lights," Elizabeth instructed the girls.

The old door creaked when she pushed herself in. "I could have sworn this light was on when I . . ."

As she walked into the dark kitchen, Elizabeth stumbled on the contents of an overturned wastebasket. Her fingers fumbled along the wall until she located and clicked on the light switch.

Elizabeth froze. Cabinet doors and drawers were thrown open, some emptied onto the counter and floor. The refrigerator and freezer were unlatched, their contents scattered about, melting in the heat. Kitchen and dining room chairs were upended, and the potted plants in the dining room had been shattered on the floor.

"Can we come in? The mosquitoes are getting me," Mince yelled.

"No, get inside the truck cab. Don't come in until I say so," Elizabeth said.

She walked through the house. No room was left untouched, no closet or storage left intact. In the living room, the old, worn couch had been slashed to its wire coils, the television smashed, the drapes torn from their hooks. Upstairs, mattresses and beds were overturned, clothing torn and strewn, possessions trampled underfoot.

When she was certain the intruder was gone from the house, Elizabeth allowed Mince, Carol Jean, and Lucky inside. There was no way to soften the blow, and they walked through their damaged home in shock.

"Who would do something like this to us?" Carol Jean asked.

"Why would they do such a horrible thing?" Mince wondered.

Elizabeth had the disturbing thought that she knew why this had been done, but who was responsible was a troubling mystery. What she did know was that she had to move her daughters out of the house to safety now. She ushered Carol Jean, Mince, and Lucky back outside and into the old truck. Then she remembered the bag she had hidden.

"Wait here," Elizabeth said. "Lock the doors and roll up the windows."

She hurried inside and down the basement steps to where the laundry chute emptied into a large wicker basket. Rummaging through the dirty laundry, she was relieved to find the bag, filled with her research. Elizabeth grabbed it and departed the ransacked house.

At the police station, Elizabeth reported what had happened. She left with the officers to return to the house, but she would not allow the girls to accompany her. Their grandparents had been called, and the girls would go home with them until Elizabeth could be sure it was safe. When that would be, Elizabeth had no idea.

The officers asked questions about whether the house was locked, how long she had been gone, had she seen anyone suspicious in the neighborhood. Inspecting every room, the men took notes, checked for jimmied windows, and searched for clues.

"Mrs. Dembrowski, I know this might be difficult to answer, but after walking through the house again, did you notice if there was anything of value or significance that might be missing?" the officer asked.

"It's such a mess, it's hard to tell. We don't own anything that has any value," Elizabeth said. The only thing of value their family possessed was inside that gunnysack, locked in Jasper's truck.

Four hours later, the two policemen completed their investigation. Elizabeth had answered their questions and was told to report to the station in a few days to sign the account of the break-in. She walked the men out, listening to their orders about keeping her doors locked, and when they pulled away, she retrieved her research from the truck, more determined than ever to uncover what was going on.

In the living room, damaged and tossed like a tornado had blown through it, Elizabeth sat on the floor and leaned against the disemboweled couch. She emptied the sack and scattered its contents around her. The map of her town was at the top of one pile, the "X" marks like headstones in a cemetery, each one representing a loved one, now gone. There, in the center of them, was the mark for Nona.

Nearby, their family photos were scattered, and the picture on top of the pile happened to be one of Nona. She was smiling up at the camera, eyes twinkling, her arms wrapped around Lucky's neck, pulling him close. Staring at the image of her beautiful, lost daughter, Elizabeth's grief was unbearable, but this time she did not allow the tears and sorrow to overtake her. They would have to put her in the ground before she would stop searching for those responsible for Nona's death.

DISCOVERY

DAYLIGHT WAS REACHING THROUGH LOW SLUNG clouds as Elizabeth left for the factory. Mondays were bustling work days, with trucks lined up to dump loads of late season pickling cucumbers. There was no time to fret over the house she had left in disarray, and for that, Elizabeth was thankful. During her lunch hour, she used the pay phone outside the main office to contact her parents, who had picked up the girls from the police station.

"They are still pretty shook up," her father said. "Seems like a good idea for them to stay here until you get this thing straightened out."

"Thank you, Dad. I think that would be the best thing for them."

"What did the police have to say? Any idea about who did this or why?"

"Not really. There haven't been any other break-ins in the neighborhood, but that doesn't mean anything. Someone may have heard Eddie is in jail, leaving a houseful of females, or it could be random. It can happen anywhere, anytime." Elizabeth was on the verge of revealing her suspicions when the lunch buzzer rang. "Gotta go, Dad. Give the kids my love. I'll check in at the end of the day."

Clay called to Elizabeth as she was walking away from the phone.

"I heard you had a break-in last night. Are you and the girls all right?"

"Yes. It was fortunate we weren't home at the time. How did you hear about it?"

"Hard to keep anything secret in this town. Where are you staying?"

"I'm still at the house, but the girls went with my folks to the farm until things settle down. I need to get back to work, Clay."

"How are your folks holding up after the barn fire?"

Elizabeth noticed her conversation with Clayton was drawing the attention of the other shift workers returning from lunch. Without replying, she left and eased into the flow of workers, catching their suspicious looks.

"The boss doesn't think I should be using the phone on my lunch hour," she said to no one in particular. "I thought break time was ours to do as we want."

After work, with an hour until the end of business hours, Elizabeth drove straight to the Court House. The person at the information desk in the lobby directed her to the Clerk of Courts office on the second floor. As she climbed the stairs among the businessmen, lawyers, and well-dressed secretaries, Elizabeth, in her worn and pickle-stained clothing, felt like running in the other direction, but she steeled herself from their dismissive, superior glances.

In the Clerk of Courts office, the busy woman at the counter pointed Elizabeth toward the shelves of statute books, offering no assistance. With only an hour before closing, the task of wading through the volumes, covering one entire wall, overwhelmed Elizabeth. Having no idea where to began, she opened the most recently published book and browsed through the Table of Contents. There were countless sections divided into types of laws, not to mention the chronological order of passage of the laws.

The volumes containing environmental statutes had many subsections, including one on water pollution related to industry, so

Elizabeth started reading there. At closing time, she had only begun to cover the pages, finding nothing that provided any help to her.

Descending the marble stairs of the Court House, Elizabeth was rummaging through her thoughts, trying to figure out how to proceed. The data she had collected was circumstantial, with nothing concrete to connect people's deaths to Northland or anyone else. Where was the proof?

At the bottom of the steps was a water fountain tucked into a recession between two display cases, and Elizabeth stopped for a drink. Bent over the stream of water, she heard a familiar voice coming up the stairway behind her. She turned to see Julian with Richard Jordan, the Northland attorney she had met at the jail. Elizabeth remained bent over the drinking fountain, somewhat hidden in the alcove, sipping water and hoping the hair falling along both sides of her face would help conceal her. She watched the men approach the main floor of the Court House from the lower level, so deep in conversation, they passed without noticing her. When they were a safe distance down the wide corridor, Elizabeth lifted her dripping face and followed them.

"No one can know I am involved in this," Julian said.

"We're in this together, so whether anyone knows it or not, you're involved," Attorney Jordan replied.

Elizabeth eased herself around the corner, out of sight of the two who had stopped to share a cigarette lighter.

"With everything that's been going on, it's only a matter of time before someone connects the dots," Jordan warned. "Fix this, Julian, and get it done soon."

When she heard their footsteps receding down the hall, Elizabeth peaked around the corner and saw the two attorneys leaving the building. Looking through the glass entry doors, she watched them cross to their reserved parking places and drive away.

In Jasper's old truck, Elizabeth rammed through the gears and headed toward home. The conversation of Julian and Richard troubled her, seeming to link Julian to Northland. Were the dots Richard did not want connected the same as those on Elizabeth's maps, the ones she was struggling to connect? Her research proved the deaths represented by those marks were publicly misreported and that the causes were similar but not identical. Northland had provided medical assistance to many of the patients, and those physicians' diagnoses happened to be the ones in the obituaries. Many, but not all, of the deceased had presented symptoms or were ill before their deaths. In addition, there were the addresses of the people who had died, some located close to Northland, the river, or both, but some not.

When she arrived home, Elizabeth sat parked in the driveway, unable to face the mess inside. She could hear Lucky's frantic bark, so, for his sake, she summoned her courage and turned off the truck, pulling the keys from the ignition. The ring was heavy in her hand, crammed with not only the truck keys, but others of various sizes and shapes. Examining them, Elizabeth noticed that inscribed on each key was the word "Northland." These were keys that belonged to Jasper, keys he had copied and stolen from the mill.

MEMORIES AND MADEIRA

IT TOOK ELIZABETH AND LUCKY MANY HOURS TO CLEAN up the ravaged house. Countless things were beyond repair. It was painful to lose dishes and linens she had inherited, or furniture from her family or that her father had made for them. The last place she worked through was her bedroom, where a pale yellow sundress lay crumpled on a pile of clothes that had been tossed to the floor. It was the dress she had worn to greet her new husband when he returned from the university. She picked up the dress, her mind traveling to that moment.

After their brief wedding ceremony, Elizabeth had stayed with her parents at the farm, while Eddie left for the university. Because he had a full scholarship, the school required his attendance at early football practices. Eddie drove back from college that same day, arriving home earlier than Elizabeth expected. When his truck pulled into the yard, Elizabeth, wearing a new, yellow sundress, ran to greet him, throwing herself into his embrace.

"I've been so nervous, waiting to know how things went," she said. Looking into Eddie's eyes, she could tell something was not right. "What is it?"

Eddie pushed her away, his hands holding her shoulders. "They rescinded the scholarship, said they didn't want me."

"I don't understand. You worked so hard to raise your grades and pass those exams. What about the agreement you signed with them?"

"Yeah, well, it seems they had the right to back out because of something called a 'morality clause'. I guess getting a girl pregnant is not considered good, moral behavior."

"But did you tell them we're married, that we are doing the right thing for our baby? Doesn't that mean something?"

"It means I set a poor example for the other players. A married guy with a family is not the type they want representing the university. It says that in the papers I signed."

"What if I stay here with my folks and the baby, and you go by yourself. Would they take you then?"

"Too late . . . they already know I'm morally corrupt. Can't put the toothpaste back in the tube." He laughed at the irony of his comparison.

"What will we do now? There isn't any way we can move there and have you attend the university without that scholarship."

Eddie pulled her close and pressed his lips to her hair. "Before I came here, I stopped to talk to Jasper. He's going to get me in at the mill, knows the guy that does the hiring and says they want strong, young guys in the tougher jobs."

"Work at the mill? No, you can't give up your dream and go to work at the mill." Elizabeth looked up at Eddie. "You seem so calm, like it doesn't matter."

"I've had awhile to adjust to the whole thing. Believe me, it matters. That life, the one I thought we'd have, isn't going to happen. I guess we have to be grown-up about this and make the best of things."

Eddie started at the mill the next day, working second shift at the steam vats and filling in on the loading docks as needed. They lived at the farm until Carol Jean was born, and when she was two months old, Eddie rented a one-bedroom apartment downtown. It was on the second floor of a store purchased that autumn by a new attorney in town, Julian R. Prince, and his wife, Madeira.

Madeira, Elizabeth thought, laying the faded yellow sundress on the bed. She would go to Madeira, a woman she trusted, and the smartest person she knew. If anyone could help her, it would be Madeira. Elizabeth gathered her notes and charts and organized them as best she could, going over in her mind how she would lay out her findings for her longtime friend. With any luck, Madeira would be home alone tonight.

Madeira and Julian lived in the third story apartment above her store downtown. They had long since given up the idea of building the grand colonial home Julian always wanted, choosing instead to enjoy the convenience of living above Madeira's business and a short distance from Julian's law office. It was late in the evening, and Elizabeth considered pulling over to use the pay phone near the store to call ahead. She was certain Madeira would not mind Elizabeth visiting, no matter the time of day, but Julian's whereabouts were an issue. If he was somehow involved with Northland, Elizabeth needed to conceal from him what she had researched.

The streets were deserted. Elizabeth parked down the block from Prince's store and walked to the back, where a garage had been built to house Julian's current favorite car. When she saw his Cadillac was not there, Elizabeth climbed the back staircase to the third story, where lights shone from several windows in the apartment.

"Madeira, it's me, Elizabeth. Can we talk?" Elizabeth alternated between knocking and ringing the doorbell, but there was no response. She was about to leave when the door flung open, and Madeira pulled her inside.

"What are you doing here at this late hour? I heard about the break-in. Don't tell me they came back. My goodness, are you all right? Come in and tell me everything."

"I'm okay, and the house is safe, for now. The girls are at the farm with my parents."

"You all must have been terrified. Stay here tonight, maybe for a few days, to be safe."

"I appreciate the offer, but I came here for a different type of help. I realize it's late, but I have to talk to someone. I've been gathering information I think might prove why so many people are sick and dying around here."

"This sounds serious. Let me get us some coffee, and then you can start talking."

"First, I know it sounds crazy, but I need to be sure you are here alone."

"Yes, I'm alone. This is Julian's poker night, and it's a late one for him. You do know you can trust Julian, as you can trust me," Madeira responded from the kitchen.

"I know. I don't mean to sound suspicious and untrusting. For right now, I want as few people as possible to learn about what I've uncovered."

"That's good enough for me." Madeira set a cup down for each of them. "Now, what is this about?"

Elizabeth spread out her notes, charts, and map and began explaining. For a long time, Madeira listened, nodding but saying nothing. When Elizabeth stopped, her friend picked up the map and placed her finger on the "X" that was Nona's.

"It's no secret that mill has done damage to our community. Why, in the thirteen years we've been here, the fishing industry has disappeared, and so has most of the water recreation."

"Losing fishing, boating and waterskiing is one thing, but having people die is a whole new level of damage."

"You are right. It's frightening to think what all of this might mean. The only thing missing is the definite link to Northland. What did they do and when? Was it done with negligence and disregard

LONG TIME COMING

for the health and safety of the people here? There are an awful lot of unanswered questions, Liz."

"I know. I'm trying to figure out what to do next. Maybe I could interview additional people or talk to the local doctors who first treated the patients. Even so, that wouldn't provide any concrete proof of Northland's involvement," Elizabeth said.

Footsteps on the stairs stopped their discussion, and Julian entered, smelling of cigars and whiskey. Madeira met him at the door with a warm embrace, while Elizabeth pushed her research back into its folder.

"You're home early, Jules. Did you win enough to buy me that new diamond ring you've been promising?" She laughed, flashing a square-toothed smile that stretched across her face.

Julian chuckled, but his smile dimmed when he spotted their visitor. "What a surprise, Elizabeth. It's sort of late for a social call. Is everything all right?"

"Julian, how rude. Elizabeth came at my invitation."

"After all that has happened with Nona, Eddie, the fire, and then the break-in, I needed to talk to someone, and lucky for me, Madeira is a good listener."

"You have been through so much these past months, and I want to make assurances that you can count on both of us to help whenever you need us." Julian walked to the couch where Elizabeth was sitting and parked himself next to her.

"Madeira, I could use a cup of coffee, and bring along some of that dessert you've been hoarding," Julian said.

He patted Elizabeth's knee. "Liz needs a refill, Darling, and perhaps a slice of that dessert, too."

When Madeira was gone, Julian said, "I have heard some unsettling talk around town about you, Liz."

"About me? Oh, right, the fire! I'm guessing people are having a field day about that."

"That's part of it, but several folks have complained you are harassing them and meddling in their private affairs."

"Complained to whom?"

"I'd rather not say. When you ask questions concerning someone's personal business about painful things that have happened, people are going to be upset and uneasy."

Elizabeth felt the beads of sweat dotting her face, and she held tight to her coffee cup to stop her hands from shaking. "It's a free country, Julian. I can ask whatever questions I feel like asking."

"Absolutely, you have every right to do that." His icy blue eyes locked on her face. "Despite everything that's happened, you seem to be doing well, better than expected. I can understand why that would be, knowing what your life was like and how difficult it can be living with a man like Eddie. It must be somewhat of a relief having him out of the house."

"The girls and I are coping and making the best of the situation."

"You will have most of the foreseeable future to do so, since it looks like Eddie will be out of the picture for awhile, unless . . ."

"Unless what?"

"It might be another rumor floating around the Court House, but after so many folks were upset by all this dredging up of the past, I've heard Northland is having second thoughts about pressing charges against Eddie. Seems they don't want to create any more bad feelings in the community by punishing one of their own for what was a very small offense."

Julian reached over and traced a cool, slender finger along Elizabeth's face. "That was quite the accident you had. I can still see faint shades of purple and yellow around the eye."

"Here's the coffee," Madeira said, bustling into the room, "and that dessert Julian's been panting over all day."

Elizabeth had risen and was walking toward the door. "Thanks, but I should go. Perhaps another time."

Madeira followed, taking hold of Elizabeth's elbow and leaning into her ear.

"Stay in touch," Madeira whispered, "and please be careful."

Before Elizabeth could close the door behind her, Julian was there. "I forgot to ask how Jasper is doing. I had heard the pneumonia isn't good, and that he's in and out of consciousness."

"He's doing okay," Elizabeth said, hoping her surprise at this bit of news did not show on her face.

REVEALING VISITS

EXHAUSTION PULLED ELIZABETH TOWARD HOME, BUT at the last minute she turned onto a side street leading to Denton Avenue, where the hospital was located. She and Jasper had never been close, not even friendly, throughout her marriage to Eddie. It was no secret the old man blamed Elizabeth for ruining his son's chance for a better life, away from this town and the mill. Thinking back, she could not recall a time when Jasper had said or done one kind thing to her.

Visiting hours had long since ended, but the nurse walked Elizabeth to Jasper's room anyway.

"You are the first person to visit the old guy," the nurse said, padding along in her rubber-soled shoes. "I think it'll mean a great deal to him that you're here."

At the doorway, she added, "He probably won't wake up, but you could hold his hand and talk to him. They can sense when someone cares."

The room was dark and still, its quiet punctuated by the clicks and beeps of machines lined up beside Jasper's bed. He was curled up like a child, his body shrouded in a blanket tucked around him.

Elizabeth approached the bed and took one of Jasper's hands in hers, surprised at how smooth and soft it was. His wrists were slender as twigs, their translucent skin loose and crinkled along the bones, and his face was shriveled and gray, the eyes sealed, and the mouth sunken into its toothless gums. Tufts of sparse, silvery hair sprung from his speckled scalp and escaped from his large, leathery ears.

Despite the years of enduring Jasper's anger and hostility, Elizabeth's heart filled with an inescapable sadness for this man and his empty existence. He had lost his wife early in their marriage and had spent the remainder of his life alone, raising his son, and working at a hard and thankless job. Elizabeth chastised herself for not trying harder to break Jasper's armored exterior. After all, he was her girls' grandfather and part of the family.

Still holding Jasper's hand, Elizabeth began talking, recalling stories of when her girls were little and life held so much promise. She told of their apple tree and how they climbed it to adventures every day. Their family had once shared good times, like summer picnics, winter sled rides, and card games that lasted for hours. Although it was difficult, Elizabeth spoke of Eddie, the boy Jasper had raised with love and pride, and the young man who became a star athlete.

At the mention of his son, Jasper moved his head, squeezed Elizabeth's hand, and struggled to speak. His words were garbled and interspersed with fits of coughing. Elizabeth leaned in closer, hoping to make out what the old man was attempting to say.

"Keys . . ." He stopped to cough, the rattle deep in his chest. "My keys. . ."

"I have your truck keys right here." She patted the hand she held, trying to calm him. "I want you to know you were a good father to Eddie, and he appreciates how much you cared about him." Elizabeth wasn't certain that statement was true, but, for Jasper's sake, she hoped it was. Everyone deserved to believe their life meant something to someone.

He was agitated now and the coughing resumed. "Take keys. . . "

Jasper's coughing became severe, and Elizabeth left to locate the nurse, who was already hurrying down the corridor towards his room.

Rushing to her patient, the woman spoke to Elizabeth. "You should leave now."

At the door, Elizabeth hesitated, looking back at Jasper. The nurse continued, "He'll be all right for now. Come back again tomorrow."

Back home, Elizabeth sat with Lucky on the front porch watching the stars winking throughout the hazy night sky. Sleep was what she needed, but her racing mind would not allow rest. She had been physically attacked, which was frightening enough, and the barn burning down was tragic, but the fact that their home and her girls had been threatened was terrifying. In addition, there was the night Julian had the girls in his car and his questionable ties to Richard Jordan. Tonight, his talk of Eddie's release sounded like a threat, and she could not forget the feeling of his cold finger tracing the fading bruises on her face.

Was she being paranoid? Maybe she should let the whole thing go and move on with their lives for the sake of Mince and Carol Jean. Reaching into her pocket, she extracted the metal ring with Jasper's truck keys. On that same ring were several keys labeled with Northland's name, the keys to where the skeletons were buried, as Jasper had put it. They lay heavy in her hand, their weight cast in metal, but also in potential. Jasper had wanted to make sure she had the keys.

In bed, after tossing and turning for hours, Elizabeth fell into a troubled sleep, then awoke with a jerk, discovering she was late for work. Wasting no time, she dressed, grabbed her lunchpail, and jumped in the truck. Without warning, a hand tapped on her window, nearly sending her through the roof. Peering into her windshield was the face of Wayne Nelson.

"I want to talk to you," his muffled voice said into the glass.

They sat facing one another at the picnic table, Wayne's enormous hands folded, resting on the rough boards. His plaid shirt was open at the throat, revealing the white skin of his chest untouched by the sun, bordering the deep, reddish tan of his weathered face and neck.

"When you came to my house the other day, it was the first time I talked about Patrick in months, maybe years."

"I'm sorry to have dredged up those painful memories."

"What's even more painful than losing Patrick, is that we covered up how he died. It wasn't the car accident that killed him."

"What happened, Wayne?" Elizabeth asked, heart pounding, attempting to sound calm.

"There was a car accident, but Pat was sick weeks before that. We went to our doctor here in town, even took him to Madison. The doctors there questioned whether he had been exposed to some kind of poison or chemical."

"What was wrong with Patrick?"

"First, he had what we thought was a cold, lots of coughing and stuff in his lungs. Then, his temperature rose so high he was delirious, sweating and freezing."

"What about the accident? How did that enter the picture?"

"Patrick was getting worse, and we were driving him to the hospital. Our car was rammed in the backend by another car. We spun around, hit the ditch, and by the time we climbed out, the other vehicle was gone. It took a long while for the police to arrive, and when the ambulance delivered Patrick to the hospital, he was unconscious. He never woke up."

"Wayne, I am so sorry. Did you ever find out who caused the accident?"

"Nope, police found nothing. Didn't seem like they tried all that hard, and, after a few months, they ended up saying it was a hit-and-run accident, but I knew different. Didn't matter anyway, because Patrick was gone."

"What do you mean, you knew different?" Elizabeth held her breath.

"Patrick's mother and I weren't in our right minds after he passed. My wife and I couldn't sleep, couldn't eat or work. The farm was going to hell and the bank was pestering us for payments, when this attorney shows up with what he called a compensation settlement. All we had to do was agree to release the driver of the other car, if he was ever located, from any negligence on his part in the accident. To tell you the truth, I didn't care what I signed."

"You agreed to a compensation settlement releasing the driver from all responsibility, for the car accident that precipitated Patrick's death? Who offered the settlement?"

"Didn't know or care who was offering the settlement. I signed that paper, and we took the money. We paid off the bank and the rest of our debts. I ain't proud of it, but, to tell you the truth, it didn't matter. Nothing mattered because our son was gone."

"I don't suppose you remember the name of the attorney who contacted you to sign the release?"

"Some slick fellow, fancy dresser and fancier car. Can't recall his name."

"Would you check the papers you signed to see if the attorney's name or law firm is shown on the documents?"

"I could do that. Anyway, that's not all I came to say about Patrick."

"What did you want to tell me, Wayne?"

"That boy spent every spare minute he had fishing and swimming in the creek, from the time he was old enough to hold a fishing pole. That last year, there was more dead fish belly up in Copper

Creek than was swimming in the water. There was something wrong, but we ignored it and didn't hear what our son was telling us." Wayne's hands tightened into two stoney fists.

"That's why it didn't matter that we signed that release about the car accident. It wasn't the car accident that killed Patrick. It was Copper Creek."

Elizabeth felt a shudder run through her body, the blood pulsing in her ears. This was the link, the person who could connect the water of Copper Creek to the death of someone.

Elizabeth extended her trembling hand to Wayne, who grasped it and held on.

"I don't know if one person can take on something like what's been going on here," Wayne said, "but I hope you succeed. I hope you make them pay for what they done."

After he left, Elizabeth sat at the picnic table thinking about Wayne's revelations. Copper Creek ran along the back boundary of Wayne's sixty-acre farm, and then snaked its way through the northern one-third of John Hohlfeld's place. Before it reached the edge of town where the high school sat, Copper Creek fed into the Oconto River, and along that river loomed the Northland Paper Company's factory. By Wayne's account, Patrick's death was caused by the condition of Copper Creek, which was linked to the quality of the river, and that had everything to do with Northland.

Elizabeth also realized there might be another connection. Was Northland's attorney, Richard Jordan, the slick fellow who brokered the fatal accident release from the Nelsons, or could it have been Julian Prince?

THE LAW AND THE PLAN

BECAUSE OF HER CONVERSATION WITH WAYNE, Elizabeth was more late for work than ever. She should have driven straight to the factory, but instead she drove to Madeira's and parked along a side street, one block from their apartment. A short time later, she saw Julian's Cadillac back out of their driveway. When his tail lights disappeared into the morning haze, she rushed up the stairs to the third floor, the smell of coffee drifting from Madeira's apartment.

Madeira answered the door in a black dressing gown, her hair wound in a tight french twist, and her makeup magazine perfect. Inviting Elizabeth inside, she offered her a place on the window seat and put a steaming cup of coffee in her hands.

"From the expression on your face, it looks like something's happened," Madeira said.

"Not something. . . someone. Patrick Nelson's father." Elizabeth relayed all that Wayne Nelson had told her, leaving out her personal suspicion that Julian might have been involved in the deal.

"Okay, so another death not as it was portrayed to the public, but you already were aware of that. What's changed?"

"What's changed is the fact that Wayne Nelson has admitted his son died under questionable circumstances, with a possible connection to the water of Copper Creek, which could have something to do with the pollution there. That pollution could lead directly to Northland. Add to that what might be called coercion or bribery or something illegal in obtaining the release from the Nelsons, maybe by Northland's own attorney."

"I don't know, Liz. Those conclusions are based on possibilities and maybes. Don't get me wrong, I think you are on to something, but the solid proof isn't there . . . yet."

"There are all these puzzle pieces that look like they should fit together, but too many parts are missing to form a picture I can recognize."

"I have about an hour until I need to get downstairs to the store. Let's go over all your notes and charts again, in case something was overlooked."

They spread Elizabeth's pages across the kitchen table, then over to the counters, ending up on the window seat cushion. Madeira began at one end of the trail of papers and Elizabeth at the other, making notes and questioning each other when needed. In the end, they were no further than when they started, except that both were more certain than ever that the deaths were linked to each other and to Northland.

"It's bad enough if the mill unknowingly damaged the town by dumping stuff into the waterways and killing the fishing and recreation industries. It's a whole different story if they had the knowledge that what they were doing was deadly to people and did it anyway." Madeira tapped her finger on the county map Elizabeth had marked. "There must be some kind of laws that govern what companies can and cannot do to the air, land, and water. If there aren't, there should be."

Elizabeth broke into a smile, something she hadn't done in awhile. "I knew you would think of a different way to approach the issue. Instead of looking at what Northland did, maybe I should look at what they didn't do. If there is a law they didn't follow, I'm going to find it, even if I have to break into Northland myself. That information is hidden somewhere."

Leaving her friend's apartment, Elizabeth was on her way to Landers, when she began considering another visit to the Clerk of Courts office. The jammed parking lot indicated the Court House was bustling with people, and it was possible she could run into Julian or Northland's attorney, or others who might be suspicious or resentful about her activities. Passing the library, its "Open" sign beckoned her, and she turned in. The parking lot was empty, and the rooms of the library were devoid of patrons. Inside, the librarian was more than willing to show Elizabeth the location of the state and federal statutes in countless volumes filling one complete section of an entire room.

"This is the main library in our county, so we are fortunate to house volumes of federal statutes going back about fifty years. Any more than that, and we would have to add a wing to the library." She laughed and pulled out a volume. "There are sections with types of laws, but laws are also listed chronologically based on the session in which they were passed, regardless of when the bill was introduced."

Elizabeth thanked her and was left alone to tackle what seemed like an insurmountable task. Since she had been attacked after hours near this same library, Elizabeth chose a table facing the open door and the clock. Many hours passed, and she was close to quitting in frustration when she came across an index listing for a law passed in 1899, the Rivers and Harbors Act. Its section 13, called the Refuse Act, prohibited the discharge of materials into a navigable waterway without a permit from the U.S. Army. Lacking such a permit, a company was liable for the harm done to the environment and endangerment to the public health. Did Northland have that permit?

"Elizabeth, there you are!"

The voice startled her, causing Elizabeth to knock over a stack of law books piled at the front of the table, sending them crashing onto the floor.

"Clayton, what are you doing here? You scared me half to death."

"I'm sorry. After all that's happened, I became worried when you didn't show up for your shift. I saw Jasper's old truck parked in the lot, so thought I'd check on you." Clay was bending over, retrieving the books. "Didn't mean to scare you."

"I was so deep in thought, you startled me, that's all." She began to help him with stacking the books.

"Forgive me for butting into your business, but, like I said, I was worried."

"It's me who should be apologizing to you," Elizabeth said. "First, for not being at work, and then for not stopping in to tell you everything that's been going on."

Elizabeth was certain her old friend could be trusted, and she needed another ally to assist her.

"Sit down, Clay, and I'll fill you in on the details."

She talked all the way through to the law she had discovered that might be the linchpin to her entire investigation. "Now, I need to find out if Northland had a permit, and whether they were ever charged with breaking that law, permit or not."

"How do you propose to do that?"

Elizabeth pulled out Jasper's ring of keys and placed them on the table. "By going right to the source."

The two spent the next fifteen minutes arguing over Elizabeth's plan, but Clayton was unable to dissuade her. "All right, if you are adamant about breaking in, and, by the way, it is still breaking in even if you have keys, then, I'm going with you."

It was agreed that night was as good as any. They left the library together, and Clayton walked Elizabeth to Jasper's truck.

"I'm going to follow you home, to be on the safe side," Clay said.
"That's not necessary."

"Humor me and allow me to play the gallant knight." He placed his hand over his heart and bowed low.

Back at her house, Elizabeth turned into the driveway and spotted Lucky, sprawled out on the front porch. Clay parked behind her and the two walked to the porch, where they were greeted by Lucky.

"What are you doing out here?" Elizabeth said to the old dog, petting him. "Lucky was inside when I left this morning, and no one else is home," she told Clayton.

Clay crossed the porch and checked the front door. "It's open to the screen, Liz, and that's not locked either."

"I overslept this morning and was in a hurry. I didn't have time to check all of the doors," she said. "Lucky has always been able to push the screen, and considering what a long day this must have been for his old bladder, I'd guess he nudged the door open to get outside."

"Do you want me to go in and check the house for you, in case?"

"No, it'll be okay. The police promised to check on our house whenever they were in the neighborhood, and I have Lucky to keep me safe." Elizabeth patted Lucky's soft head. "Plus, whoever broke in the last time knows we have nothing of value. They won't be back."

Their plan for the break-in at Northland became the topic of their conversation. After that, the two sat in silence, until Clayton spoke.

"You know, Liz, you were my best friend in high school. I wish I had told you that, but I never had the courage."

Elizabeth felt a smile spread across her face. "You were my best friend, too, Clay, and I should have recognized that."

"It's odd how smart we become as the years pass. There were lots of things I should have realized and didn't until it was too late."

"Regret is a funny thing, isn't it?" Elizabeth's voice was subdued. "The other night, when I was running water for a bath, it came to me how much Nona loved to take a bath, begged to take a bath every night. I was overcome with regret for not always doing such a simple thing for her when she asked."

"You were a wonderful mother to Nona, and she adored you. Don't ever doubt that."

"I tried so hard to be a good mother to her and her sisters. It's been difficult to keep our family together and make it all work. For awhile, things were going okay, but with Eddie and his drinking, the mill closing, and Nona . . . I'm not sure I want to try anymore. I'm so tired of it all."

Clayton moved next to Elizabeth on the porch step and put his arm around her shoulders.

"Feels like old times, huh? Making out in the front seat at the quarry on a sultry summer day."

"I don't think we ever did anything at the quarry," Elizabeth said.

"No? Oh, right, that was all in my mind. Wishful thinking, I guess."

"You're saying that to make me feel better. Despite us being close friends, even best friends, we were just that, friends, and nothing more."

"Talk about regrets!" They both laughed, and Elizabeth turned her head in such a way she was almost facing Clay. Without hesitation, he leaned into her and kissed her smiling lips.

"I should go inside. Thanks for being here for me," she said.

"Wouldn't have it any other way. Go on in and remember to lock the door."

HE'S BACK

LUCKY LEAD THE WAY INTO THE HOUSE, THE FRONT hall dim in the fading daylight. Running her hand along the wall, Elizabeth located the light switch and snapped it on. Lucky growled, a deep, threatening sound, and Elizabeth froze.

"Evening, Lizzie. Long day at the pickle plant, I guess." Eddie was standing at the end of the hall, beer bottle in hand. The air felt stagnant, stale, furnace hot.

"You don't seem happy to see me." Eddie's voice was cold and razor sharp.

"I'm surprised, that's all, since we couldn't afford to pay your bail. Don't tell me you broke out of jail."

Eddie walked closer until he was face to face with Elizabeth. "The charges were all dropped. Disappointed?"

"No. What happened?" Elizabeth felt the sweat trickle down her temples, her hands damp and shaking.

"What happened is Northland wanted to show they care about everybody here."

"I thought they were going to make an example of you."

"That's where you come in. Seems your digging got folks upset, so Northland felt sorry for them and me. They dropped the charges on the condition you stop snooping around."

"How is your release going to stop me?" She tried, but Elizabeth couldn't keep the anger from creeping into her voice.

"It's going to stop you because I gave my word it would. If you don't stop, I'll be back in jail. Before they put me away again, I'll put you out of your misery."

Eddie was standing very close and when he raised his hand, Elizabeth flinched out of habit. Instead of striking her, he touched her hair, smoothing the dark tangles tumbling over her shoulders.

"You always had nice hair, Lizzie, real nice. First thing I noticed about you was that damn hair. I used to love its smell," he said, sniffing along the top of her head, "but now it's covered with the stench of Clayton Landers and his pickles." Without warning, he seized a large handful, yanking it until she bellowed in pain.

A flurry of barks from Lucky was the only warning before the dog plunged his teeth into Eddie's calf. Eddie thrashed and kicked at the animal, freeing himself from the dog. Lucky continued to snarl and snap, until the rabid man backed the attacking creature out of the house, slamming the door. Elizabeth, who was too stunned to move, somehow was able to find her voice.

"Let's not fight, Eddie. Can't we sit down together, have a beer and talk?"

"Yeah, let's do that, like you and Clay, sitting on the front porch."

"We were talking."

"Too bad you're such a dumb ass, Lizzie. I saw you kissing that clown. What else you been doing, huh?" His voice was like a severing chain saw, cutting Elizabeth to pieces.

Eddie grabbed her by the hair with one hand and twisted. Elizabeth struggled to gain a foothold, to grasp Eddie's wrists, to somehow secure control of her own body, but he was too strong. He hurled her against the wall with such ferocity her teeth slammed down, slicing her tongue and rattling her head. She felt queasy and faint, her eyes losing focus, her ears ringing.

"Don't do this, Eddie," she slurred, the blood seeping through her teeth. "Please, I'm begging you to stop and think."

"Oh, I'm thinking, all right. I'm thinking you and your buddy Clayton Landers have been having a good time. While the cat's away, the mice will play, so to speak."

With one swing of his fist, Eddie demolished Elizabeth's nose, fracturing it like dry kindling. Blood ran from her shattered nose and wounded mouth as her head sagged to her chest. On the verge of losing consciousness, Elizabeth dredged up the strength to speak.

"It's not what you think, Eddie. Clayton is an old friend, and that's all."

Eddie leaned down into Elizabeth's face. "You're not a good liar, Lizzie. In fact, you're a piss poor liar. I can smell him on you, like skunk spray on a dog."

He stood erect and pulled Elizabeth up by the front of her blouse, her legs wobbling beneath her. When his grip loosened for a moment, she was able to steady herself, leaning her back against the stair railing. Eddie laughed and lunged for her once again.

Elizabeth grasped the banister post, kicking her husband in the groin with enough force to double him over and send him stumbling backward into the wall. As he struggled to stand again, she reached down to the floor where she had dropped her metal lunchpail. She snatched its handle and swung the pail hard, connecting with Eddie's skull above the temple, the hollow thud like a stone plunging into a deep well. He dropped face first and unconscious at her feet.

Elizabeth fought to catch her breath as she stared at Eddie's body sprawled in the center of the hall. She kicked him hard in the ribs, but he didn't move. A thin ribbon of blood trickled from the split in his head, winding its way to join the blood leaking from the corner of his open mouth.

Stepping over Eddie's body, Elizabeth stumbled to the kitchen and leaned into the sink, splashing water from the tap into her bloody mouth and onto her broken nose until the liquid ran clear. Still groggy, she peered up at the window above the sink, the window without the lace curtains.

The sky was pristine, colored in shades of rose and orange, fading into the coming night. Gone was the usual opaqueness streaked with thick, murky clouds. As her head began to clear, Elizabeth realized she preferred seeing the world through a window unadorned and free, and she was grateful there had never been enough money to have those curtains.

BREAK-IN

WITH LUCKY IN THE TRUCK BESIDE HER, ELIZABETH drove away from the house, leaving Eddie unconscious on the floor. Unsure of her destination, she drove through the empty streets, turning right or left or not at all. Eddie was free and back in their lives, something she had not anticipated. The fact that he demanded Elizabeth stop digging so he could stay out of jail was more motivation for her than ever to continue. Breaking into Northland and searching was a beginning.

Elizabeth worried that despite having Jasper's keys to gain entrance to Northland's offices, their chances of finding what she needed were slim, considering the size of the place. Besides, it was unlikely a company would keep damaging records stored where anyone entering the offices could have access to them. Circling back to Denton Avenue, Elizabeth decided to visit Jasper in the hospital again. If he was conscious, and if he was willing to help her again, the old man might be able to shed some light on where she and Clay should look.

Inside the hospital, she found Jasper in the same location with a nurse attending him. The woman looked at Elizabeth's battered face with concern.

"You should get that looked at right away."

"I'm on my way. I thought I'd stop for a quick visit with Jasper first."

"All right, but keep it short, for both of your sakes. Mr. Dembrowski, someone is here to see you." The nurse touched Jasper's hand, then spoke to Elizabeth. "Please try not to upset him. He is very weak and becoming agitated could cause another coughing attack."

Elizabeth thanked the woman and leaned over the frail, withered figure. "Jasper, it's Elizabeth. Are you able to hear me?"

Although his eyes remained closed, Jasper turned his head toward Elizabeth.

She took the keys from her pocket and swung them like a bell. "Thank you for the keys. Could you tell me which one to use and where to use it?"

Jasper's eyes fluttered open, and he focused on what she held. With a trembling hand he touched the keys, his fingers fumbling from one to the next until he held firmly to one key. Attempting to talk, his words were tangled in a fit of coughing.

"Can you tell me what this key unlocks?" Elizabeth asked.

Jasper didn't answer. Instead, his coughing became uncontrollable, and he struggled for air.

"I think Northland did this to you and many others, Jasper. With this key, somehow I will find out for sure," Elizabeth whispered, touching Jasper's hand.

The nurse came in, checked the monitors, and asked Elizabeth to leave. She stepped out of the room and watched another nurse rush in, scurrying into action, as Jasper's machines flashed and beeped.

Elizabeth left the hospital, surprised at the tears forming in her eyes for the father-in-law who hated her. Though he had been unable to give information about what the key opened, Jasper had provided the means for them to enter the exact location they needed inside Northland. For that, she was thankful.

She and Lucky drove off towards the Court House where Clayton would meet them. The bells of the tower chimed nine o'clock as Elizabeth entered the parking lot. Clay's car was there in a dark corner of the lot, and Elizabeth stopped next to him.

Elizabeth started to climb out of the truck when Julian's silver Cadillac halted with a jerk behind her. Julian was visible through the open driver's side window, and he waved her over to his vehicle.

"Elizabeth, glad I caught you. Eddie is . . ." Julian stared at her battered face. "Looks like you already know that Eddie is out of jail."

"I saw Eddie. Let's just say it didn't go well."

"I'm so sorry. I thought I'd have time to warn you, but I was held up in court."

"Don't worry about it. Eddie and I had to work things out ourselves anyway," Elizabeth said. "I have to get going. Thanks for your concern."

"Be careful, Liz." Julian drove away, and Elizabeth and Lucky walked around to Clay's car.

"I thought, actually, I hoped, maybe you had changed your mind about tonight," Clay said, throwing open the door for them.

Before Elizabeth could respond, Clayton saw her injured face, noticeable even in the dim light. "What happened? Don't tell me someone's attacked you again."

"I'll explain once you start driving. Let's go."

They rode in silence for a short distance before Elizabeth spoke. "Eddie's out of jail. The District Attorney decided to drop the charges. Northland did the same, provided I stop searching for the causes of death for Nona and the others."

"That sounds like blackmail or collusion or something. Are you sure they can get away with it?"

"Not only can they, but it's already done. In case I had any ideas about not cooperating, Eddie gave me a little extra incentive."

"That bastard. Where is he now?"

"Last I saw, he was unconscious and lying face first on the hall floor at our house."

"Maybe we should rethink this. If Eddie figures out what we're doing, no telling how he'll react or what he might do to you if he finds you."

"I'm not afraid of Eddie," Elizabeth said. "The only way to know what's been going on is to get those records, and that means getting into Northland. Are you still with me?"

"Whatever you say, Miss Sloan. I was always a sucker for a take-charge kind of girl. What did Julian Prince want?"

"He wanted to warn me of Eddie's release. That I already knew." Elizabeth touched her broken nose, swollen and throbbing, and leaned her head back against the seat.

They were a block from the Northland complex when Clayton pulled onto a side street lined with trees and older houses. Elizabeth rolled all the windows down halfway for Lucky, locked the doors, and ordered him to stay in the car. She and Clay walked the short distance to Northland, Elizabeth's hand gripping the keys deep in her pocket, while Clay carried flashlights.

The north side of the mill provided the easiest access to the offices, except for the locked gate connecting the seven-foot chain link fence surrounding the entire complex. Elizabeth tried Jasper's key and every other key as well, but none fit the gate's metal lock.

"Someone's coming," Clay whispered. "Get back here, out of the light."

Elizabeth scurried backward and fell against Clay, who pulled her further into the shadows. A single flashlight beam bounced its way toward them, accompanied by the grinding of gravel beneath heavy boots. The guard waved his light around the gated area and beyond, jiggled the locked gate, and swept the light's shaft once again outside the gate. He paused, holding his position, staring into the shadows. Then, he moved along.

"We need to hurry before he comes back," Elizabeth said, gazing upwards at the towering fence.

"What's your plan?"

"Climb the fence. I think I can make it if you give me a leg up." Elizabeth was already reaching high on the fence, working her fingers to gain a firm grasp of the chain links.

"Here goes nothing." Clay cupped his hands into a stirrup and launched Elizabeth upward, supporting and pushing her feet as she clawed her way to the top. The crest of the fence was jagged and ripped at her hands, but she managed to throw one leg over. Easing her body up across the ridge of the gate, Elizabeth's clothing caught on the razor-edged wires protruding at sharp angles along the upper edge. As she struggled to release them, she lost her balance and fell seven feet to the ground below, inside the Northland complex.

For a few moments, Elizabeth struggled to breathe. The wind had been knocked out of her, and her ankle was injured. Clayton tried multiple times before he was able to scale the fence and drop to the ground beside her.

"Liz, are you hurt? Please, say something."

Elizabeth pulled herself upright to a sitting position and inhaled deeply. "Had to catch my breath, but I'm all right. Help me up."

Standing, Elizabeth tested the ankle, which was painful but tolerable. Without hesitation, she set off limping toward the first building where the company offices were housed.

Elizabeth wiggled each key on Jasper's ring into the door's lock, but not one fit, nor did any fit the enormous padlock securing the heavy chain looped through the door's handle as an extra precaution. She slammed the padlock against the door in frustration and looked through the office windows, reinforced with steel mesh. The rooms were dark, but spot lights installed along the roof outside laid down patterns of light on the interior floors, revealing at least the front office had been cleared out. Clay grabbed her arm.

"Move over here, now!" He pulled her away from the front of the offices to the shadows on the east side. "The guard is back."

They hunkered down in the alley along the concrete block wall, and the guard passed, flashing his light in their direction for a moment before he left. Elizabeth breathed a sigh of relief, then dropped the key ring with a clamor that reverberated within the concrete walls. On her hands and knees, Elizabeth scrambled to locate the ring, and then the two scurried to the far end of the building, as the guard's light once again lit up the alley. The man, dressed in a uniform, pulled his gun from its holster and walked part way into the alley, flashlight darting. After stalling to listen, he was gone.

They held their position for a brief time, and, as they did, Elizabeth glanced over her shoulder, noticing a second entrance, tucked away and a few feet from where they were hiding. Crouching low, she scurried toward the steel door and began working the keys in its lock. At last she came to the key Jasper had singled out, and it turned with a click. Clayton joined her, grabbed the door knob, and turned it. The door swung open.

Clayton handed Elizabeth a flashlight, and the two began scanning the windowless room. When she located a light switch, Elizabeth flipped it up, triggering the flashing of lights throughout the room. Rushing past her, Clay dove for a metal box located near the door. Holding his flashlight in one hand, he used the other to flick a switch that disarmed the system and shut off the lights again.

"That was close. How did you know what to do?" Elizabeth asked, flashlight focused on Clayton's face.

"We have the same setup at the pickle factory. The system sets off flashing lights as the first level of the alarm, and if that is not shut off, the sirens go off. It's a pretty common setup."

"Are we all right with the lights on or will the alarm sound again?"

"I disarmed the alarm in this section, so the lights are okay." Clay switched on several ceiling fluorescent panels and started for the filing cabinets lined up along the concrete walls.

"I don't think this room is part of the front offices, do you?" Elizabeth asked.

"No, the concrete walls are thicker and there's no connecting doorway between the two parts of the building. This was definitely used for something other than office work."

Elizabeth was pulling drawers, rifling through sections of files. "Anything?"

"Not sure what I'm looking for." His fingers fumbled along the file name tabs.

"Stuff that has to do with chemicals, discharging effluence, legal references, that sort of thing. Also, if there are any maps of the area, they might have some significance."

Elizabeth had worked her way through three file drawers before coming across a memo dated several years ago.

"Here's something, Clay. Do you remember back when we were in high school, the stink that became noticeable in town? The fumes were so strong, the paint on some of the buildings along the river bubbled and peeled off. I remember because the Dairy Queen is next to the Third Street bridge, and their DQ sign's paint fell off in long strips."

"Not sure I remember that happening, but I'll take your word for it. So what?"

She continued. "According to this memo, that was around the time the mill shifted to manufacturing higher value paper. It says pulpwood was getting scarce, so they began using less wood, but more chemicals. Lower costs, more expensive paper, bigger profits."

Elizabeth continued. "According to these figures, that shift caused a huge increase in the amount of highly toxic discharge. Two to three million gallons of liquid waste went into the Oconto River and the bay every single day."

"That happens wherever factories are located. Communities accept some residual effects when allowing industries to use their resources. In return, the people get good jobs," Clayton said.

"Think about the thick sheets of bacterial slime at the bottom of the river. We used to have bass, perch, bluegill, and walleye, but they couldn't survive in that environment. They were replaced by carp, suckers, and catfish. I've watched even those poor creatures swim in circles with their heads reaching out of the black water, trying to stay alive by gulping air."

"They're fish, Liz. Not that big of a deal."

"No fish means no commercial fishing jobs. Our trees, farms, and gardens are ruined because the water and soil are bad. Even the air we breathe is bad, causing people to wheeze, cough, and maybe die."

"I think you're reading a lot more into what was a move on the part of the company to remain in business, be competitive, and save jobs."

"Sure, they stayed in business and made more profit, but at what cost? Besides, I told you, there's a law that made it illegal to discharge materials into a waterway, unless the factory had a permit."

"What makes you think Northland didn't have a permit?"

"We have to know for sure. Let's keep digging."

Elizabeth returned to the files lined up in front of her, Clayton's comments shaking her confidence. He was mumbling and muttering as he read file names to himself, making little progress. She proceeded through several more cabinets, and then she approached one whose lock was engaged.

"Clay, this file cabinet is the only one so far that is locked."

"How about using one of the keys?" he asked with a hint of sarcasm in his voice.

"I've tried. They're all too big and won't fit. Let's jimmy it with something." Liz hustled about the room, searching for any sort of tool or sharp instrument, while Clay checked containers and drawers for anything they could use.

"Here, this might work," he said, walking over with a letter opener. Forcing the blade into the lock, he worked to pry it out. "I need something solid and hard, like a rock or brick, better yet, a hammer."

"I don't know about a hammer, but I did notice there were rocks piled outside," Elizabeth said, striding toward the door. "I'll be right back."

Flashlight in hand, she walked outside toward the back of the building until she found stones used under the downspout. Kneeling down, she set her flashlight near her feet and started wrenching loose a large, flat rock when someone struck her from behind, knocking her to the ground. Elizabeth felt herself falling, but was unable to stop her body from collapsing and the blackness from overtaking her. She came to in semi-darkness, face pressed against damp, cool concrete, her skin sticky with blood from the wound at the back of her skull. Her head throbbed with pain. Battling to remain conscious, she concentrated on the rumbling she heard in the distance, like the idling of a diesel engine overhead.

EXPLOSION

AFTER SEVERAL DIZZY MINUTES, ELIZABETH REALIZED she was not in the building she and Clay had been searching. The dank, musty air choking her was laced with the unmistakeable smell of chemicals. Whether it was her recent head trauma or the chemical-laden air, Elizabeth was overcome by nausea that made her gag each time she tried to stand. Belly crawling her way to the nearest wall, she managed to pull herself up to a seated position, where she leaned back and closed her eyes. Based on the way her head and body felt, Elizabeth guessed she had sustained a concussion, and somehow she managed to stay awake by thinking of the girls. When the waves of nausea subsided, she opened her eyes.

Blackness surrounded her. Struggling to focus in the darkness, she noticed a faint light on one end of the room and the glow of an exit light on the other end, appearing to be about thirty to forty feet apart. Moving her hands over the surface behind her, Elizabeth determined the walls were concrete block, and the absence of light along the perimeter walls indicated there were no windows. What filled the enormous interior of the building she could not tell, deciding her best option was to crawl ahead and find out.

In the darkness, she scraped along on her hands and knees until she encountered the first of what she determined were metal drums. Taller than Elizabeth, they were lined up in rows like sentinels and wrapped with thick wire mesh. Gripping the wire, she pulled herself up to a standing position and continued to shuffle along the queues of barrels. There were hundreds of them filling the room.

As her eyes became accustomed to the dark, Elizabeth noticed labels and stamps on each drum, but without a flashlight, deciphering them was impossible. Determining her location was a storage room in the paper mill, it wasn't a stretch to conclude that inside these drums were the chemicals used for making paper, the same chemicals, she suspected, that were responsible for poisoning her town and Nona.

Without warning, the door at the front of the building screeched open, accompanied by the scuffling and scrambling of feet against the concrete floor. Placing her hands along the wall, Elizabeth felt her way deeper into the darkness to hide, as voices echoed in the building. The door slammed shut, leaving behind the sound of heavy breathing and someone locked in the building with her.

"Clayton, is that you? It's me, Elizabeth."

"Isn't that like you to call for your boyfriend, Lizzie? Surprise, it's me, your loving husband. Hate to disappoint you, seeing's how you left me for dead."

Elizabeth followed the outer wall to the doorway. A narrow sliver of light from the outside ran along the bottom of the double doors, illuminating the entrance. With that faint light fanning out along the floor, she could see Eddie, slumped nearby, hands tied behind his back.

"Eddie, what are you doing here?"

"I'm locked up, same as you. Looks like you didn't quit your digging, like I told you."

"I couldn't quit, not when so much is at stake."

"That worked out real good for you, didn't it? Now get over here and untie me."

Elizabeth did not move.

"We gotta get out of here," Eddie growled. "I know this building, and the stuff in here is explosive. There's dimethyl sulfide, powerful stuff, used in pulping. Plus hundred of barrels of sodium sulfide and sodium hydroxide, both poisonous and unstable."

"Building's been here for a long time. It's not going to explode by itself."

"Maybe not, but we still need to get out of here. Untie me, and I'll open the door."

At that moment, the door did open, and a man entered, flashlight in hand, scanning the room, honing in on Eddie's face.

"I don't know how the hell you think you're gonna get away with this, Landers." Eddie squinted into the light. "Untie me and let me outta here."

"Only you, Eddie? Should I keep Elizabeth locked up in here?"

"I don't give a damn what you do with her."

"Isn't that touching? Did you hear that, Liz?" Clayton scanned the room with the light, locating Elizabeth. "Eddie has once again demonstrated what a stand-up guy he is."

"Clayton, what are you doing?" Elizabeth was filled with shock and disbelief. "What's going on? I thought you were helping me."

"I am helping you, because I'm going to get rid of your useless husband for you."

"I worked my ass off for my family all these years," Eddie said.

"You never deserved to have a family at all, considering how you lied about your football scholarship being withdrawn when you two married because Liz was pregnant."

"Shut up, Landers."

"Liz, listen to this revelation." Clayton walked closer to Elizabeth, the light focused on her broken face. "There was no scholarship, because Eddie failed to meet the academic standards required.

Marrying you was a convenient way out, and he could blame you all these years for ruining his life."

"What a load of bull. No one's gonna believe your lies," Eddie snarled.

"Eddie, you're about to meet your maker. As good a time as any to come clean."

"Is it true, Eddie?" Elizabeth asked. "You fabricated the whole story about losing the scholarship?"

"It's all lies. He's making me out as the bad guy to impress you."

"You're wrong, as usual, Eddie," Clayton said. "If I'd wanted to impress Liz, I could have said something long ago, because I've known the truth from the beginning. You forget, I attended the university and with a little digging, I learned the truth about you and what really happened."

"All these years," Elizabeth said, "you lead me to believe you gave up everything for me. What a horrible thing to do. Our entire life together was based on lies."

Elizabeth felt engulfed by the betrayal and evil of what Eddie had done, magnified by what Clayton had not done.

"Clay, since the beginning, you knew the truth and didn't tell me."

"Not my place to fix your mess of a life, Liz. You chose this bum, and you had to live with that decision. Big mistake," Clay said.

"When I get outta here, you are going to pay, Landers," Eddie threatened.

Clayton approached Eddie and swung his heavy flashlight, connecting hard with Eddie's face.

"More bad news, I'm afraid. You're not getting out of here." Clayton switched on the auxiliary light in the building.

"Why are you doing this?" Elizabeth asked.

"Haven't you figured it out, Liz? A brilliant sleuth like you?" Clayton smiled. "Let me tell you a little story to enlighten you. When

I met Audrey, she had recently inherited Northland, a company she turned over to me soon after we were married. A match made in business heaven."

"So everything you did was all about money? When you pretended you cared about the girls and me, when you said you would help me, that was all about protecting your company's profits?"

"For the most part, although, I have to admit, I was enjoying your flirtatious attention and playing your little games. In the end, business is business."

She lurched toward him, but Clayton caught her arm and pinned it behind her. He bound her wrists and shoulders with a thick rope and shoved her onto the floor. From the container he had carried in, Clayton removed a gas-soaked rope which he snaked through the barrels, from the front of the building to the back.

"I do love a barbecue," Clay said as he worked. "Pay attention. This method will take a bit of time, but it is guaranteed to do the job." Reaching into his pocket, he withdrew a cigarette lighter, snapped it open, and flicked it until a flame appeared.

"I want to thank you both for solving a multitude of problems for me. The probing into all that pesky pollution business and dead people will be buried, no pun intended. The mill will be damaged beyond repair, resulting in an enormous insurance check to cover my losses. Oh, and here's the good part. The world will be a much improved place without Eddie Dembrowski."

"You're gonna regret this," Eddie said, trying to stand. Clayton kicked him to the floor, Eddie's head bouncing against the concrete.

"One thing I never suffer from is regrets, Eddie. Now stay conscious, or you're going to miss the barbecue."

Elizabeth's mind was racing, scrambling for any lifeline possible. Listening to Clay, it was obvious this amoral, disturbed man was enjoying himself. She needed to keep him talking, anything to give her more time.

"Clay, satisfy my curiosity. Would I have been able to prove the case against Northland?"

"You're giving yourself too much credit, Liz. What you found was circumstantial at best. The proof was locked away where neither you, nor anyone else, could access it. After tonight, it'll disappear up in flames." He stepped closer to the raveled end of the rope near their feet and reached down to ignite it.

"Wait. Tell me about Copper Creek, by the Nelson's farm. I couldn't figure out how that location, so far upstream from the mill, tied into what Northland was doing."

"A smart girl like you? Ever hear of outfall pipes? They're hidden underground and lead away from the plant, spilling into a distant water source, like Copper Creek. Voila, problem solved."

"What your company did was deadly, not to mention against the law, Clay."

"Shame on me," he said, laughing. "Laws are written for the little people, the nobodies of society. The world of business is allowed to do whatever is necessary for the good of the owners and shareholders. It's too bad you're a nobody, one of the little people."

"You used to be like me, a nobody in high school, but we never minded because we had one another. Don't you remember those happier times?"

"Happier times? We were the oddballs of the school, the losers, tolerated at best, but mostly ignored and teased. A pathetic story, but lucky for me, marrying Audrey earned me a promotion to the winning team. Unfortunately, your pathetic story continued on and is about to have a very unhappy ending."

"Think about my girls, Clay. They need me. I promise I'll stop my investigating and will forget everything, if you let me go."

"I'm afraid I can't do that, Liz. Don't take it personally, because, like I said, business is business."

He flicked the lighter again and connected the flame to the rope. It sizzled and hissed, then began a slow burn toward the barrels through which it zigzagged.

"Good-bye, little people." Clayton touched Elizabeth's face. "Such a waste," he said, then left the building, the door clanging shut behind him.

Eddie scrambled to his feet and rammed himself against the metal doors, screaming and cursing. After several attempts, he crumbled to the floor.

"This is your fault, Lizzie. Because of you and your lunatic boy-friend, we're dead meat."

"Shut up, Eddie."

She stumbled forward, trying to reach the ignited rope, but lost her balance. In the midst of the barrels, there was a snap, like the crack of a whip, followed by what sounded like thunder off in the distance. Elizabeth looked toward the rear of the room to see a ripple of fire moving in slow motion, ricocheting from barrel to barrel.

Outside, something slammed against the door, and Elizabeth screamed for help. Then, the deafening explosions of the deathly steel drums, like a freight train rambling in the building, blocked out every other sound. As the unbearable heat rolled over the room, Elizabeth staggered to the door, struggling to breathe, the thick, chemical-laced air choking her. She pounded and pounded on the door until she nearly blacked out.

The door gave way and swung open. Air, light and clean, enveloped Elizabeth, and she felt herself being pulled out of the building and along the ground.

"Liz, was there anyone else inside with you?" a muffled, faraway voice asked.

"No . . . nobody," she whispered, trying to open her eyes.

An enormous blast reverberated, and Elizabeth allowed herself to drift away, the roar closing around her. Upon awakening, she felt a presence beside her. It was Lucky, licking her hands and arms. A deep, crackling cough rattled Elizabeth's chest and ravaged her raw throat. She forced open her stinging eyes and witnessed the explosion of the building that had held her prisoner, detonating a flood of ignited chemicals and barrel shrapnel. She pulled Lucky close, as that first blast blew away the rear of the building, shattering concrete block and metal. When a second, larger explosion catapulted the roof into the air, Elizabeth pushed Lucky down, covering his body to protect him, as a maelstrom of flames and toxic liquids rained down within feet of where they were. Elizabeth and Lucky huddled together, the fire crews arriving in trucks with lights flashing and scattering to surround Northland's compound. As a nearby building erupted in flames, its roof ignited from the showering of burning debris, a rumble overhead caused Elizabeth to gaze above the burning mill. Enormous rolling clouds threatened, lightning stabbed the sky, and the heavens opened up with a deluge of silvery-white rain. Elizabeth lifted her face, the raindrops trailing down her cheeks in coal-black streams, washing away the terror and helplessness Clayton and Eddie had inflicted on her. She had survived.

Sitting with Lucky in the rain, she lost count of how many explosions occurred throughout the factory's complex. The blasts were strangely synchronized, tumbling adjoining buildings like dominoes in a hellish game. To Elizabeth, the detonations lasted for an eternity. Later, she learned it had taken less than three hours to level the buildings of the Northland Paper Company.

She hoped the mill had taken Clayton and Eddie down with it.

IT WILL TAKE A LITTLE TIME

AFTER THE EXPLOSIONS AND FIRE, ELIZABETH WAS hospitalized. Fifteen stitches closed the wound on her head, her many burns and contusions were treated, the sprained ankle was wrapped, and a wide bandage crossed the bridge of her nose beneath two swollen, black eyes. Her mouth and throat were singed and sore, and her hearing had not fully returned, but she was allowed to go home the following afternoon. Rain and wind battered them as Carol Jean pushed Elizabeth's wheelchair from the hospital, and Mince wrangled an enormous umbrella over their heads. William drove them home through the flooded streets, lightning continuing to flash across the churning clouds.

Marta and Lucky met them in the driveway, both drenched but relieved Elizabeth had returned home.

"This dog would not rest without you. He fretted and paced from window to window, watching for you," Marta said.

"They told me he saved my life," Elizabeth said, as she hugged Lucky. "You are my hero."

"There are several more heroes in the house waiting to see you," Marta told her.

The family went inside where Madeira, Julian, and Art waited. One by one, Elizabeth pulled her dear friends to her in a grateful embrace. "I don't know how you did it, but you rescued me from the fire. You saved my life."

They gathered in what was left of the living room, drinking the last of Eddie's beer and piecing together what had happened.

"When you left the Court House that night," Julian said, "I was concerned because you were with Clayton, about whom I had my suspicions. Eddie was on the loose, and I was even more worried about what he would do."

"I never suspected Clayton," Elizabeth admitted, feeling embarrassed and betrayed. "I can't believe I thought he cared about me and wanted to help me."

"Don't blame yourself. You two had been friends for a long time," Julian said. "It's only because I had been doing some investigating into the ownership of Northland, that I began to suspect Clayton. When Audrey's family name turned up buried in the paperwork, I was certain Clay was involved with the mill."

"I never liked Clay," Art said. "Pretended to be a regular guy, but he hung out with all those big shots, here in town and up at the capital."

"How did you manage to find me at Northland? The complex is enormous, and there were so many places I could have been." Elizabeth's smoke-damaged voice was strained.

"I have to give Madeira and Lucky the credit for that," Julian answered.

"Elizabeth, I realize you asked me not to share with Julian all you confided to me," Madeira said, "but I was so worried about you that night. When he came home and told me you had left with Clay, I felt Julian needed to know you two might be planning on breaking into the mill."

"I was looking for Eddie in every tavern in town," Art said. "Ended up over at your place in hopes of tracking him down, when Julian and Madeira showed up."

"We were searching for you and Clay, but first we wanted to locate Eddie," Madeira said.

"Truth be told, we all thought Eddie was your greatest threat last night," Julian admitted. "We found signs of a struggle in the hallway at your house, but no sign of Eddie."

"I panicked when we found the blood," Madeira said. "I knew you were hurt."

"It was Madeira's idea to go to Northland," Art said. "I had my doubts you would have the guts to break into the mill, but Madeira convinced me otherwise."

"With what you had dug up, Elizabeth, I was certain you were close to proving your suspicions. Julian agreed, and eventually, so did Art." Madeira laughed. "We, and I mean, I, decided going to the mill was your logical next step."

"I don't know if it was logical or not. More like desperate and a little bit crazy," Elizabeth said. "I still don't see how Lucky was part of all this."

"We drove across town and spotted Clay's car parked near the mill, which, by that time, was already on fire," Art said. "That's when we teamed up with Lucky, who was frantic and barking like mad. We let him out of the car, and that dog ran so fast, he nearly killed the three of us trying to keep up with him. It didn't take Lucky long to find where you were locked up."

"Elizabeth, there's something I wish I could have told you before, but Julian swore me to secrecy." Madeira reached for her friend's bandaged hands.

"Although Julian was the union's legal counsel in the unemployment compensation case, he was also trying to prove damages to the community by Northland. That's why he was researching into the ownership of the mill," Madeira said. "You tackled the issue from the environmental and human side of the problem, while Julian was analyzing how Northland and its owners broke the law."

"Together, we could have proven their guilt." Elizabeth shook her head in dismay. "If only I had waited until I had more proof, instead of charging headlong into a disaster that destroyed the evidence we needed."

"But, because of what you did, you proved Clayton was responsible," Madeira said.

"There was no way anyone could have guessed we were close to nailing them, so close Landers was willing to destroy everything to protect himself and the corporation," Julian reassured her. "Even though their records went up in smoke, we have the evidence you researched. I am confident we will be able to link the mill to those deaths, especially with you as a witness to Clayton's final words and actions at the mill. With my legal documentation, it will be enough."

"Did they find Clayton?" Elizabeth asked. "Did he survive the fire?"

"His body was located in a large storage room behind the main offices," Art said.

"That's the place where Clay and I started digging, the room with all the files."

"Based on what was left of the area, the fire chief thought Clay was setting up a second combustion site when the fire flashed through the building, setting off the incendiary devices he was planning to use. He was probably killed by his own explosives," Julian added.

"I'd say he got what he deserved," William said.

"I would have enjoyed seeing him brought to justice in court," Julian said.

"Was anyone else hurt in the blaze?" Elizabeth asked, fearing the answer.

"There were two other bodies found, but they haven't been identified yet. One guard was on duty, and he sustained minor injuries," Julian responded.

"Clayton introduced me to a couple of his friends who worked at Northland. They were at Nona's funeral and several other funerals in town, too. I could supply the authorities with their names and descriptions, in case the bodies they found are theirs," Elizabeth offered.

"The police would appreciate any information you have," Julian said.

"Here's some information I'd appreciate, Julian, and it's about you," Elizabeth began. "I overheard a conversation you had with Northland's lawyer, Robert Jordan, and it worried me."

"What was the conversation about?"

"It was about you two working together on something, but you wanted your involvement to be kept a secret. You were talking in the Court House, and Jordan demanded you fix the situation and get it done soon."

"Oh, that," Julian said, laughing. "Robert and I were on the committee to purchase new pews at church. We didn't want the rest of the committee to know we were donating the money for the renovation. The other members were talking about taking out a loan, and, of course, that wasn't necessary."

"I guess that will teach me to eavesdrop. I even suspected you were working for Northland, too," Elizabeth admitted.

"In your shoes, I probably would have thought the same thing," Art said.

"I'm sorry I doubted you, Julian," Elizabeth said. "I was starting to become paranoid after all the things that had happened."

"No one could blame you for being careful and suspicious," Julian said. "You were attacked, your house was ransacked, and your family was threatened."

"I'm guessing our barn fire wasn't an accident either," William said.

"Probably not," Julian answered.

"So much devastation," Marta said. "What a terrible waste."

"What will happen to the mill now?" Art asked.

"The whole area looks like a war zone. My guess is they will come in with bulldozers and level the place."

Elizabeth looked at the faces of her family. "You have been through so much these past few months. I hope we can put this all behind us and start a new life together."

"What about Pops?" Mince asked. "If he's out of jail, does that mean he will come home again?" Elizabeth could hear the anxiety in her daughter's voice.

"Your Pops and I have decided it would be best if he stayed away," Elizabeth said. "He thought he would get a job working the boats on Lake Superior, to get a fresh start."

As she said the words, Elizabeth was overcome by a feeling of tranquility. Eddie was gone, and if no one was looking for him, he would be entombed in the destroyed mill and never be found. Better still, the Northland Corporation would be held accountable for what they had done. There would be justice for Nona and the others.

"We should go, because you, Elizabeth, are exhausted and were sent home to rest and recover," Madeira said, hugging her friend.

"Take it easy, Liz," Art said as he was leaving. "I'll stop by tomorrow."

"You've done so much for us. I don't know how I will ever repay you."

"Forget it," Julian said as he and Madeira walked out the door.

"If you want us to stay for awhile, we will," Marta said, gathering up the beer bottles.

"Go on home. We are going to be fine," Elizabeth said with a smile.

She and the girls walked her parents out of the house. "I'll call you in a few days, when I get the phone reconnected."

A loud cheer exploded from Carol Jean and Mince, too. Elizabeth predicted having a phone was a small step toward starting over again, at least for her daughters.

"Girls, go upstairs and open some windows. Make sure the rain isn't coming in."

Elizabeth stood alone in her shabby kitchen. Her gaze wandered upward to the bare kitchen window, and with both hands, she pushed against the frame and forced it open, ushering in a cool, damp breeze.

"Come on, buddy," Elizabeth said, patting Lucky. "I need to be outside."

Like so many times before, the two planted themselves on the back porch, its faded boards dappled with raindrops. Elizabeth stroked Lucky's ears as he leaned against her, resting his nose on her knee. The rain and wind had subsided, and overhead what remained of the storm clouds was being replaced by glimpses of blue. Across the yard, meandering in the distance, Elizabeth could see the river, a silver ribbon that would one day run clean again.

Elizabeth breathed in the misty air, a hint of the cool autumn days to come. "The mill is gone, and I think the air feels better already," she told Lucky.

Staring past the remnants of her garden, Elizabeth said, "I don't believe it."

She and Lucky walked across the yard, its grass now flecked with pale green blades. On the edge of the river stood the stump of the girls' old apple tree, its life severed by Eddie's murderous ax.

Sprouting from the tree's root flare, infant shoots had risen, a gift of the recent rains and the promise of a new beginning.

"This is for you, Nona," Elizabeth said, her bandaged hands caressing the delicate leaves. "Someday it will be another beautiful apple tree for young girls to love. It will only take a little time."

History of the Northland Paper Company & Northland Worldwide Industries Regarding the Oconto River and Green Bay Water Pollution

1956 - Nearly two million gallons of waste water, only partially treated, are discharged into the Oconto River.

1957 - More than three million gallons of partially-treated waste water leak out of a mill outfall pipe into nearby wetlands that drain into Green Bay.

1958 - A dumping site leachate collection pond overflows for longer than four days, spilling a half million gallons of liquid chemicals into the Oconto River which feeds into Green Bay.

1959 - Eight tons of dioxin-laced sludge from Northland Paper Company breach a container dike and come to rest near the Oconto River that runs into Green Bay.

1960-1962 - Northland and the state of Wisconsin dispute over a 300-acre mass of sludge (20 feet thick in places) that Northland had deposited on the bed of Green Bay. Northland refuses to admit that the sludge bed, on the floor of the bay and extending into the Oconto River, is their responsibility, despite the fact that the mill dumped its effluent directly into Copper Creek which feeds into the Oconto River.

1963 - An independent researcher for the Green Bay Port Authority finds a new sludge bed, east of the Oconto River's mouth, and less than one mile from the mill's outfall pipe. The researcher said the volume of sludge would cover a football field to a depth of eighteen feet.

1967 - The Wisconsin DNR and other state agencies file charges against Northland Worldwide Industries, alleging that their facility (Northland Paper Company, destroyed by fire in 1964) discharged toxic waste water which state officials said had triggered a massive algae bloom in the Oconto River during the summers of 1959 and 1960. Sources close to the case stated that NPC agreed to pay a fine of more than $100,000 to resolve the allegations. The money is slated to go to the residents living along the river and the adjacent bay shoreline.

1970 - Approximately 450 landowners file a class action lawsuit against Northland Paper Company/Northland Worldwide Industries for damaging their property values and causing personal injury and a decline in health.

1979 - A $2.5 million class action settlement provides damages to landowners and residents along the Oconto River and adjoining bay shore area. Under the verdict, the plaintiffs would likely split the damage award equally, at about $4500 after legal fees.

1980 - Northland Worldwide Industries pleads guilty to five felony counts and pays $2.8 million in federal fines for illegally storing, treating, and disposing of hazardous waste and making false statements to regulators. The infractions occurred at the company's Northland Paper Company mill. According to a release by the U.S. Department of Justice, NWI pleaded guilty to three violations of hazardous waste laws under the Resource Conservation and Recovery Act (RCRA) involving the generating, storing, treating, and disposal of hazardous waste without a federal or state permit. The fourth and fifth felony counts charge that NPC officials knowingly made false material statements to federal and state environmental authorities that the NPC mill did not generate, store, treat, or dispose of hazardous waste, and that the mill had only one outfall to the Oconto River, when, in fact, it had three. According to the Justice Department, this was the largest fine, criminal or civil, ever assessed in Wisconsin for environmental law violations and was the second largest criminal fine to that date ever collected in the U.S. for violations of hazardous waste and water pollution laws.